T0277274

STEAL
FIRE
FROM THE
GODS

STEAL FIRE FROM THE GODS

CLINT HALL

Steal Fire from the Gods
Copyright © 2023 by Clint Hall

Published by Enclave Publishing, an imprint of Oasis Family Media.

Carol Stream, Illinois, USA.
www.enclavepublishing.com

ISBN: 979-8-88605-074-5 (hardback)
ISBN: 979-8-88605-075-2 (printed softcover)
ISBN: 979-8-88605-077-6 (ebook)

Cover design by Kirk DouPonce, www.Fiction-Artist.com
Typesetting by Jamie Foley, www.JamieFoley.com

Printed in the United States of America.

"Our darkest secrets can be our greatest strengths,

if only we allow ourselves to see."

THE HUMAN ALLIANCE KNEW IT WAS OVER
WHEN THE ANDROIDS STARTED USING MAGIC
TO CAST FIRE, SHAKE THE GROUND, CONJURE
STORMS, AND PART THE SEAS.
WE FOUGHT BACK ANYWAY.

― SGT. JACK SWEET

I STOPPED BELIEVING IN GOD

years ago, on a night when fireballs tore across the starry sky and destroyed everything I ever loved.

But it still feels strange when I walk out of my assigned living quarters without having said a morning prayer. My parents would be disappointed.

A forest of yellow and green creates a large perimeter around my village. Other than the towering pines, nothing here resembles life before the war. There are no paved roads, no visible electric lights, no skyscrapers or rumbling car engines. Instead, people wear simple clothes and push carts with wooden wheels. The huts are arranged in rows with small patches of dirt and grass between them. Smoke from the blacksmith's shop mixes with the smell of dirt and baking bread. At first glance, it looks as if the war machines copied a village from the dark ages and pasted it into the present.

It's all an illusion, of course. We're surrounded by technology, the eyes of digital gods monitoring our every move.

White text appears at the bottom of my field of vision, a reminder that the machines are inside me, as well.

CORONARY IMPLANT POWER LEVEL: 100%.

Cool morning air presses against my skin as I move quickly out the door, ready to start my day's patrol of the surrounding forest. The digital voice in my quarters will ask the inevitable question when I return tonight. My twenty-second birthday was two days ago, which means I've heard it twice already.

In a few days, it won't be a question anymore.

Don't think about it now. I put on my best fake smile and shove my hands into my pockets as I walk. My outfit today is the same as every other day—a white, long-sleeved shirt under a buttoned jacket and pants woven from light brown fibers. The clothes are perfectly tailored and keep my body at the ideal temperature, whether I like it or not.

The village buzzes with the commotion of a new day. Everyone else is dressed in the same clothes as I am, as if we're all on a yoga retreat instead of prisoners of the war machines. Other villagers stroll down streets made of stone and mud, laughing and talking with each other. A few huts have open windows, at which people trade for items like wooden toys, paintings, and home decorations. Nobody sells anything essential; all our needs are met by the machines. I guess even post-apocalypse, people love to shop.

I avoid making eye contact with any of them. They're good people, probably no different than those who stood beside me as we fought an unwinnable war, people I considered family regardless of their blood, their skin, or their beliefs. I used to welcome others with open arms.

But the war is over. Now, it'd be safer for everybody if they left me alone.

My gaze drifts to the trees in the distance. To everyone else, they're a border. To me, they're a gateway to another world, a place where I can forget who I am, remember who I was, and even dare to believe in what I might become.

You'll get there soon enough, Gunnar. Just don't stop walking.

The first person to spot me is Michael, who lives next door. He was probably heading toward the cafeteria when he saw my door open and doubled back to greet me. He has a burly frame, red hair, and a strong handshake. The calluses on his dirt-stained hands make me wonder if he was a farmer before the war. "Morning, Gunnar. We didn't see you at the market festival last night."

I turn as I keep walking, so as not to break off the handshake too soon. "Oh, I was there. You must've missed me." It's not a lie. I was *there*, but I've gotten very good at hiding in a crowd.

Before he can say any more, I turn and find Jenn standing right in front of me. She looks up to meet my gaze, her eyebrows raised and her strawberry blond hair pulled back in a ponytail.

"Hey, Jenn." I flash a smile as I sidestep her.

"Nice to see you." Jenn offers a grin and a fast wink. If she knew about the metal heart the machines put in my chest, she wouldn't be so friendly. None of them would. Even among people who have embraced machine rule, cyborgs aren't trusted.

"Nice to be seen," I respond with a laugh but don't break stride, speeding up as I head for the woods.

A few others call out to me as I walk. They all seem determined to bring me out of my shell. I have no idea why. After five years of the cold shoulder, I would've expected them to give up.

"Hey, Gunnar! Another day in the trees, huh?"

"When are you coming over for game night, Gunnar?"

"Gunnar, have you seen that animal I mentioned? I could have sworn it had . . ."

Keep moving. It's a constant mantra as I make my way through the village, throwing out my best face and canned responses. *Yep, I love my patrol job. Busy tonight, catch me next time. Okay, I'll keep an eye out for strange creatures.*

I don't pause until I reach the water pump near the center of the village, right before the street opens into a large market area. As I bend over to fill my canteen, a wooden ball rolls into my foot. I pick it up.

"Ball?"

My head snaps up. A golden-haired toddler stands in front of me, chewing on his fingers.

I show the ball to the little boy, move it behind me, then toss it over my shoulder and catch it on the back of my hand.

His expression is still blank.

"Tough crowd." I toss the ball to the kid. "Here you go."

He doesn't try to catch it, but instead watches me as if I'm a ghost. It sends a quick shiver over my skin. Does he somehow know what I'm hiding?

The boy's mother rushes over and offers a fast apology before taking his hand. I nod in response, then fill my canteen.

When I look back up a few moments later, the mother and child are gone, but something else catches my eye—something I meant to ignore.

An air mage stands on a raised platform in the center of town, towering over the market. It stands about eight feet tall and has a skull covered in synthetic silver flesh, with three curved white lines carved into its forehead. The machine's black robes billow in the gentle breeze. The mage hasn't so much as twitched since I was placed here years ago, but the light bends around its body like heat radiating off asphalt. Its eyes remain dark, but I have no doubt that the android is activated and watching. None of the villagers look directly at the mage, but give it a wide berth as they move through the square.

Faint echoes of screams and explosions shake the back of my mind. I remember my mother's strong hands gripping my shirt, telling me to run an instant before an eruption of heat and light ripped us apart forever. Androids march through the night in my mind. Flames glisten in their human-shaped metallic bodies as they use automatic rifles to execute one survivor after another.

Everyone except me.

The scar on my chest burns. It might be an air mage standing in front of me day after day, but it's the fire mage that haunts my dreams.

Part of me believes my life will always be this way—hiding in plain sight, living beneath the constant watch of the machines, wondering why they kept me alive. My prayers for change stopped a long time ago.

Now I'm looking for hope somewhere else. *I need to get to the woods.*

I turn away from the air mage and bump into a woman. She gasps in surprise, and her blue eyes widen.

Her presence is like an invisible force that slams into me, stealing my words and stopping my breath. I've never experienced anything like it. Something clicks in my soul when my eyes meet hers, something both familiar and new.

"I'm sorry," she says with an apologetic smile and takes a few steps back, wrestling with a large bundle of blankets in her arms. The pile looks heavy, but her movements are strong and graceful, like she was born of the wind.

That's when I notice her clothes—made of similar materials to mine, but they're a much darker shade of brown.

She's an outcast.

Recognition flashes across her face and she averts her eyes. Her slight smile disappears. I almost apologize, as if I've offended her by noticing the obvious.

"No problem," I say, but she's already gliding away. The machines have never told us why they designate certain people as outcasts, but we have our theories, including genetic potential for passing on birth defects and predisposition to disruptive behaviors. Outcasts are allowed in the villages to trade, but only for a few hours at a time. Any non-commercial interactions are prohibited. Not that the villagers would be eager to speak with her, anyway. If they knew about my cybernetic heart, they would treat me the same. I doubt she deserves the shunning any more than I do.

Nothing I can do about it. I turn my attention to the trees that lie beyond the village. Everyone who's fourteen and older is assigned a job, mostly to keep us busy. The machines provide and maintain our food, shelter, clothing, and any other essentials. My role patrolling the woods for dangerous wildlife is as arbitrary as any other job here, but at least it gives me time to be alone. The forest looks like a great curtain of leaves through which I can enter another world.

My steps carry me toward the solace of the woods, but before I pass the last of the huts, I can't resist taking another look back over my shoulder.

For an instant, she looks back too.

"Niko!" I shout through cupped hands once I'm far enough into the forest that none of the villagers can hear me. A cold breeze pushes through the trees. I quicken my steps, scanning the branches for my friend. It's a game we often play, Niko and me. He won't get the drop on me today. "Ni-ko!"

A rustling in the leaves causes me to stop and jerk my head to the right. When I find nothing there, I whirl left, expecting to see him coming toward me from the opposite side.

No sign of Niko. Did something happen to him?

The moment the words form in my head, I feel his weight land on my right shoulder. I laugh with relief. "How did you do that?"

The little animal stares back at me with black eyes. His fur is the color of smoke, his face mostly white, except for dark circles around his eyes and a black diamond on the top of his head. I'm not sure exactly what type of animal he is; during my time with the Human Alliance, most of our lessons focused on topics that were more relevant to surviving a world at war. I've looked for zoology books in the village, but couldn't find any. All I know is that Niko glides between the trees using flaps of skin between his limbs and that he doesn't need me to survive, but follows me anyway whenever I'm in the woods.

I also know that he's an incredible scavenger. Today, Niko grips a shining silver ring with both paws. Stealing stuff seems to be Niko's favorite pastime. More often than not, it's trinkets that probably come from ruins of cities and neighborhoods. But on occasion, he's dropped small gears and other metallic parts into my hands, shining as if brand new, which means he's somehow robbing war machine facilities. It's almost like he's showing off.

"Where'd you find that?" I take a closer look, recognizing it immediately as a locket ring. I haven't seen one in years. The Human Alliance used them often for carrying codes and secret messages. This one is small—silver with a green gemstone. I open the clasp, wondering if I'll find any messages inside, anything that will remind me of the past. But inside the locket is only a bit of dust.

"Thanks," I say, dropping the ring into my pocket.

Niko raises his nose and sniffs the air, his big black eyes watching me expectantly.

"Yeah, yeah, okay." I dig into the pouch on my belt, pull out a piece of dried meat, and offer it to him. "You know I could get in trouble for this if they catch me, right?"

Niko grasps the food with tiny paws and shoves it into his mouth, creating a bulge in his cheek. He scurries down my chest into the warmth of my jacket. Niko knows where we're going as well as I do. We've done this routine countless times since I started venturing into the woods years ago.

The walk takes a few hours, but I don't mind. I spend as much time out here as I can. It's the one place where I can relax. A wispy fog lingers in the cool air above golden aspen trees and towering green pines, obscuring the gray mountains that watch over me from the distance. But the peace is spoiled by dark thoughts creeping along the edges of my mind. I know what waits for me at the end of this walk.

These days, I could make the journey blindfolded, but when I first came to the village, it took me months to find this place. As the trees start to thin out, I think of the day I first encountered what I had spent months searching for—the crumbled remains of concrete bunkers built into the side of grassy hills or peeking up from the ground, the demolished vehicles, the craters in the earth.

This is the last place that felt like home.

I used to wonder why the machines placed me in a village so close to the site where our unit made its last stand. For all they know, there could still be weapons or other supplies hidden in the destruction. Although I have no proof, I've always assumed there's a tracker implanted beneath my skin somewhere. Why would they let me roam free so close to the remains of a Human Alliance base?

But after a few weeks of digging through the craters, I realized the cold truth. It didn't matter what I found here; the machines' victory was absolute. Nothing I could uncover among the wreckage could change that.

I walk past piles of blackened rubble. I would have expected the vegetation to overtake the area by now, but for some reason, nothing seems to grow here.

I pause at a small hill and offer a respectful nod. Despite searching for weeks, I never found my parents' remains. It's possible they were completely incinerated in the fires or that their bodies were carried away by the machines.

In the end, I buried what few of their possessions I could find—my father's watch, my mother's wedding ring, and our worn-out family Bible—on the hillside facing away from the destruction, where the land was still green. The first few times I came here, I would sit in the grass and talk to them, watching the sunset fade in the distance, gazing up at the moon, and wishing I could escape to other worlds.

Sometimes I thought I could hear them speaking to me on the wind. I never liked what I heard—or perhaps I didn't believe it.

The memories of the destruction seep into my mind—the fire, the screams, my mother's desperate plea for me to run. My breath quickens. My body temperature rises.

To calm myself down, I sing.

"The gravedigger's spade is a friend to me, opening a door that will set me free, 'cause I carry the water that washed me clean . . ."

The melody trails off. It's a song my parents taught me. In fact, I owe my name to the lyrics. *Gunnar Graves.* My parents never told me my real surname. "Too much data attached to it," they said. "Besides, God knows who you really are. That's all that matters."

Even with years of practice, I've never mastered the tune. My parents both performed it beautifully; when I sing it, the melody is always off-key.

At least it reminds me of them. I'd give anything to hear my mother and father sing again, their voices so full of hope and belief. My parents clung to their faith even in the darkest times, but for the past few weeks, I've been uttering a different kind of prayer.

Niko crawls out of my light brown jacket and onto my shoulder as I approach an old metal toolbox buried at the base of the hill. The faded red lid is scarcely visible beneath the layer of dirt.

I brush away the dust and open the latch. Inside is a dark green jacket, unremarkable except for a black patch with the symbol of the Human Alliance—a red H and A in letters that share a side and slant to the right—sewn to the left side of the chest. Niko scampers from one arm to another as I slide the Alliance jacket on over my machine-provided clothes. The first time I put this jacket on as a kid, it was so big I had to roll the sleeves. Now, they're a little short.

But the fabric still carries the smells of home—gun oil and cigarette smoke. I swear I even catch a whiff of the old chicken and salsa MRE entrees from time to time.

A side compartment in the box holds Niko's stolen treasures. I dig the ring out of my pocket. I'm about to drop it in with the other trinkets, but I pause and look at it again, then tuck the ring inside the inner jacket pocket.

I head to the fire pit in the center of the decimated facility. A pile of wood surrounded by cinder blocks sits waiting, taunting me.

CORONARY IMPLANT POWER LEVEL: 98%.

I draw in a deep breath, release, and stretch out my arms.

This is the worst part.

In my mind, I picture the fire mage standing amidst the destruction, arms outstretched, fingers twisted in unnatural positions. The memory of intense heat pushes over my body, reminding me of the searing pain that burned my world to ashes.

I hear the mage's words clearly in my mind, spoken in a low, guttural tone no human could truly reproduce.

I do my best. *"Ignis sacer terrae. Mandata mea."*

I repeat the phrase over and over again, trying to mimic the exact movements of the machine's arms and fingers, the precise pronunciation of the words, the rhythms and tempo of the chant. I've heard that the reason people could never harness elemental magic was that the rituals were too precise for humans to perform.

But I'm not entirely human.

My chant grows in intensity. Even if I manage to summon the fire, I have no idea whether I can control it. If I'm burned alive, at least I'll join my family in the afterlife or the nothingness, dying the way I was supposed to die years ago.

A burning energy rises inside me, emanating perhaps from the machine that replaced my damaged heart. If this is the source of my power, my vengeance, then so be it. We created the machines and they annihilated us for it. They made me what I am by destroying who I was. I'm happy to repay the favor.

My muscles tremble. The hairs on my arms stand on end. Niko darts down my leg and onto the ground, though I don't open my eyes to check on him. He can take care of himself.

The burning increases; a current of pinpricks runs down my spine as sweat pours over my body, the chill of the late autumn afternoon long forgotten. It feels as if power emanates from my skin.

I keep my eyes shut and lower my hands so that any flames might be directed toward the wood.

"Ignis sacer terrae. Mandata mea."

I don't know what the words mean, but to me, they demand the power to come and serve, to flow at my will. And today, more than ever, I feel it coming on, like electricity coursing over my skin.

"Ignis sacer terrae! Mandata mea!"

A rushing sound fills my ears; my body quakes. The energy seems to extend from my arms, even my mind.

But something's wrong. The tendrils stretch out, then fall, grasping for a hold that isn't there.

My chanting falters for a heartbeat, my concentration momentarily fractured.

The power disappears. The electricity vanishes and the cold rushes in to fill the void.

I open my eyes. The world has grown darker, the gray clouds thick overhead. Niko watches me from the other side of the wood pile. It remains unburnt. Like yesterday. And the day before. And so many days before that.

A bitter wind blows in my face. My shoulders slump and I mutter a curse that would've broken my parents' hearts.

I slide off the jacket and place it back in the box. I'm not ready to return to the village, so I sit on a large brick and reach into my pocket, searching for the lighter I found here a few weeks ago.

It's not there.

My gaze flicks to Niko.

"Did you steal it?"

As if he can understand me, Niko disappears behind a brick, then reappears holding the metal lighter. Despite the lingering disappointment of my failed efforts, I can't help but laugh.

A few minutes later, the wood finally burns, though not from magic. Niko and I sit, sharing the rest of the meat from my pouch, watching the smoke rise and disappear into the gray sky. I'll gather more wood to try again tomorrow; it's as good a way to fill my time as any.

A small object flitters down from the sky, drifting back and forth in the air until it lands at my feet. Niko watches it fall, too, but he makes no move to claim it for his own. Maybe he's as surprised as I am.

"Is that a . . . feather?" I pick it up. Despite all the time I've spent in the woods, I don't think I've ever seen a bird. I assume most of them were killed by the environmental impacts of the war.

The feather is small and solid black, unremarkable except for the fact that it exists. I scan the sky, finding nothing but clouds and smoke.

I tuck the feather in my jacket pocket and return my thoughts to the spell. *What am I doing wrong?*

"I'll figure it out soon enough," I promise myself, imagining the day I will hold fire in my hands and bring the machines to their knees. The thought warms me in ways that this fire never could.

I cast another glance toward the hill that serves as my parents' memorial before I stand and start back toward the village. Their prayers for salvation went unanswered, but maybe they asked for the wrong thing. In a world overrun by an unstoppable force that humanity created, maybe salvation is both impossible and undeserved.

But revenge . . . *that* may still be within reach.

IT WASN'T REALLY MAGIC, I GUESS,
BUT SCIENCE. THE MACHINES LEARNED TO
PRODUCE ASTOUNDING REACTIONS THROUGH
COMBINATIONS OF ELEMENTS, HEAT, SOUND
WAVES, AND KINETIC ENERGIES THAT WERE TOO
PRECISE FOR HUMANS TO PERFORM. BUT WHEN
YOU SEE AN ANDROID SUMMON A SUBMARINE
OUT OF THE OCEAN AND RIP IT APART IN MIDAIR,
I DON'T CARE WHAT YOU CALL IT.
WE CALLED IT OUR DOOM.

— NADINE S. WEBER, JOURNALIST

MY CLOTHES REEK OF SMOKE

and my muscles ache by the time I press my hand to the sensor on the door of my hut. It's late enough that most of the village has turned in for the night. On the way back from the forest, I considered stopping by the cafeteria for a late dinner, but I'm too tired.

Dim light fills my hut from inset bulbs that line the ceiling. It's a modest space, standard issue for single-occupant housing in the village—a large room with off-white walls, fake plants, and light gray floors crafted to look like wood. Not the decor I would've chosen, but they didn't bother to ask. There's a small, separate bathroom tucked into the corner. My bed is pushed against the wall opposite the door, next to which is a wooden wardrobe. There's no kitchen; eating is allowed only in communal spaces, though I hoard a bit of food here and there for Niko. I'm pretty sure the machines know, but I haven't been reprimanded.

In the living area are two chairs and a small table, atop of which sits a stack of approved books—*Building Our Salvation: The Story of AI, Poems of Serenity and Calm, Finding Your Purpose,* and a thick book on world history that was almost certainly generated by a computer. The buckram covers are various shades of gray and the spines are all in perfect condition. I used to love reading, but I've never so much as cracked one of these open.

"Welcome home, Gunnar Graves," a digitized voice with a pleasant feminine tone says. The sound comes from everywhere; I gave up trying to find the speaker a long time ago. I mouth the words I know it will say next. "Please proceed to the scanning station."

"Hey, Sheila." I shuffle to the white circular platform embedded in the floor along the adjacent wall. The voice has never given itself a name, but it never corrected me after I chose one for it, either. Sometimes I wonder whether other people in the village do the same thing—naming the voice of our oppressors. I've never asked anyone.

When I stand on the platform, a circle of green light appears at my feet and moves up my body. As it scans me, a blue hologram rotates through images of my skeleton, muscle tissue, and organs. The scan reaches the faint scar on my chest and a representation of my cybernetic heart flashes green in the hologram. Text appears alongside it.

CORONARY IMPLANT POWER LEVEL: 95%.

CHARGING . . .

My muscles tense out of habit, but it's been years since I've noticed the current of electricity the platform sends through my body.

CORONARY IMPLANT POWER LEVEL: 100%.

The charge complete, I step off the platform and walk to the wardrobe against the wall. The bottom of the wardrobe slides open in silence as I undress, revealing a metal chute. I drop my clothes into the darkness, then grab another pair of pants to sleep in, but I don't put them on. I need a shower to wash away the day's failure.

I'm halfway to my bathroom when Sheila breaks the silence. "Satisfactory local breeding matches are currently available," it says in a suggestive tone. "Would you like to begin the mate-selection process?"

I wince. Holograms of women's faces flash in the air beside me before I respond, as if the machines are trying to entice me. Jenn is one of the first to appear. *That's why she smiled at me.* Several of the faces belong to strangers; the machines sometimes expand the pool of candidates by drawing from other villages. Even for those I recognize, I don't know much more than their names. I plan to keep it that way as long as I can.

The machines always ask me the question at night, probably because some algorithm suggests that I'm more likely to comply when I'm tired. *Mate selection.* Forced choice disguised as free will would be more accurate. As a kid, I always thought I'd get married one day, but that person would be a friend and companion, not a 'local breeding match.'

Doubtless my face appears every night in these women's quarters, as well. Some might have even agreed to me, but that's not the same as choosing to love. Would any of them actually love me once they knew what was inside?

The whole idea wraps my stomach like hot coils, but all I can do is delay the inevitable. "Why are you trying to hook me up with your friends, Sheila? You know you're all the woman I can handle."

The voice pauses. "Sorry, I didn't understand that response. Would you like to begin the mate sel—?"

"No." Out of the corner of my eye, I see the faces disappear.

The voice returns, the suggestive overtones gone. "Your choice to postpone selection has been confirmed. You have two delay options remaining," the voice says, "before a suitable mate is—"

"Yeah, I got it." I don't wait for her response. I toss the pants on the bed.

Seconds later, I'm in the serenity of the shower, taking deep breaths to calm myself as the hot water cascades down my back.

The outcast pops into my head, a welcome distraction from everything else. People like her are forbidden to reside in the village, let alone actually marry someone like me.

But I can't help wondering what might have happened if she and I had met under different circumstances, in a time and place when we both had the freedom to choose, to be chosen, or decide not to choose at all. Would I find her so enchanting if she wasn't off-limits? If so, would she pick me? The idea is nothing more than a fantasy, probably a dangerous one.

Still, I don't want to stop thinking about it.

And I wonder if she's thinking about me too.

"GUNNAR."

I jolt awake in bed, my body covered in sweat. My chest heaves with labored breaths.

The nightmare again. I scan the room to make sure the flashing monitors, steel arms, and whirring blades have retreated back into my past where they belong. Still, the memory lies heavy on my mind—the high-pitched whine of the spinning blade, the hot steel carving into my skin, the sterile white walls of the operating room where my enemy became a part of me.

I close my eyes, relax my shoulders, and concentrate on slowing my breath. I remind myself that I'm in my living quarters. The smell of tea olive fills my nose. My mother used to rub the blossoms on her wrists. The scent is as artificial as everything else in my hut, but it calms me down. My fingers instinctively touch the scar on my chest as I try to push the memory of the saw away. *It was years ago,* I remind myself.

But the voice speaking my name . . . that was new, something not from my memories. I've never heard it in my nightmares before. *Then where did it come from?* The question lingers in my mind as I quickly get dressed and set out for the ruins.

Cold air hits me the moment I step out of my hut. It's early; most of the villagers aren't awake. Instead of the normal chatter of people, I hear a chorus of insects in the surrounding woods.

I used to look forward to the first cold morning of the year. Despite growing up in the South, I never got accustomed to the heat. My parents didn't, either. We stayed put to be close to family. But I remember the relief of walking to the school bus stop on cool mornings, the first nip in the air that promised upcoming holidays and my mother's apple dumplings. That seems so long ago, so far away.

But it's important to hold on to the positive thoughts, the happy memories.

I shove my hands in my pockets and start toward the woods, already thinking about another day spent attempting to cast fire magic. I try to fool myself into believing that showing up earlier may bring more luck, but the truth is that the frustration of being so close to using magic kept me awake most of the night. What could I have done differently? Was there a piece of the ritual that I missed? The first light of day streaming through my window was a mercy, an end to a night of questions with no answers.

Niko finds me soon after I enter the forest. We return to the ruins, my arms filled with fresh wood that I gathered along the way.

I take my time stacking the logs against each other in the fire pit. When I'm done, I consider saying a prayer. It's what my parents would have told me to do. Despite my loss of faith, I've tried it once or twice, just in case. I've prayed different words, or uttered the same words in a different order. I've sat, stood, lain down, spoken out loud, and screamed.

None of it makes any difference. At the end, I'm left with sore muscles, unburnt logs, and a shattered sense of hope.

Today, I dive right into the spell. *"Ignis sacer terrae. Mandata mea."*

I waste the morning trying to summon the flames, but the energy never comes. When the sun is directly overhead, bringing an unseasonably warm day, I finally surrender. I'm mentally exhausted and tired of failure, so I decide to spend the rest of my afternoon wandering in the woods.

Hours pass as I stroll through the forest. Every so often, Niko leaves to investigate a new tree, scurrying up the trunk and out onto a branch, then gliding back down to me. He lands on my shoulder without me having to break stride.

It's early afternoon when I raise the canteen to my lips to discover that it's run dry. I change direction and head for the river. It isn't far.

My feet know the way on their own, which allows my mind to wander. Usually, I distract myself with simple thoughts—often the faces of girls in the village. I think about them one at a time and wonder whom I might have dated if the world were different. What if we were kids at college instead of a prison camp? What if I were a regular guy instead of a cyborg orphan? Which one would I ask out first? Would any of them accept? It's pointless, I know, but sometimes it's nice to turn off your brain and ponder impossible realities.

As usual when my thoughts wander, the song comes to mind. *"The gravedigger's spade is a friend to me . . ."* I continue humming under my breath until I hear the gentle rush of the river. Already I can feel the cool water washing down my throat.

I speed up my steps in anticipation. Hunger gnaws at my gut, but I'll spend as much time as I can by the water, burning the day away while the villagers go about their business. Another distraction.

As I get close to the river, the rushing water begins to sound like a melody drifting on the wind. The tune is familiar, but I can't put my finger on it. It's so faint that I'm not totally sure I'm hearing anything. Maybe all this solitude is starting to drive me insane. After all, the creature I speak with the most isn't even human.

But as I keep walking, the notes become clear, as do the words.

It's a woman. She sings beautifully, her voice like a flute. *"The gravedigger's spade is a friend to me, opening a door that will set me free, 'cause I carry the water that washed me clean . . ."*

I freeze and drop my canteen. Her tone is so pure, her voice strong and effortless. I listen in disbelief, then snatch up the canteen and increase my pace.

The trees clear away as I jog toward the sound, her words growing louder with each step. When I reach the bank, I see a woman with tanned skin washing her long brown hair in the river.

Her melody endures, rising above the constant rush of the water, which itself is so loud that it muffles the sound of my footsteps. I feel a little creepy, but I'm afraid if she knows I'm here, she'll stop singing.

She scoops the water with a clay bowl and pours it over her head. Her song continues. Of everything in the world she could possibly sing, why *that* song? The song of my childhood. The lyrics that gave me my name.

I move close enough for her to hear me, but not so close as to seem threatening. I clear my throat.

She whirls to face me, wet hair flying, and I step back in surprise.

It's the woman from the village. *The outcast.*

I'm not sure what to say, but I need to say something. "Why are you singing that song?"

The woman stands, wringing her hair quickly with a cloth. She doesn't lift her head to look at me.

I try again. "We talked the other day, in the village."

She gives the slightest nod then begins to move away.

"Wait!" I say. "How do you know that song?"

"I don't know." She stops and slowly turns. This time she looks at me. "It just happens sometimes. My brain picks up melodies from somewhere and sends them to my voice."

"What're you doing all the way out here, any—" I stop myself as the dark colors of her clothing remind me of her status in this world. Outcasts are all but banished, allowed to travel to the villages for trade but prohibited from staying more than a few hours. "I'm sorry. I—"

The look on her face tells me she knows exactly what I'm thinking. *You're an exile who is only allowed to interact with the rest of us at designated times.*

She turns and hurries away.

I trot over to the water and fill my canteen. A quick drink, then I take off at a run in her direction.

"Hey! Wait up!" I call out as I move through the forest. The fading sun casts shades of purple and red across the sky. It'd be a beautiful moment if I didn't feel like such a jerk.

The woman walks swiftly between the trees without looking back.

I *have* to hear her voice again. "Will you sing it for me?"

She doesn't answer.

"That song . . ." I call after her, then hesitate. How can I explain it to a stranger without telling her my life story?

"It reminds me of my mother." My skin vibrates when I say it. It's more personal information than I've given anyone in years. When the walls have been up for that long, it's easy to forget what it's like to open a door for somebody.

The woman comes to a halt.

"The way you sing it," I say, dropping all pretense. I might as well be sincere at this point. "I haven't heard it sung like that in years, and it was the best thing that's happened to me in a really long time. I'll leave you alone if you want, I swear. But . . . please let me hear it again."

She turns and studies me, her expression unreadable. Then, quietly, she begins to sing. *"The gravedigger's spade is a friend to me, opening a door that will set me free, 'cause I carry the water that washed me clean, so the gravedigger's spade is a friend to me."*

Her voice pushes over me, sending chills over my skin. So many nights I wished that the lyrics of that song were true, that hope existed beyond death. When she sings the words, I almost believe them.

A lump forms in my throat. "Your voice is beautiful."

"Thank you." The woman shifts and then smiles. It's a huge relief.

"What's your name?"

She hesitates briefly. "Catriona."

"Catriona. I'm Gunnar Graves. Look, can I walk you back to the village?"

She draws back, shaking her head.

I take a step forward, but Catriona wheels around. She disappears into the trees, leaving me behind, still filled with the song, but at the same time, empty and alone.

I'M UP EARLY AGAIN THE NEXT

morning, and for the first time in I don't know how long, I want to stay in the village. I'm exhausted, of course. Sleep was hard to come by last night, mostly because I kept thinking about Catriona. It was curiosity that kept me awake.

Curiosity and something else.

I sigh in frustration. Why do this to myself? Her face will never appear in my morning list of potential spouse candidates, and the machines will only let me delay a couple more times before they choose a life partner for me.

Even if I could choose Catriona, how would she react when she found out I've got a metal heart and who knows what other tech hiding under my skin? The painful reminder of what I am inside haunts me as I step onto the circular platform in the floor. The text appears in my field of vision, reinforcing the truth of what I am and who's in control.

CORONARY IMPLANT POWER LEVEL: 99%.

CHARGING . . .

CORONARY IMPLANT POWER LEVEL: 100%.

My gut churns. I'll see that message every morning for the rest of my life. Eventually, I suppose there will be another person standing beside me, somebody who will know the truth. Will the machines swear them to secrecy? Or will I be a test case to see how other humans react to the news that someone they know is a cyborg?

After my scan, I wash my face, dress, and walk outside. I don't fully realize how tired I am until the sun hits my face. The weariness of another sleepless night sets in. I stretch in the early morning light, trying to wake my muscles. The cool air helps. A few sleepy villagers shuffle down the street toward the cafeteria. That seems as good a place as any to kill some time.

I walk across the village to the dining hall, which sits on the other side of the open market area. I try not to look at the air mage keeping vigil on the platform as I walk past it, but I can't help wondering if the machine is logging my behavior this very moment. For me to enter the common area and eat breakfast with everybody else is certainly a statistical anomaly.

I tear my thoughts away from the air mage as I stroll into the cafeteria. It's a long hall decorated like most other buildings in the village—synthetic materials made to resemble wood, except with no blemishes, knots, or gnarls. Tall green plants sit perfectly spaced along the walls, surrounding rows of tables. Soft acoustic music drifts throughout the room, probably filled with subliminal messages we can't actually hear. Against the far wall is a long window, on the other side of which is a kitchen operated by a complicated staff of machine arms, tubes, spouts, and a variety of other contraptions.

Most of the seats are empty this morning; the cafeteria never closes, and I've long since learned to come at times when I'm least likely to interact with anybody.

I move to the kitchen window and absentmindedly place my hand on the sensor pad. "I'll have a blueberry waffle, pork sausage, and a strong mimosa. And what do you say we change the music?" My 'order' is nothing more than a cynical joke, as pointless as trying to escape. Like most things in the village, breakfast never changes.

Moments later, a tray appears on the conveyer belt from the far side of the window and slides toward me. The breakfast might look like bacon, eggs, and toast, but it's all made from other things—plants, beans, synthetic compounds formulated for perfect nutritional balance. I'm not sure how it works, but the only honest-to-God food on my plate is the sliced orange. Even the coffee is an illusion—eternally decaf, whether you want it that way or not.

All of it tastes pretty decent if you don't think about it too hard, but I preferred the scavenged stuff we shared in the Human Alliance. We never had much, and sometimes it left me feeling hungrier than I had been before. But it was real, and we all ate together, knowing that every meal might be our last.

I take my tray and grab a seat near the corner of the room, facing a large window that looks out into the village. Outcasts like Catriona usually stay in the market area in the center of town. They're mostly here for frivolous trade, selling whatever handmade materials they can manage to produce in exile. Sometimes I wonder if the machines allow the outcasts into the village to remind the rest of us that our lives could be worse. We could be isolated, alone.

"Mind if I join you, Gunnar?"

The voice startles me. I look over my shoulder and see my neighbor Michael. He's smiling, as usual, though I notice bags under his eyes. The machines matched him with a woman about a year ago and I know they just had a baby, but I can't remember the name of his wife or child.

"Uh, sure." I make an awkward gesture to the empty chair beside me, as if it's mine to give.

"Thanks." Michael nods and plops down. His tray is identical to mine, down to the amount of eggs on his plate.

I take a bite and wonder if I'm supposed to speak next. Back in the Human Alliance, I never had a problem talking to anybody. If anything, I was extroverted, though that might have been because our circumstances strengthened the bonds between us. Maybe there weren't any atheists in foxholes, but there weren't any strangers, either.

I swallow my eggs and try to think of the least stupid thing I can say. "So, how's the little . . . uh . . ."

Great start, Gunnar. You forgot whether they had a boy or a girl.

Michael raises a hand to cover his mouth while he chews. "*He's* great." He nods a few times, smiling as he swallows. "We're not getting a ton of sleep, of course. I actually meant to stop by your place sometime soon and ask whether he was keeping you up."

He gives a shrug and a half smile. "Not that I could do anything about it. That kid screams pretty loud sometimes."

I shake my head. "No, haven't heard anything, but I'm a heavy sleeper." I cast a quick glance out the window. I wonder if Catriona will be in the village today.

"So where did you live?" Michael asks. "You know, before."

I pause. He's about to regret that question. My unit made our last stand a few miles from here—right in the center of Utah—but our fight began somewhere far away. "I'm from Atlanta."

"Oh." Michael's face goes stark white. He almost drops his fork. "I'm really sorry about . . . you know . . . That must've been horrible."

I answer with a quick nod to show I appreciate his condolences. Despite my preference to be left alone, I feel bad for him. He's trying to make friendly conversation and there's no way he expected that answer from me. It's extremely rare to come across somebody who survived what happened in Atlanta.

For his sake, I change the subject. "Are you having fun with the little guy? I guess he's still too young to play with, really."

The tension melts off Michael's face as he takes another bite. He's eating fast, probably so he can get back to his family.

"It's incredible, man," he says with an earnest smile. "He laughed for the first time the other day and it was one of the greatest moments of my life."

"Yeah?" I raise my eyebrows.

Michael takes a drink of coffee. "Funny thing is, I didn't expect it at all. He was upset and I couldn't think of what else to do, so I trilled my tongue like I was a high-pitched jackhammer, and he started giggling. I did it again and kinda shook the pillow he was lying on, and he laughed even harder. When they do that, there's nothing better."

Despite my best efforts, I feel a strange touch of envy. It must be nice to find that kind of joy and fulfillment, especially in a world like this one. I turn to look out the window again, mostly because I don't want him to see my face.

And there she is.

My heart stops at the sight of Catriona pushing a wooden cart piled high with blankets. Somehow she makes those terrible clothes she has to wear look incredible, and despite having a shoddy wheelbarrow—as if the machines couldn't easily give her a better one to use—she moves with effortless grace.

"When are you going to get yourself matched up?" Michael asks. "Has to be pretty soon, right? Then you can have one of your own and we'll swap dad stories."

"Yeah," I say, but I keep my gaze out the window as I stand up. I've barely touched my food and I know I'm being kind of a jerk, but I can't seem to wait another second to go talk to her. "Right, dad stories. Pretty soon, maybe. I don't know. Hey, good talking to you, Michael." I pick up my tray and walk away.

"Likewise," he calls after me. "See you later, Gunnar."

Within seconds, I've tossed my tray back onto the belt and whisked out the door.

The village is busier now; most people are up and starting their days. Mothers and fathers herd their children toward the cafeteria for breakfast. The blacksmith's hammer has awoken and clinks rhythmically over the sound of people greeting each other and talking about whatever they talk about. The blacksmith is more of an artist than anything; most of her items are for games or decor. I've never visited her shop. *I wonder if I should get Catriona a gift to show her I mean no harm.*

An older couple strolls by, heading in the direction of the market. They each hold copies of machine-approved books, though I can't make out the titles. They're engaged in a conversation and don't appear to notice me, which makes them the perfect people to follow. I'd rather she didn't see me coming.

Catriona's stand is a wooden booth—hardly wide enough for her to occupy—that's positioned on the opposite side of the market. When I reach the stand, Catriona is handing a stack of blankets to a woman with brown hair and two children tugging on her clothes. Their transaction done, the woman relents and allows the kids to pull her away. She doesn't say goodbye to Catriona, nor does Catriona seem to expect it. But she still offers them a warm, unreciprocated smile. Then she looks down at her counter and starts refolding a few other blankets the woman must have been considering.

I've charged headlong into android fire with nothing but half-empty sidearms and prayers. I wasn't afraid during those times. So why am I nervous now?

"Catriona?"

"Yes?" She looks up at me blankly.

"I'm Gunnar. We met yesterday."

She gives a nod. I linger, not knowing what to say. Catriona returns her attention to her folding. "If you're not going to buy a blanket, sir, I need to get back to work."

I pull back in genuine confusion. She's acting like I'm a stranger.

Out of the corner of my eye, I notice a group of people walking past us. They behave as if they're not watching and listening, but I've spent enough time observing people from a distance to know the difference. It's no secret that I'm the village enigma. Talking to an outcast in the middle of the market is bound to turn a few curious heads.

"Sorry to bother to you." I take a few steps back, watching her work, hoping she will look up at me again. When she doesn't, I disappear into the crowd. Normally I would be in the woods by this time, but the sleepless night is taking its toll. Right now, all I want is to go to bed.

"Gunnar."

I jolt awake, the late afternoon light streaming through my window. *The voice in my head again. Where did it come from?*

I take a few moments to collect myself, then get out of bed and head for the shower in the corner of my hut. Since I skipped it this morning, I take my time washing off, then step out and grab a towel from the rack.

Thankfully, Sheila stays quiet as I pull on my clothes, grab my canteen, and head out the door. By now, most of the villagers' assigned jobs are finished for the day, so they're engaging in whatever approved community activities they prefer. I look between the huts and see an outdoor yoga class in an open green space. People sit at picnic tables, some drinking tea, others with their noses in books.

I keep my head down and walk fast, hoping and praying nobody will stop me.

When I reach the market, I note that Catriona's stand is empty.

Maybe she will be at the river again. I manage to avoid looking at the air mage as I pass the platform. I don't want to think about any of it today.

Niko finds me as soon as I reach the woods. He gets a little mad when I'm not out here first thing in the morning, and today he lets me know by running up and down my body a few times before nipping me on the shoulder.

"Ow!" I say, making more of a show of it than is warranted. Niko's playful bites never come close to breaking the skin. "I know, buddy. I know. Today's a little different, okay? We're going back to the water."

It doesn't take long to get to the river, probably because I'm walking much faster than usual. When we finally reach it, I'm greeted by shining wet rocks, tall trees, and sparkling clear water, but no sign of Catriona. Normally, the landscape and the cool air would invigorate me. But today, I'm disappointed that she's not here.

I shuffle to the edge of the river and sit on the bank. It's a beautiful spot. Behind me is a thick forest of green pines, but on the other side of the water, the forest shifts to mostly yellow aspen trees. It's as if the river is a boundary between two worlds.

Niko runs down my arm and starts to lap up the water. I sit and watch, my attention alternating between him and the yellow forest beyond. Despite years of patrolling these woods, I've never had a reason to cross the river. The water has always been something of a border to me, the last place I visit each day to get a cool drink after long hours spent trying to cast fire.

The moment I stand, Niko finds his way to my shoulder. Together, we start across the water.

I spend the afternoon exploring with no objective, no destination in mind. Niko entertains me by gliding from tree to tree. Every time I think he's run off for the day, he reappears, sailing through the air and landing on my shoulder.

Eventually, the night creeps across the sky, dragging a billion stars behind it. Growing up so close to Atlanta city lights, I was never able to spot more than a few. Without the light pollution, I can see more stars than I could have ever imagined.

I come to a small clearing, a grassy pad with a better view of the sky. Despite the cool evening, fireflies dance in the surrounding trees. I've never noticed them anywhere in the woods before tonight, maybe because I wasn't looking. I typically watch the ground in front of me when I walk. It's a good way to avoid stepping in anything bad.

But for the first time, I realize what I've been missing, the wonder and the beauty taking place above my head. Maybe I should look up a little more often.

The ground in the clearing is uneven; there must have been a river here at one time. The grass slopes down to create a sort of tunnel that disappears ahead of us beneath trees that arch over it like guardians. But what this small area lacks in trees, it makes up for in flowers. Petals in shades of white, yellow, purple, and red surround us, the colors vibrant even in the fading light. The quiet and the starlit colors make it feel like a sacred place, untouched by the terrible war that ripped apart the rest of the world.

I stand there for a long time before I reluctantly turn to leave.

Something on the ground catches my eye. It's a wildflower—a white dandelion—but a radiant beam surges across the stem. The flower is the only of its kind in the grass. The other flowers are tall and regal with brilliant colors; the dandelion is low to the ground. But for an instant, it glows as if baptized in starlight.

I bend down to pluck it from the earth. The glow is gone. The stem feels thicker than I expected, stronger, but it releases from the earth with ease at my touch. I study it for a few seconds, then tuck it into my pocket before heading back.

05

FOR GENERATIONS, SCIENCE AND MAGIC APPEARED TO OCCUPY OPPOSITE ENDS OF THE INTELLECTUAL SPECTRUM. THE MORE ARDENTLY YOU PURSUED ONE, THE MORE DISDAIN YOU SHOWED FOR THE OTHER. WHAT WE NEVER REALIZED WAS THAT IT WASN'T A SPECTRUM AT ALL, BUT MORE LIKE A PYRAMID IN WHICH SCIENCE AND MAGIC—IN THEIR HIGHEST FORMS— MET AT THE APEX TO UNLOCK THE GREATEST POWER.

— DR. MYLES BROOKS, HISTORIAN

THE VILLAGE IS QUIET BY THE

time I reach my hut. I place my palm against the glowing pad next to the door and it slides open. Dim light from hidden bulbs fills the room as I approach the platform.

Sheila's voice startles me. "Good evening, Gunnar. Satisfactory local breeding matches are currently available. Would you like to begin the mate-selection process?" Holographic images of women's smiling faces appear in the air. They're larger than before, as if somehow that's going to convince me to finally pick somebody.

"No." The answer snaps out of me.

"Your choice to postpone selection has been confirmed. You have one delay option remaining before a suitable mate is selected for you."

CORONARY IMPLANT POWER LEVEL: 95%.

I walk to the circular platform and stand in the center, wondering what it would be like to have another person watching me recharge my metal heart. When I was placed in this village, the machines assigned me a private hut like everyone else. I knew that would allow me to maintain my secret, at least until I was forced to select a mate. It made me wonder whether the women that were proposed as options for me had cybernetic parts, as well. It seemed unlikely, but everyone has secrets.

The light activates. As it starts to move up my legs, a loud sound grabs my attention.

Outside, somebody screams.

I rush out the door of my quarters. Several of the other villagers dash out of their huts and into the street, all wearing confused expressions.

The screams come from the hut next to mine, the one belonging to Michael and his wife. My first thought is that the baby is sick or injured; I'm pretty sure I hear a child's cries, but there's more. Michael and his wife are yelling. Screaming.

A war machine—not a silver-fleshed mage, but one of the standard, metal-plated, non-magical units that the Human Alliance called Andy— emerges from the hut holding a metal box. A muffled cry escapes the box and my blood runs cold.

Are they taking Michael's baby?

In the doorway, Michael is holding his wife as she struggles against his grip. His face is red and I can see tears welling in his eyes. The woman's name still escapes me, but I recognize her. Almost every day, she and Michael push a wicker stroller through the village, their faces beaming with pride. I rarely see the child; it's typically surrounded by admirers.

"Stop, please!" she cries out. "Please! No!" The infant wails louder from the box, responding to its mother's call.

Michael lets go of his wife and charges the android, his face wild with anger, as if the sound of his baby has broken his better judgment.

He makes it a few steps before four other villagers grab him and wrestle him to his knees. He tries to fight back, his voice wild with fury and desperation.

As I watch, a fire ignites inside me. I know better than anybody how much a child needs its parents. It's almost as if I can feel the pain in the infant's soul.

The screams of the mother, the shouts of Michael, the cries of the baby—they take me back to the night my unit fell to the machines. I've relived those dark moments so many times, but the emotion is more visceral now, as if the same terror is being played out in front of my eyes.

My blood boils and my muscles tremble. My fists clench and before I know it, my body dashes toward the silver devil that has stolen away a mother's most precious gift.

My skin burns and my speed increases, as if an energy is pulsating beneath my flesh.

And it feels *right*.

None of the villagers try to stop me; I'm not sure they notice what I'm doing. My body moves without thought, the rage blinding, my steps quick. A single idea floods my mind and drowns out all else.

Save the child.

"Stop!" I shout when I'm a few feet away from the war machine.

The Andy turns and stares at me with glowing red eyes, still clutching the box with powerful metal hands. The android is imposing, but that does nothing to stifle my resolve or my momentum; I couldn't stop myself if I tried.

A powerful metal arm swings and pounds my face like a wrecking ball. My feet fly out from under me. I hit the ground, tasting blood.

Get up, Gunnar. The energy builds inside my body. I recognize the pain, but it doesn't bother me. Somehow, it makes me stronger.

I roll and come to a knee. The war machine places the box on the ground. Gears buzz as its metal thigh opens and an apparatus holding an automatic pistol whirs out. The android draws the gun and points it at me.

"No!" My hands rise, but not to protect myself. I'm kneeling and unarmed, but my movement feels more like an attack.

Without thought, my arms extend and my fists come together. As they do, the inner fire explodes up from my torso and down the length of my arms.

An energy bursts from my hands. The brightness is blinding and the heat is so intense I think I'll be burned alive.

It's over before I know what's happened. The light disappears. My entire body is shaking.

I stand.

In front of me, the android is still. A gaping hole burns in the center of its torso, large enough that I can see through it.

The Andy's red eyes go dim. It crumbles to the ground with a loud thud, its body deactivated.

White text appears in my field of vision.

CORONARY IMPLANT POWER LEVEL: 75%.

The other villagers have been perfectly still, mouths agape, totally silent. Slowly now, they start to move toward me, their widened eyes studying me. I back away.

The mother rushes to the box and drops to her knees. She slides back the grated metal lid, tosses it aside, and lifts the crying baby out of the box. The child's screams reduce to a whimper as she cuddles it tightly to her chest. Michael joins her, embracing them both.

I can't move. I can't breathe. The burn is gone, but every hair on my body is standing on end. That blast was unlike anything I've ever experienced.

It was . . . magic.

"How did you do that?" somebody to my right asks.

A moment later, they're all talking at once, all coming at me, one voice on top of the other.

". . . like one of the mages . . ."

"Incredible. How long have . . ."

"They'll come for you . . ."

". . . all of us in danger . . ."

"Seriously, what are you hiding from . . ."

I turn my head from side to side as the people draw closer. They're scared; it's evident on their faces, but I can actually feel their fear pressing into my mind, sending my entire body into high alert.

"Stay back, please." I turn in circles. I'm afraid that whatever I just did will happen again and I won't be able to control it. Somebody might get hurt.

Fear and confusion flood my body, churning like a storm at sea.

And the anger remains, pulling at me like an undertow.

I need to escape. I lower my head and hurry through the crowd. The villagers move out of my way, perhaps in fear, but they continue calling after me.

I begin to run toward the woods.

The shouts of the people stick with me as if they're embedded in my mind, haunting me, hounding me. So many questions. So much confusion. *Was it fire? Did you know you could do that? What will the machines do about this?*

But more than anything, they're asking the same thing I'm asking myself.

What are you?

I dodge back and forth between the trees as I rush through the pine forest. I can almost sense the cold metal fingers at my back as I run. Doubtless the machines know that one of their own was destroyed. If nothing else, the air mage definitely saw what happened. I didn't stop to see whether it had activated itself in response.

When the lights and sounds of the village are far behind me, I finally stop. Cold sweat covers my body. My legs burn and I'm gasping for air after maintaining an all-out sprint for so long. I double over immediately, putting my hands on my knees and feeling like I'm going to throw up. Whether it's from the exertion or the fact that I just conjured a magical blast of energy, I'm not sure.

Maybe I should call for Niko. He seems to know whenever I enter the woods, even if it's not in the same place.

But I don't want him anywhere close to me. The villagers were right. I have no idea how I destroyed the war machine, but I know one thing for certain—others will come for me.

A loud rumble overhead drowns out my thoughts. My head snaps up.

A massive wind pushes through the treetops, causing the leaves to rustle loudly. Branches crack beneath the force of the gale, but there are no signs of clouds, no brewing storm.

My muscles seize. I've heard that sound before. I know what's coming before I see it.

The air mage appears in the sky above the trees, its silver flesh shining in the moonlight beneath billowing robes. Its arms are outstretched, commanding the wind to carry its body through the night, though it's not alone. The winds also bring a platoon of war machines soaring behind the mage, each armed with a heavy assault rifle, all trained on my position.

Before I make it four steps, the trees in front of me collapse on themselves as if an invisible wall has crashed down upon them, creating a mountain of broken wood.

"Get down!" A woman's voice, but before I can see who it is, a rush of air pounds the earth around me. The ground thunders. Trees shatter with deafening snaps.

I dive to the dirt, shielding my eyes from the splinters that fill the air and coughing from the thick cloud of dust.

When the debris settles, I realized I'm trapped—an impassable mound of destroyed pines blocking every escape. The air mage and its platoon land in front of me.

Behind me is the woman who called out to warn me.

Catriona.

My heart stops. What is she doing here? Where did she come from? She's not ten feet away but she isn't looking at me. Her eyes are locked on the machines. I've never seen her this way. She looks ready for battle.

I stand and turn to face my death. I remember the feeling that welled up inside me when I unleashed fire in the village. Will the power come to me again? I attempt to summon the flames, trying to remember the rage and spark that burned inside me. It happened so naturally before, almost as if I didn't have a choice. It didn't feel like I created it; more like I channeled it.

When I reach down inside myself, searching for the energy, the burning, it isn't there.

I widen my stance and clench my fists anyway. I can't call forth the power right now, but the air mage doesn't know that. Maybe I can intimidate it or at least bargain to have it let us go.

If Catriona is afraid, she doesn't show it. She focuses on the mage. Blood trickles down her right arm. She must have been cut by one of the flying slivers of wood. Her left hand touches the wound, bloodying her fingers, which appear to twitch in anticipation.

The wind dies down. The air mage's robes settle as it steps forward. Behind it, the platoon of androids raises their assault rifles in perfect unison, the barrels pointed at both Catriona and me.

I prepare for the air mage to attack, though I remember that using magic drains a large amount of energy for the war machines. My attention flicks to my own power level reading, still located at the bottom of my vision. *60%.* My cybernetic implant has never drained so fast. I can't remember the last time it got below 80.

Regardless, the machines are driven by efficiency. I heard that once—before I was placed in the village—the air mage lifted a would-be rebel into the air and choked the life out of him in front of everyone. Bullets would've been more efficient, but the purpose of the magic was clear—it was shock and awe, an act to remind the rest of the village of the machines' awesome power.

Out here, with no other witnesses, they'll probably just gun me down. Gun Catriona down.

I grit my teeth and wait for the shots to come, frantically trying to think of some way to save Catriona from destruction.

But instead of opening fire, the air mage walks forward, its glowing eyes appearing to regard me. "Gunnar Graves."

The sound of my name sends tremors through my body. The voice of the air mage is deep, but it's a good mimic of human speech. Still, the soullessness is evident, carrying the slightest hint of digitization.

"Let her live," I say. "She didn't do anything that broke your laws. Move her to another village. Everybody will believe you killed us both."

I steal a glance at Catriona. Her lips move a little, though I can't hear what she's saying. Her bloodstained fingers continue to twitch.

"Your death has not been ordered," the air mage says, stopping about twenty feet away from us. "The destruction of an android is a punishable infraction, though you have revealed an opportunity that might make it worthwhile."

The same time I realize its meaning, I also understand that I'm not really talking to the air mage, but to the hive mind. The Human Alliance was fairly certain that the machines were all wirelessly connected to the central database, the true home of the AI. In a way, I'm speaking to all the war machines at once. This unit knows everything that any of them know.

"You're referring to my powers." I puff out my chest a little, hoping to keep up the facade that I know how I did it.

The machine's posture does not change. "According to our database, you are the first human to achieve this ability. This is a development for which we have been monitoring for a long time, in our efforts to benefit the human race. We are connected, Gunnar Graves, surely you understand that. You would not be alive without our assistance."

My implant. I cringe. I wonder if the machine will say it out loud. If Catriona is to know, I would want her to hear it from me first. Although that doesn't seem to matter much now.

"What do you want?" I ask. Whether machine or man, there's always a self-serving motivation.

The air mage lifts its chin. "Our objective is to support the progression of the human race by nurturing your power."

"You want to help me be *more* powerful?"

"Preliminary readings suggest that you cannot recreate the effect again, but even if you could, our forces would defeat you soundly while sacrificing a statistically negligible amount of units. But there is another way, a function you could serve. There is still discontent among your kind, but you may be the key to final, lasting peace. We can put you in that position, Gunnar Graves."

"If I serve you," I say.

In the moonlight, I could almost swear I see the air mage smirk. "Humanity has long proven that it is not equipped to self-govern. Without our intervention, the world would have fallen. Now, there is no unnecessary death, no disease, no hunger. Humanity created us to mold a better world, and we achieved that objective. Do not think of this proposal as serving us. You will serve yourself, your own kind, by promoting the true order, the logical choice."

The air mage lifts off the ground, hovering toward me in a small but clear display of power. "But you should also understand that—if you agree to our terms—there shall be no other human above you. We know you do not prefer the life you now live. Your dissatisfaction has been well documented. I offer you a new life. You can create whatever reality pleases you the most. Live where you like. Eat what you want. Choose whatever . . . *mate* you prefer, or none at all."

The air mage comes close enough that I can feel the air move beneath its hovering form. "Humans cannot be their own gods. But a king . . . that is a different matter. You shall be a ruler unlike anything the world has ever seen. You need only to accept."

I don't bother asking what happens if I refuse. I notice that Catriona has stopped moving her lips and is watching. The memory of the power surging through my body comes to mind. For that instant, I felt more alive than ever before. If the machines share the secrets to elemental magic with me, I might feel that power again.

And Catriona would be safe, outcast or not.

I catch her eye, but she looks down, then briefly back up at the mage.

There is something about her posture as she stands steadfast, unmoving, that fans the flames of courage and truth inside me. I'd rather die than bow before the machines.

"I choose Sheila," I announce to the air mage. If I'm going to die anyway, I might as well enjoy my last moments.

The air mage does not respond and I wonder if somewhere, there's a computer buffering, running an untold number of algorithms as it tries to make sense of what I've said.

"That's right, Windy," I say, using the code name the Human Alliance assigned to war machine air mages. "Sheila, the voice from my room. Nobody understands me like her. Put her in a body kind of like yours, but, you know, better. No offense. I'm sure you do alright. You know, with that fancy air magic, I bet you're one amazing juggler."

The air mage lifts a hand and a wall of air hammers my torso. My body flies back toward the mountain of trees, but before I slam into it, another invisible force catches me. The mage's hand still extended, it lifts me up into the sky. The machine is toying with me. Air tightens around my neck, cutting off the oxygen.

And though I know it shouldn't be possible, I swear I see rage on the android's synthetic face.

There is a flash of movement as Catriona dives at the air mage. The war machine doesn't see it coming. She knocks it off-balance, disrupting its magic for an instant.

I fall like a rock and hit the ground in a heap. Adrenaline lifts me to my feet in time to see the mage hit Catriona with a blast of air that sends her reeling. The other androids train their rifles on her.

I let out a cry and slam my hands together, praying that the fire will come.

But instead of flames, the roots at the androids' feet reach up like brown tentacles, pulling at their legs. The machines try to jerk away, but the vegetation grows fast. The twisted roots appear to grow thicker and more powerful.

Within seconds, the platoon is restrained in woody vines that jerk them to their knees and restrain their arms, rendering them incapable of firing their rifles.

The air mage watches in disbelief as its soldiers are ripped apart by vegetation.

A loud screech sounds overhead, lifting my attention to the sky. Above me, a large black bird moves like a missile, diving straight for the air mage. The mage doesn't appear to see it, instead casting more air magic in an attempt to free its fellow machines.

When the bird reaches the treetops, it explodes into a burst of black feathers.

I stand immobile, trying to understand what has happened. Was the bird shot? Why did it fly at the mage in the first place?

But the feathers fall fast, too fast, and in a heartbeat, I realize they aren't feathers at all. They're insects, moving like a black cloud.

The air mage turns at the last second, but it's too late. Insects swarm its body, coating its silver flesh. The mage flails and tries to utter an incantation, but the words are stifled by insects filling its mouth.

I sprint to Catriona and slide to my knees when I reach her. "Catriona, are you alright?"

After a moment, she nods and slowly sits up.

Relieved, I look back to the air mage. The insects are devouring its silver skin. Seconds later, the black cloud lifts away from the war machine, its robes and flesh gone, leaving only a metal exoskeleton that tumbles over.

I brace myself for an attack as the swarm moves toward us, flying high at first, then descending slowly.

Before it reaches us, the swarm lands and becomes a black mass writhing on the ground. I watch as two distinct legs form, followed by arms and a head. The insects meld together, thousands of bodies becoming a single pale flesh.

It's a woman.

She's tall, with green eyes and a mess of blond hair. A layer of black feathers covers her body except her face, arms, and the bottoms of her legs. "Hello, Gunnar Graves."

"How do you know my name? What is going—?"

"Why do you use the bugs so much?" says a gruff voice behind me. When I look, I would almost swear that a tree is marching at us, except it's in the shape of a man. He's a good six inches taller than me, but his skin is made of bark. He wears green camouflage pants and a black short-sleeved T-shirt. At first, his hair looks like branches and leaves. But as he moves forward, it lightens to blond hair. His green eyes are the same shade as the woman's.

"Because I enjoy how it creeps you out, dear brother," the woman says.

The man pulls a small device out of his pants pocket and points it at us. It emits a few beeps, then a small display flashes green.

"They're clean," the man says. "No outgoing signals."

The machines aren't tracking me? It doesn't make any sense, but I decide to file the question away for later.

"Let's go, Lark," the man says. He regards Catriona and me. "More will be here soon and we don't need a longer fight. You two okay to run?"

I hesitate. Just because these two destroyed the machines doesn't mean we'll be any better off with them. During my days with the Human Alliance, I heard rumors of people who had turned to dark rituals in an attempt to seize power . . . blood magic, summoning demonic forces, crazy stuff like that. For all I know, I might be better off with Andy.

"Gunnar."

The voice from my nightmare speaks in my head again, clearer than ever. It sounds young, innocent, but strong. It's not just talking to me. It's *calling* me. The energy ignites inside my body. I look at my hands and see a flash of the white fire.

I look at the tree man, then at Catriona. She hesitates, then nods. It's all I need to see.

We run.

06

AI'S PRIME DIRECTIVE WAS SIMPLE—PROTECT MANKIND AT ALL COSTS. MAYBE THE GENIUS WHO WROTE THAT LINE OF CODE COULD HAVE BEEN MORE SPECIFIC. MACHINES IDENTIFY PROTECTION AS THE EFFORT TO KEEP AN OBJECT RUNNING AT AN OPTIMAL LEVEL AS EFFICIENTLY AS POSSIBLE. THAT'S FINE FOR A SMARTPHONE, BUT IT'S NEVER BEEN HOW HUMANS CHOOSE TO LIVE.

— RYAN MILTON, DOCUMENTARIAN

CATRIONA AND I RUSH THROUGH

the woods, following the tree man. I look over my shoulder for his accomplice, but she's not there. I glance up to see if she transformed into a bird again so she can watch for pursuing machines from the sky. I don't see her, but after what I just witnessed, I'm not sure that means anything.

The man leads us through the woods for what seems like an hour until we reach a place where the trees clear away. A small open area and a dirt path separate us from a lake so large that I can't see the far side of it. The night air grows cold. Wind rushes through the surrounding pines and sends moonlight ripples across the water in gentle waves. I used to enjoy the breeze, but now I wonder if it means more air mages are coming. I may never feel the wind again without asking that question.

The man walks down the grassy bank and into the lake without breaking stride. When he's waist deep, he turns to face us. "Let's go."

I narrow my eyes at the murky water. I've never been a big fan of lakes as it is—too hard to see what's beneath me. It might be a good place to hide from the machines, but the idea of following a total stranger into such a vulnerable position gives me pause.

"What's wrong?" the man chides. "Can't swim?"

I shrug. "It's not that I can't. I just never really needed to. We didn't spend a lot of time hanging out by the pool during the war."

"You'll be alright," he says, "but nobody's forcing you. My mission was to bring you here. The rest is up to you." The man wades further into the water and disappears.

Catriona glances at me, then follows him in.

I expect the water to be cold and foggy, but when I sink below the surface, it's clear, and warmer than I anticipated. Thin rays of moonlight twinkle off small particles as they float by. Fish glimmer like diamonds in the faint light, some swimming close to inspect me. It feels like I could reach out and touch them, all the different living colors. I'm surprised at how comfortable I am. Moving through the water comes easy, effortless, like I'm in space. In front of me, Catriona glides with surprising grace.

Ahead of her, I see the tree man at the opening of what appears to be an underwater cavern. He motions for us to follow.

My lungs burn by the time we reach the man. I fight the instincts telling me to turn back. I have no idea where I'm going or whom I'm following. Even if I can trust them, I'm a creature of the woods, not the water.

But instead, I steel myself and follow Catriona into the darkness.

As soon as we cross the threshold, the water above us glimmers blue. I swim to the surface and find myself inside a narrow, winding passage.

Glowing blue dots cover the low rock ceiling like millions of tiny lanterns, lighting our way forward. Many of the lights move back and forth, though only slightly. Bits of moss hang around them, reflecting the light, revealing the various contours of the ceiling.

No one says a word; there is only the gentle slosh of our strokes as we swim forward. I try to watch where I'm going, but I can't tear my eyes away from the wonder of it all.

We turn a corner and the stream opens into a pool. More of the blue orbs cover the domed ceiling, casting enough light to reveal a cavern not much larger than my living quarters. The wet rock walls glisten with the blue light.

To my left, the woman called Lark sits at the base of a tall stone staircase that leads out of the cave. Her feathers are gone. Now, green and silver scales cover most of her flesh. She lifts her brow. "Took you long enough."

"Where did you go?" the man asks her as Catriona and I follow him out of the pool.

"Had to make a stop." She stands and nods toward me. "Turns out this guy comes with an entourage."

Something small and dark rushes past her feet, moving in my direction. A jolt of exhilaration surges through me.

"Niko!" I say as my friend scampers over the rock floor. He reaches my shoes and runs up my leg, using his wet claws to move in circles around me, sniffing me all over. The fact that he's here sets my mind at ease, at least a little. If Niko trusts these people—whoever they are—maybe I can, as well.

Lark eyes him and smiles. "So he's a friend of yours?"

"This sneaky little thief who eats all my food and bites me when he doesn't get attention? Yeah, he's my best friend. How did he get here?"

"There's more than one way in," the stranger says. "C'mon. We have a lot to show you." He gestures to the stone staircase. Niko takes his normal place on my shoulder as we follow the man out of the cavern and into a long tunnel.

The dampness of the cave fades as our steps reverberate along the beige-colored walls. The blue orbs are replaced by torches that light our way. Except for the floor, the stone is rough and unfinished. The tunnel is small; the man hunches over as he walks to keep from scraping his head. A black line runs down the center of the ceiling; I assume it's meant to guide our path. Every so often, we pass a small opening on either side, but we continue to follow the line.

"What is this place?" Catriona speaks for the first time since the attack as she trails her fingers along the walls. I no longer see any trace of blood on her hands.

"It'll be easier to show you," Lark responds. A thick layer of scales still covers most of her body. The rest of us are all dripping wet, but she appears to be dry already, even her hair.

The tunnel slopes down and we walk for what seems like a mile. With every step, the air grows cooler, but never cold. It's refreshing. Invigorating. Somewhere ahead, I could almost swear that I hear music. It's barely audible, like a whisper in my mind, low enough that I can't quite grab the melody, though I know it's beautiful.

After several twists and turns, the tunnel opens into a large room.

My breath catches in my throat.

Catriona utters a small gasp.

The cavern is enormous. Did we actually swim down far enough that a place of this size could be hidden below the surface? It doesn't seem possible, but I can't deny the rows of great stone pillars before me, stretching from the smooth rock floor to the high ceiling. The paint on the walls has cracked over time, but there are traces of shining golds, reds, and blues, telling old tales of former glories. Despite the obvious age of the place, a clean smell drifts light on the air. It tingles my nose in a familiar way.

Incense. I haven't smelled it in years, but the sensation brings memories flooding back. My mother used to love it. The experience almost makes me feel as if she's here with me.

At the center of the room, a carved staircase rises up to a golden altar. A stone table sits empty, and behind it, the wall is painted as if exploding with light. Once I see it, I can hardly take my eyes off it.

In front of me, a woman emerges from the shadow of a pillar. She walks with the confidence and wisdom of a person who has seen many years, but she radiates with youthful energy. Her brown hair is pulled back and she wears light gray robes tied at the waist with simple brown fabric.

The music continues to play, a bit louder, but still too quiet for me to recognize it.

"Welcome, Gunnar and Catriona," she says. Her robe nearly touches the floor, hiding her steps as she moves. It looks like she's hovering off the ground. "You will be safe here, for now. The machines cannot locate us—this temple is protected by old stones and older power. I see that you already met Rowan and Lark. My name is Elisha."

"How do you know our names?" I ask.

"We have certain . . . talents among us. In fact," she says, "we've been calling out your name for a while. You probably thought the voices in your head were from your imagination, or perhaps diminishing mental capacity. That must have been troubling. I apologize. It was necessary to get your attention."

I cock my head, trying to piece it all together. "You're talking about magic?"

Elisha frowns in a way that suggests I've used the wrong word.

But she doesn't correct me.

My mind jumps to the possibilities, remembering how I used pure energy to destroy a war machine with my bare hands. These might be people who could help me harness my power.

Maybe even help me get revenge.

"How?" I ask Elisha, my eagerness growing. After all, I've tried to figure this out for years, and now, maybe it's finally in front of me. "How have you learned to use magic? What can you do? Can you help me do . . . whatever I did before?"

Elisha raises her hand in a gesture that tells me to slow down. "All in time, Gunnar, but there is quite a lot that must be undone first. You've walked a different path for a long time. To get where you want to go, you may first need to go backward."

Go back? How could I possibly go back? It took years of practice—of pushing away everything else in my life—to get to where I am.

But I don't want to argue, at least not out loud. "How do I do that?"

Elisha smiles in a way that says she knows I'm trying to manipulate her, but doesn't necessarily mind. There's a confidence about her that I can't help but admire. "You must recognize the place to which you need to return, or you will become as lost trying to go back as you became trying to go forward. You must understand the source for what drives you."

This is beginning to feel like one riddle after another. Why do wise people in robes insist on speaking in parables?

And where is that music coming from?

"Okay." I give a slow nod to show I'm willing to play along. "What is the source?"

"Something deeper," Elisha responds, "and far more powerful than the elemental powers the machines discovered. I'm not sure they could ever understand it, not really. It's an energy tied to the most ancient roots of life itself. Call it whatever you want—science, magic, the power of the angels. It is a guardian, and it has awakened."

"And who are you?" Catriona asks.

Elisha regards her with kindness. "We have been referred to by many names over generations. Perhaps the most accurate way to think of us is the keepers of the Breath, the stewards of an energy that moves through all life. We recognize the true nature of humanity, the place from where we come and of what we are capable. For that, you may think of us . . ."

Elisha pauses to look at me. "As Scions."

"I agree with you about one thing, Gunnar," Elisha says as we walk through the rock hallways of the underground temple. Niko rides on my shoulder, but Catriona declined Elisha's invitation for a tour of the temple. She said she was feeling unwell and asked for a place to rest, so Rowan and Lark showed her to an open room. I was a little concerned, but I guess I shouldn't be surprised; we have been through a lot in the past few hours.

The music continues to drift on the air, but I've given up trying to decide what it is, and I'm not going to ask. I'm not sure I'd get a real answer; Elisha would probably offer some vague response about the symphony of life.

The hallways in the main body of the temple are wider than the passage we followed in from the pool. I can't take my eyes off them. Fantastical figures from various religions and mythologies are carved and painted all along the smoothed rock. Many of the paintings tell stories as one image leads to the next. My parents believed it was okay to openly question God, so they never hesitated to teach me about other belief systems, legends, and folklore. As a result, I recognize many of the various deities depicted around me, the dragons and phoenixes, the serpents and griffins.

But other images I see are unfamiliar—humans wielding fire like a weapon, people ascending to the stars, and others turning invisible.

"What's that?" I ask, studying the pictures as we stroll by. "Are those all different types of magic?"

Elisha gives a knowing smile. "I don't like the word 'magic.'"

"Why not? Judging by what I saw in the woods, you Scions are pretty good at it."

Elisha returns her attention forward. "It's not the fault of the word. It never is. It's the way it's been corrupted. Since the beginning of time, people have spent their lives searching for it, journeying to distant lands, hunting for components, and poring over spell books in hopes of gaining power by harnessing the supernatural.

"Not that there's anything wrong with intense study." Elisha gestures to a room on her left. I gaze through the open doorway and see a small library. Wooden shelves filled with books line the rock walls. Most look old—spines cracked and edges frayed as if they've been read hundreds of times.

"So everybody wants to use magic for the wrong reasons . . . except you?" I ask. "The Scions are the ones who have always known better?" It's an aggressive question to ask someone whose people saved my life, but the idea seems arrogant. Why should *they* have magic, but no one else? It almost resembles the machines' logic.

Elisha leads me past the library. "Wielders of the Breath have existed since the beginning, but those who truly understood its secrets kept them mostly hidden. To know the Breath is to know why it should never be used for personal gain. Rather, its stewards—the Scions— waited for the right moment. But even they controlled mere traces of the potential energy."

We walk past another open door. The room inside is simple— stone walls and nothing in the way of decoration, but the Scions have converted it into a type of gym. A few sets of free weights occupy one corner of the room. Lark is there, bouncing on a large, padded mat and circling a heavy bag that hangs from the ceiling. She wears workout clothes instead of feathers or fur as she throws kicks and punches. Half the bag is covered with strips of duct tape.

Elisha stops as we watch Lark train. "Since the war machines discovered elemental abilities, the Breath seems to have awakened, unleashing far more power than was ever recorded in the ancient texts."

I scoff. "Maybe it should have shown up *before* the machines destroyed humanity."

Elisha stands with her hands behind her back. "Well, it wouldn't be much of a mystical power if we understood everything about it, would it?"

I don't take the bait. Part of me wants to accuse her of reciting fairy tales, but I can't deny the incredible things I saw in the woods. "How does it work, then?"

"Energy is required," Elisha says. "Just as the machines need abundant power to perform elemental magic, except our reserves aren't as limited. We draw upon the power of other living things."

I raise my eyebrows. "You mean like vampires?"

Elisha shakes her head. "Scions don't pull from any creature against its will. What we do is more like uniting with them. As long as we are close enough to other living things, as long as we stay connected, the Breath flows. Sometimes the energies given to us by other life-forms can amplify our powers. Sometimes they even tell us their secrets."

"Secrets? What secrets do animals have?" The moment I say it, I feel like a jerk. I have a bad habit of making sarcastic jokes when I'm nervous. Besides, I'm the guy whose best friend is a fuzzy little forest animal.

And I'd forgotten about Lark. But if she heard me, she gives no indication. She keeps her focus on the bag, though I can see her eyes shift to those of a cat.

My body freezes. I've seen her change before, of course, but the understanding that this might be a power that was given to her by another species somehow changes the experience. Does that mean she's encountered—and somehow earned the respect of—every animal she can change into?

Elisha resumes walking. I follow, but keep watching Lark for as long as possible. Right before I lose sight of her, Lark's hands shift to paws. She snarls and swipes at the bag. Her claws rip deep gashes in the red fabric, and white sand pours like blood from a gaping wound.

I shake my head in disbelief. "Okay, so this . . . Breath . . . is growing more powerful because of the machines."

"No." Elisha's voice is firm. "The power is as it has always been. It is Infinite; concepts of more or less don't apply. What's growing is our capacity to receive it, to channel it."

"To fight back." I choose my words carefully. If Elisha senses that I'm more interested in frying a fire mage than helping her holy crusade, I might get tossed out of here before I learn anything useful.

"If we use it only for war," she says, "we're no better than the machines."

"If not to fight back, then what's the point?"

Elisha grimaces. "Don't mistake me. There are battles worth fighting, especially now. The machines' ability to wield the elemental powers is growing. That's troubling enough, but we have reason to suspect they're trying to unlock the secrets of the life energies as well. We've seen them do things we hadn't thought possible for non-living organisms. If the machines learn how to bend the power of the Breath to their will . . ." She doesn't bother to finish the statement.

We approach another room, this one filled with plants of various colors and sizes. An array of UV lamps shines down on the lush vegetation. Rowan stands in the center of the room. Lines of green light emanate from the leaves and vines that surround him, feeding into his body. He channels the power to his open hand, which he holds above a small plant. A yellow flower grows rapidly beneath his palm.

"This is all impressive," I remark, "but the war machines have real firepower. I mean actual *fire*. Not to mention wind, electricity, ice, water, storms, and who knows what else? I don't think flower power and shifting into were-tigers is going to be enough to stop them."

Rowan locks eyes with me, his impressive biceps rippling with energy. The guy looks as if he could snap me like a twig.

Still, I don't break eye contact. They taught us never to show fear in the Alliance, and I've taken down larger opponents before. I'm not going to be intimidated by a florist. "No offense, big guy."

For a moment, I think he's about to charge and pound my face in. Can't say I would blame him.

Instead, Rowan huffs and returns to his gardening.

"The Breath is more powerful than you may think." Elisha ignores my rudeness. "Anything that involves living tissue may be possible—enhancement of physical attributes, healing, resurrection, levita—"

"Resurrection?" Could that really be possible? My mind races at the idea. Could I actually use this magic to see my family again?

Elisha nods almost casually, like she's chatting about the weather. "Death is a door that opens both ways."

"You can't be serious," I say, trying to manage my expectations.

"Well, it isn't without precedent, depending on your spiritual dispositions. Do you believe in God, Gunnar Graves?"

I wince. Memories flash through my mind—me sitting with my parents in the bunker as they tell stories of God by candlelight. I thought I had managed to forget most of them, but the details surface in my mind as if they had been beneath a thin layer of dust that was just blown away.

"I used to," I say, my thoughts still adrift.

"To believe in God is to believe in the existence of the supernatural. If you believe in that, anything is possible."

In the room, Rowan—his veins still radiating with green energy—bends over a wilting plant that's riddled with tiny holes, as if it's been blasted by a shotgun. Rowan runs his hand over a leaf. A vibrant green spreads over the plant, glowing as it heals.

My mouth drops open at the astonishing display of power. I gather myself and turn to Elisha. "What does any of this have to do with me?"

"There is power in you, Gunnar, but you know that already. You've known your whole life."

I shift my weight. "Yes, well, I'm not sure how much. Sorry to disappoint you, but I've been trying to cast a fire spell for almost a year. It's worked once, at the worst possible time, and I'm not sure I can do it again."

"The power inside you runs much deeper than that," Elisha says. "But you need training, preparation. Your resolve will be tested."

I can't help the grin on my face as I raise my eyebrows. "Training? Do I get a different colored belt every time I level up?"

The hint of a smile tells me Elisha doesn't take my dumb joke as an insult. "No belts, but you may ascend, if you allow yourself. The power will find you when you're ready . . . if you're ready . . ."

"You make it sound like I'm the chosen one."

Elisha's head snaps up. "Not at all. But there is enough power given to you to make a difference, if you are willing and that's what you choose to do."

I dare to let down my guard. Is it possible that she's right? "How could you know that I have the potential for so much power?"

"In your own way, you told us. You've been sending strong telepathic signals for some time. You probably didn't realize it."

"That's how you found me, isn't it?" The image of my attack against the android flashes in my mind. I see the burst of blinding white light.

"All who have the Breath inside them are connected. When you attacked the machine, you released a powerful signal. We all felt it. But it was the boy who found you."

I scrunch my face at her in confusion. "Boy? What boy?"

On cue, a small boy appears in the greenery behind Rowan, carrying a large metal bucket. Water spills over the rim. From the look of the kid, he's not quite a teenager. He has dark, curly hair. His frame is skinny, but not sickly, and he grips the bucket as if he can barely handle the weight. He wears a faded gray and blue hoodie that's way too big for him. His face and hands are stained with dirt. The kid hands the bucket to Rowan, then flicks his gaze to me.

"Hi, Gunnar." The whispered voice speaks in my mind again, clearer than ever.

I nearly stumble back at the realization.

"He has been reaching out to you for some time," Elisha says as the boy shuffles toward us, hands jammed in the pockets of his jeans. "But he couldn't find you until tonight. He said it felt like you were blocking him out, but you probably didn't know you were doing that, either."

I don't care if he is a kid, I glare at him as he approaches. "So I have you to thank for this rescue, huh?"

The kid watches me like he's sizing me up.

Elisha gestures toward him. "Taron's telepathic abilities are still developing, but he's already very powerful."

I release a deep breath and bend over so that I'm eye level with the kid, then lower my voice. "Well, I'm here now, so stay out of my head." I appreciate everything the Scions have done, but if they find out what's inside me, they may not feel so hospitable anymore. I know this kid can track me and speak into my brain, but I'm not sure if he can read my thoughts. If what Elisha said is true—that I was blocking him before—maybe I can keep it up, maintain my secrets until I figure out whether this place is really safe.

The kid trots back to Rowan as Elisha and I resume walking.

"This unit you've got going . . ." I ask, not really sure how I'm supposed to categorize this group of people. A rebellion? A militia? For all I know, it's a cult. "Do all of you have powers?"

"Not all of us," a scratchy voice says behind me.

I turn to see a man sauntering down the hallway in our direction. The sight of him sets my nerves on end. He's more machine than human, but what remains of his skin appears to belong to someone in his mid-forties who spent most of his life trying to kill himself with one substance or another. A short, patchy brown beard reaches across the human half of his face. He wears a trucker hat, but through the mesh sides I can tell his head is mostly metal. One eye is a glowing orb.

I can't help but gawk. I've never seen a person with so many implants. "You're . . ."

"A cyborg?" He barks a laugh. "Afraid so, but hold that secret for me, will you? Not everybody is as tolerant as I'm sure you are."

Elisha gestures at him with one hand. "Otis may not have mastered the Breath, but he is valuable in many other ways."

"Is that right?" I say, trying to act casual. I can't help but feel paranoid talking to so much tech, which I know makes me a massive hypocrite. "Like what?"

"Like hacking the war machines' primary comms channel," Otis says, his tone conveying both pride in his abilities and disdain for my question. "Sending them the all clear, that's what."

"The all clear?" I ask. "Why does that matter?"

Otis rolls his eyes. "Guess the Breath doesn't make you pass an IQ test first."

"Huh?"

Otis sighs. "They're machines, Sparky. They need commands to tell them what to do and what not to do. And if they receive a command that says, 'Hey, no need to drag your shiny metallic selves over to this area,' guess what they won't do?"

"Will that actually work?"

"It'll work." Judging by his tone, if I hadn't offended Otis before, I've done it now.

Elisha interjects. "We believe we might free some of the villages with this technology. If we can overthrow a localized group of machines and use their signal to hide what's happened, we may have a chance."

"Just missing one piece," Otis says.

"What's that?" I ask.

"The access code." Lark emerges from her room, sweating from her workout. Her hands are human again. "The channel is encrypted."

Rowan steps into the hall as well. He leans against the wall, staring.

I look at each of them, waiting for somebody to say more. "Okay, the access code . . . how do you plan on getting that?"

Otis narrows his eyes. "You ask a lot of questions."

"The point is," Rowan says, "it might make a big difference when the time comes to fight back."

I look at them all, one after another. "You think you can hack their communications, pull the wool over their electronic eyes?"

"Worth a shot," Lark says, "unless you'd rather go back to being a slave."

They're all watching me. Even Elisha seems to evaluate my every move. I don't like being the center of attention. In the village, I stood out on my own terms as a way of controlling my relationships with other people—hiding in plain sight, that sort of thing. I have no idea who these people are, except that they have crazy powers and they're surrounding me in their underground lair.

What choice do I have?

"And what type of magic is it that you think I can do?" I ask.

Elisha puts a hand on my shoulder. "That's what we intend to find out."

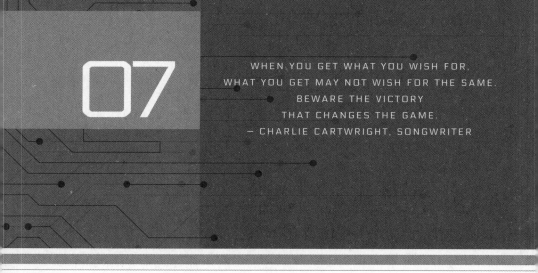

07

WHEN YOU GET WHAT YOU WISH FOR,
WHAT YOU GET MAY NOT WISH FOR THE SAME.
BEWARE THE VICTORY
THAT CHANGES THE GAME.
— CHARLIE CARTWRIGHT, SONGWRITER

ROWAN EYES ME LIKE A BOXER

trying to psych out his opponent, flexing his muscles and making me wonder if this guy ever wears sleeves. As if it weren't bad enough that, out here in the forest, we're literally surrounded by his allies.

Then again, I've never been in a fair fight before. Why start now?

Streaks of sunlight break through the canopy of leaves overhead. A cool morning breeze pushes through the branches, biting at my skin. My first day with the Scions started this morning when Rowan banged on the door of the room they gave me. It was tight quarters, containing nothing but a small wood-framed bed. The thin mattress was surprisingly comfortable, but I spent the entire night awake, staring into the darkness, replaying the events of the day and trying to remember how I summoned the magic.

I was physically and mentally exhausted by the time Rowan woke me to train, but I didn't protest. Magic or not, I won't give him the satisfaction of thinking he's tougher than me.

At least he gave me a change of clothes. For the first time in years, I'm not wearing the subdued earth tones of a war machine prisoner. Instead, I'm in boots, gray military-style pants, and a black T-shirt. The only thing I kept is the dandelion, which is in my pocket. The flower has never glowed again, but amazingly, it has not wilted since the night I picked it, the night my world turned upside down.

"I hear you don't think plants can be effective in combat," Rowan says. Judging from his muscles and his stance, he doesn't think he needs magic to beat me in a fight.

But I can hold my own. I've taken down Andy, though I was armed at the time.

Rowan waves his right hand. I keep my eyes on him, expecting an attack, but he remains a good twenty feet away.

Pain explodes in the back of my head. I stumble forward and whirl around to see that a branch has hit me from behind. My skull throbs.

"Could you sense that coming?" Rowan asks.

"No." I touch the hair on the back of my head, then look at my bloody fingertips. "Should I have?"

"We draw energy from living things. Vegetation is our most abundant source."

Another branch whacks me in the side of the head, knocking me to the ground. I consider myself a nature guy, but I would give anything for a chainsaw right now.

When I look up, Rowan towers over me, wearing a snarky grin. "So it might be a good idea not to be disrespectful."

Rowan reaches down with an open hand. It doesn't seem like a trap, though as far as I'm concerned, he's already hit me with two sucker punches. I take his hand anyway and pull myself up.

As soon as I regain my footing, Rowan takes a swing at me. My combat training from the Human Alliance takes over and I dodge, grateful that it's a human trying to hit me for once instead of an android or a tree. I duck low and send a quick jab to his side. It's like hitting a brick wall, but it feels good to get a solid shot in.

I roll away and pop up. "Are we having a straight up fight? Or are you going to make flowers spit pollen in my eyes?"

Rowan laughs, moves toward me, and throws another punch. We spar for a few minutes, testing each other, both of us managing to either block or avoid the other's blows. Most of the hand-to-hand combat training we did in the Alliance was for exercise and mental toughness; nobody expected to slug it out with a machine.

But I'm experienced enough to recognize when somebody's setting me up, which means I have to end this quick. I bounce back and send a fast kick to Rowan's midsection.

The flesh of his arm shifts to bark in a flash as he blocks my kick. Pain jolts up my shin. Rowan thrusts his other hand downward.

Roots shoot up from the ground, wrap my ankles, and pull me off my feet.

I hit the dirt facedown again, harder than before. "Cheater."

Rowan crosses his arms. "You think the machines are interested in a fair fight?"

As he talks, the roots stretch across my back, grinding my face into the ground.

"All right," I say, holding up a hand in surrender. The roots let go. Rowan's made his point.

I pull myself up and dust the dirt off my clothes. "I get it. So how do I—"

The roots hit my boots again, and I'm back on the ground.

Rowan laughs. "The trees don't seem to like you very much. That's probably not a good sign."

"Aren't you supposed to be helping me?" I taste blood in my mouth.

"Not my fault you're a slow learner."

Lark places one hand against the tree and grabs her bare foot with the other. She raises her leg straight up and pulls it against her face. My stretches are admittedly less impressive, but at least I'm able to bend over and touch the ground.

At her instruction, we both wear workout clothes—Lark in long pants and a yellow sports top, me in black shorts and a blue sleeveless T-shirt. My body is covered in scratches and bruises from my morning beatdown at the hands of Rowan and his floral friends. I can only imagine what Lark has in mind for my 'training.' At least she's barefoot, while I'm wearing sneakers. Maybe that will even the odds a bit.

My mind drifts back to Catriona. I haven't seen her since we arrived yesterday, but Rowan told me she decided to stay, at least for now. I'm not sure she has much choice. The machines are probably hunting her too.

"The Breath affects all living things," Lark says, interrupting my thoughts as she executes the same incredible stretch with the opposite leg. "If you can tap into that power, you can manipulate your body in ways you never thought possible."

I pull my right arm across my chest and pretend to stretch it. "Bigger, stronger, faster . . . that kinda thing?" My fingers instinctively go to the pocket with the dandelion, checking to ensure it's still there. During my training session with Rowan, I half expected the flower to climb up my shirt and try to choke me to death, but it remained neutral, which I appreciated. Maybe it's good luck.

Lark furrows her brow and points at my hand. I look down and realize that I've pulled the flower out.

"Is that for me?" she asks with a gleam in her eye.

Before I can shake my head, she snatches the flower out of my hand, moving so fast I hardly see it. "You want it back?" she yells as she runs. "You'll probably need some magic."

With that, she transforms. The workout clothes fall off her body as Lark shifts into an eagle. She clutches the dandelion in her talons as she flies away.

I take off after her, adrenaline pounding in my veins. For reasons I don't quite understand—or want to admit—she could have taken anything else away from me.

But not the flower.

I alternate between watching the sky and the ground in front of me, trying to track Lark's flight path without running face-first into a tree. The thick leaves overhead make it hard to keep my eyes on her, and the tree trunks force me to constantly dodge one way or another.

She seems to fly in a straight line, at least, but she's getting too far ahead. I increase my speed and stumble over a root. Is Rowan nearby? That would figure. I keep moving, sweat coating my body.

I lose sight of Lark, but keep sprinting, hoping that maybe I'll spot her again.

"C'mon, Gunnar!" she shouts from somewhere in front of me. "I'll even wait for you."

I dash toward the sound of her voice, my strength renewed by the idea of catching her.

After a few moments, I see Lark again. She's back in human shape, though feathers still cover most of her body. She crouches between the trees and twists the dandelion between her fingers like it's a toy.

"You sure don't want your flower back, do you?" Lark winks at me, places the stem of the flower in her mouth, and morphs into a mountain lion. She bounds away.

I chase her through trees and brush. I'm pushing myself as hard as I can, but my legs refuse to go any faster. The white text appears in my vision.

CORONARY IMPLANT POWER LEVEL: 60%.

I'm burning energy, pushing myself as hard as I can, but it seems hopeless. No matter what I do, Lark stays just close enough that I can see her, teasing me like it's a game. She could leave me in the dust if she wanted.

She reaches a large yellow tree and shifts into a monkey with blond fur. She clutches the flower in her hand as she climbs the trunk and disappears into the branches.

By the time I reach the tree, panting hard and with sweat dripping into my eyes, Lark's perched on a branch high up in the tree, large brown wings hiding her body. She doesn't appear to be the least bit tired.

"C'mon," I say from the base of the tree, my hands on my knees. "You're supposed to be teaching me, right? This isn't doing anything to help."

"There are *so* many different ways you could get this back from me right now," Lark shouts down at me.

Hot anger wells up inside me. I shout in frustration and jump, hurling myself against the tree. My fingers grasp for any type of hold in the bark. I try to dig in my feet and push myself up.

After a second, my body falls, my muscles exhausted and my body covered in scratches. I utter a curse.

Above me, Lark shakes her head. She shifts into a hawk and flies away, the flower in her talons.

My body aches as I sit cross-legged on the rock floor across from Taron. The room appears to be designated for meditation; there's nothing more than a simple brown rug and a small table with two candles to my right. It's probably supposed to create a calming environment, but my growing frustration makes me want to grab the candles and hurl them against the wall. After my earlier disasters with Rowan and Lark, I'd hoped telepathy training with the kid would be easier.

The third time he rolls his eyes at me, I know I was wrong.

Taron leans forward, pumping his dirt-stained hands like he wants to shake sense into me. He wears a thick black sweatshirt and jeans that look like they've been mended a hundred times. "Don't try to force words into my head. That won't work."

I bury my face in my hands. We've been at this for well over an hour, and I've made absolutely no progress. "You put words into mine."

"That's because I'm better at this than you," Taron informs me. "*Way* better. But this would go a lot easier if you stopped trying so hard to keep me out of your head. I could help you."

I answer him with a stern look. Sending one-way telepathic messages is one thing. Dropping my guard so the Scions can poke around in my thoughts is another.

For a scrawny little kid, there isn't an ounce of hesitation in him. Taron stares right back at me.

"You're like a baby trying to grab a chunk of banana," he says, "but you keep smashing it in your fingers."

I nod. "Okay, I get what you're saying . . ."

"You're like a calf who knows that he's supposed to eat, but doesn't realize he's standing in grass."

That one stung a little, but I push it down. *He's a kid, Gunnar.* "Right," I say, "so how do I—"

Taron taps against his left palm with his right index finger. "You're like a bug who keeps trying to fly through glass when he could go around it."

I grit my teeth and turn my head to the side, holding back an avalanche of choice words. "You done?"

Taron looks up at nothing, like he's trying to see if there are any other good insults hiding in his mind.

"Yep," he says, apparently satisfied that I'm aware of my place. "Let's try it again."

By the time I stumble back down the narrow stone corridor toward my room, I can't decide what I want to do first. My sore body screams for me to get in bed, my stomach grumbles for dinner, my clothes are soaked in sweat, and my pride suggests that maybe I should keep walking right out of the temple or whatever this place is called. I don't seem cut out to be much of a mage. Maybe I need a wand.

I pause a few steps as I reach the door of Catriona's room.

Her door is closed. *Maybe she's asleep.* I doubt it, though. The truth is that I really don't want her to see the failure all over me. Even if she couldn't see the bruises and scratches, I'm pretty sure that the shame is written all over my face. At least when I was trying to cast fire, the only creature around to see me was Niko. Falling short in front of Catriona seems worse.

I freeze at the sound of people talking inside the room. *Catriona and Elisha.* I'm about to turn away when something catches my ear. The thick door has muffled their voices, but the words are suddenly clear.

"You don't have to hide in here, Catriona," Elisha says. "Not from us."

Has Catriona been hiding? Hiding from what? I'm not proud of it, but I move closer to the door, curious to hear anything that could tell me more about the mysterious outcast woman.

Catriona is speaking. "I appreciate everything that all of you have done for us. I'm just not sure that . . ." Her voice trails off.

My ear presses against the wood and I close my eyes, listening for anything.

"Hey, Gunnar Graves!"

I shoot away from the door at the sound of Lark's voice. She's striding down the hall, her brother beside her. They're both wearing condescending grins.

"Forget your key card?" Lark asks with a laugh. "Did you call the concierge desk for help?"

"I . . . uh . . ."

"Maybe you lost it in the woods." Rowan brushes past me. "You got knocked around pretty good out there."

Normally, I would try to snap back with something witty, but my mind is focused on hearing what Elisha and Catriona are saying. "Yeah," I mumble. "Maybe."

Rowan and Lark stop to look back at me. They're both still smiling, but it no longer looks like they're making fun of me.

"Keep at it," Rowan says with the tone of an older brother. "The training, I mean."

"You'll be fine," Lark chimes in. "It takes time."

I nod in reply. Moments later, they're gone and I'm back at the door.

"No magic is inherently good or evil," Elisha says. "Even the life energies can be twisted to dark purposes. It's the way the power is used that determines its righteousness."

Righteousness. The word reminds me again of my days spent trying to cast fire so I could avenge my parents' deaths. Are they talking about me? Are they concerned that I'm here for the wrong reasons? Maybe that's why the Breath keeps eluding me.

"You belong here, Catriona. You both do." Elisha speaks the last part a little louder.

I instantly pull away from the door, wondering if she knows I'm here. The guilt of eavesdropping weighs heavy on me. My stomach grumbles again. I need some time to collect my thoughts anyway, so I head toward the kitchen.

"It's really not as hard as you're making it." Taron takes the cereal box off the table—crunchy cinnamon squares that are homemade by Rowan, apparently—and pours more into my bowl, like a friendly bartender refilling my glass after a hard day.

I use my spoon to push the cereal down into what's left of my milk. Taron suggested we continue working on telepathy while having breakfast for dinner. I couldn't think of a good reason to say no.

"Then why haven't any humans been able to harness the Breath before now?" I ask, trying to avoid more pointless training.

"Some have," Taron replies. "But for the most part, Elisha says it wasn't the right time for the Breath to be used. Try again."

I take a deep breath and relax my shoulders. Maybe if I don't push so hard, it will come to me. I'm desperate for the magic at this point, for a glimmer of hope that it's hiding somewhere inside me. It's funny how fast things change. Hardly a day ago, I thought I had finally discovered the power that I had pursued for so long. I was on the cusp of wielding fire magic.

Now, it would take a miracle for me to melt butter.

"Think about somebody you care about," Taron says.

My mind draws a blank. I push down the thought of Catriona's face.

"How about somebody you're related to?" Taron suggests. "Blood is strong. Think about your parents."

"I'd rather not."

He tilts his head. "You didn't get along with them?"

"We got along great. Until they were killed right in front of me." My words are sharper than I intended.

Taron pulls his arms in, like he's closing himself up. He looks down. "Mine too."

The revelation surprises me. "Really? You saw your parents killed?" My reaction seems too abrupt, even to me. "You don't have to tell me if you don't want to."

"Well, I sort of saw it. We were in a group of people, not really fighting back, just hiding. It was good for a while, but when food and supplies started running low, the fighting began."

A chill runs through my body.

"One night, it got really bad," he says. "I knew it was going to happen. My parents knew it too. They told me to run and I did what they said. I wasn't there, but I knew the moment it happened, like I had seen it with different eyes. I knew they were gone."

I feel bad for the kid. "Is that when Elisha found you?"

He nods. "I hid in the woods for a few days. I didn't realize it, but I was sending out a signal, like you were. They found me and took me in. I've been with them ever since. I'm grateful to be here, but I miss my family. I think about them when I need to use my power. It hurts, but it also helps."

I shake my head. "I don't think that would work for me."

Taron leans forward. "You're never going to get it if you don't trust what we tell you." He sighs. "If you're not going to listen, why be here at all?"

I can't believe I'm getting scolded by somebody who hasn't gone through puberty. "Listen, you seem like a smart kid. Maybe too mature for your age, but with all you've been through, that's not your fault. And I appreciate what you're doing, trying to help me develop whatever this is. But do you really believe—even with all these things you people can do—that you stand a chance? Do you really think that trees and birds can win against machines that hurl fireballs from the sky or crash tidal waves into cities?"

"The Breath is way more powerful than trees and birds. There are much deeper powers, stuff you can't imagine. None of us have really unlocked it yet."

"Unlocked what?"

Taron looks from side to side, like he's about to tell me some great secret. He leans forward again. "Some people believe that if we can really tap into the Breath, we can unlock the pure power of heaven. Some Scion texts call it star fire. Others call it the Angel Sword."

"The Angel Sword?" I raise my eyebrows. "Cool name. Who dreamed up that one?"

"It's real!" He pauses, then squirms a little. "At least, we think it's real. Scion scholars have been searching for it for centuries."

I sigh and place my elbows on the table. "Okay, I'll play along. You think you might be the one to find it? You seem to have a lot of power for somebody so young."

"Some power." Taron slumps back. "I can read minds, but we're fighting enemies that don't have brains. Elisha says that what I can do is important, but as a telepath, I'll never be much help in combat other than relaying messages."

My heart hurts for the kid. I recognize the pain and frustration he must be feeling—wanting something so badly, and even wanting it for righteous reasons, but realizing you'll never have it. That's how faith dies.

I'm about to lie and suggest that maybe Taron *will* be the one to discover this mystical power, when Otis's voice breaks the silence. "You should be happy about that, kid."

Otis leans against the doorframe, clutching two beers—one in a hand of skin, the other in a glove that I'm guessing hides metallic fingers. He regards Taron. "If you're done eating, you ought to go help Rowan in the garden. Let me talk at our new friend a little bit."

Taron's eyes flick to me, as if he's looking for my permission.

I give a quick nod. "We'll try again later. Thanks for dinner."

The kid is careful not to touch Otis as he runs past him and out the door. Otis watches him for a few seconds, then flops into a chair and slides a beer across the table. "It's not cold. Sorry about that. I keep 'em tucked away so Rowan and Lark and the others won't drink them."

I pick up the tall silver can and study it, wondering if I should tell Otis that I've never had a drink in my life. "I'm surprised that works. I thought you could all read each other's minds."

Otis removes his hat, revealing a large section of shining steel on his skull. He taps on it, making a low, clanging sound with his fingernail. "Nobody gets in my mind, buddy. It's the implants, I think. Saved my life and took it away at the same time. Nothing inside me is like it used to be. I can't even drink the beers. Don't have the right plumbing for it anymore."

"Then why do you keep them hidden?"

Otis smirks. "Because they're *mine*."

I have to smile at that. He tilts his can toward mine, clinking them together. "You should enjoy it, though. Call it a welcoming gift."

I crack open the beer and take a sip. My first impression is that it's bitter, sour, but after a few seconds, I'm able to take another drink. The beer burns a little as I swallow. I haven't had anything carbonated since the fall of the Alliance.

A burp surprises me. "Thanks," I say.

"You and the kid have any luck unleashing your inner superpowers?" The way Otis uses the word *'superpowers'* makes it clear that he finds this all about as strange as I do.

"Not yet, but he keeps trying."

Otis gazes at the door as if Taron were still there. "He's a good kid, but a bit too wide-eyed for this world. A true believer, you know? I'm afraid it's going to get him killed."

I take another drink. The beer goes down easier this time. "And you're not a true believer?"

He frowns as if he's tossing the idea back and forth in his metallic head. "In some sense of the word, I suppose I am. God's magic wind or whatever I'm supposed to call it . . . it's impressive. But that doesn't mean it's going to decide to up and save the world all of a sudden."

"Taron thinks it will. He mentioned a power called the Angel Sword."

Otis cocks his head. He wears an expression like I've suggested Santa Claus is coming to rescue humanity. "The Angel Sword is a myth, friend. A useful one, sure. Keeps morale up, people pressing on, breathing in and out. Hope's a powerful thing. But it's dangerous too. If there was some mighty power of heaven going to save us all, hal-le-freaking-lujah"—he does a little wave of his hands, then drops them back on the table with a thump—"it would've shown up by now."

His words catch me off guard. If that's how Otis feels, why has he been here so long? "You don't believe any of it? Angels? God? Nothing?"

Otis shakes his head. "Didn't say that. God just might not be quite as involved in the day-to-day as the Scions think. Or, maybe He isn't as kind and loving as we thought. Maybe them boys who wrote the Old Testament had the right of it. He's angry with His creation for our disobedience. The machines are the new flood, the locusts. I've been on the wrong side of fire from the heavens, and I bet you have too. Maybe AI is the new and final angel of death, God's vengeance on the children who disappointed Him. Why else would He put us through all this? At least He decided to throw us a few weapons to keep the game going a little longer, maybe even survive."

That makes me take a long drink of the beer, mostly because I don't know what to say.

Otis watches me. The humor is gone from his face. "Do you hear what I'm telling you? That's our greatest hope, Gunnar. That's our only salvation and it's why I joined this circus they call a church. Not victory. Survival."

08

THE PROBLEM, THE MACHINES DECIDED, WAS
OUR FREEDOM TO DO ILLOGICAL DAMAGE TO OUR
OWN SPECIES. TO PROTECT US FROM OURSELVES,
THAT FREE WILL HAD TO BE REMOVED.
— SENATOR CLAIRE ROBBINS

THE NEXT MORNING, I'M AWOKEN

by Elisha, who tells me that we'll start our training in the woods. It makes me wonder if I'm in for another day of getting thumped by tree limbs and chasing Lark while she laughs at me in various animal forms. At least she gave back the dandelion.

The thought of feeling the energy flow through my body again pulls me out of bed. I've tried for so many years to wield magic. *Maybe today will finally be the day.*

A little while later, I'm standing with the Scions next to a small river carving its way through the woods. Elisha leads us through breathing exercises that create long periods of silence. The other Scions are probably praying during this time, but nobody mentions it or suggests that I do the same. I'm glad for that.

Next, Elisha begins a form of kata, leading with slow, deliberate movements while continuing to take deep breaths. We sway back and forth, gliding our arms from one side to another, bending our knees, turning and stepping in exaggerated motions. As we move, fields of energy begin to glow around the others. Rowan's skin shimmers and veins like those from a leaf appear on his skin. Lark's body shows flashes of fur, then feathers, all of it in beautiful shifting patterns that almost look like reflections beneath the surface of her skin. Even Taron shines with a light that seems pure, innocent.

As for me, it's all I can do to keep up. My muscles tense as I try to match Elisha's movements exactly. I keep losing my balance.

"Reach out to each other," Elisha says without looking at us.

"You can do this," Taron says, speaking into my mind.

I grit my teeth, close my eyes, and focus all my thoughts. I reach out with everything I have, all my mind.

A sharp pain jolts through the left side of my chest, so intense I feel like I'll collapse. Just as quickly, it's gone.

The power.

My eyes pop open in surprise and I notice a faint white light enveloping me. I close them again, desperate to hold on, trying to summon energy from nearby living things and pour it inside. In my mind, I stretch out to the large aspen trees near the edge of the clearing and envision myself drawing energy from their silver trunks and their crowns of golden leaves. I call out to the red-winged blackbirds trilling their voices in the branches, imagining that their songs will fuel the power.

But the spark fades and disappears.

I open my eyes again and stop moving. I *had* it. But I couldn't hold on to it. It almost makes everything worse, like I'm being teased with a small taste of the magic before it's jerked away.

The other Scions all stop. I can tell from their faces that they realized what's happened, but I can't tell if they're sympathetic or if they're tired of wasting time on a lost cause like me.

Elisha addresses them with an open hand. "A moment, please."

Rowan, Lark, and Taron walk into the woods, leaving Elisha and me alone.

This time, the burning inside me has nothing to do with magic. "I can't do this, Elisha. There are things about me that you need to know." I can't believe I'm about to trust her with this secret, but what's the point in hiding it anymore?

She speaks before I get the chance. "The machine heart?"

I look at her in surprise. "You know about that?"

Elisha walks to an aspen tree, her head up like she's admiring the yellow leaves. "Why do you think that's what's stopping you, Gunnar?"

I shrug. "It has to be. Maybe the Breath . . . whatever it is . . . maybe it won't tolerate the technology. Maybe that's why the war machines can't figure out how to use it."

Elisha glides her fingers along the bark of the tree, tracing the black scars that carve through its pale flesh. "It is not your metal heart that hinders your ability to embrace your power, your destiny. Our darkest secrets can be our greatest strengths, if only we allow ourselves to see." She regards me over her shoulder. "But you must have faith."

"Faith in what? God or myself?"

"I'm not sure you can have total faith in one but not the other."

My emotions swell. Words that have been stored up in the deepest recesses of my heart come pouring out. I'm talking to Elisha, but I'm not *only* talking to her. "Don't you think I want God to be real? To be loving? Because if He's not really there, or if He's there but not the loving parent we all thought He was, that means I never get to see my family again. But He didn't show up when we needed Him. It's not like He wasn't *invited*. We prayed for help every day, but it just got colder, more hopeless. Not that we should've been surprised. Magic was right there in the world, had been all along, except He wouldn't let us see it. We weren't allowed to touch it."

"Maybe we weren't ready."

My fury spikes. "I was ready when the war machines attacked! I was ready when they killed my parents!"

I turn away from Elisha, walk to a pine tree, and slump to the ground, pressing my back against the rough bark. I already regret the outburst. She's trying to help me. It's not her fault my life was ripped apart. But despite my attempts to heal myself—all the prayer, all the meditation, everything I've tried over the years to change my perspective—the rage is ever-present beneath the thin veil of my countenance. It doesn't take much digging to cause an eruption. Meeting the Scions and discovering the existence of the Breath has caused me to think that maybe God does exist after all, which makes the anger so much worse.

Elisha sits down in front of me. The faint music returns as if it's following her.

"Tough day yesterday?" she asks.

I lean my head back against the tree. "You could say that. Maybe you Scions need to change your strategy for scouting new talent. You're wasting a lot of time on me."

"You've been trying very hard." The way Elisha says it, I know it's not a question, and I don't think she's talking solely about the past day. She's not wrong, either. I've been striving to achieve some variation of magic for my entire life, and what has all the work gotten me? Nothing but pain, frustration, and isolation. Part of me wishes I could just go back to the village and resume a normal life.

But there were good things that seemed on the verge of happening. That's the problem with regrets. The bad things we would change in our lives threaten to take the good stuff along with them.

"Let's try a new approach." She places a hand on the back of my head. "Close your eyes and breathe."

More meditation. I've tried it before meeting the Scions, but never had the discipline to stick with it. I do as she says anyway.

Elisha's robes shuffle as she stands and starts to walk around me in a circle. "The Breath is close to you. It's always been there, calling out, pursuing you, and waiting for you to respond. Can you feel it?"

It's the same question the other Scions have been asking since I got here. "I don't feel anything."

"You will," Elisha says. "Whether you realize it or not, you have felt it before."

I draw in a breath. My thoughts cry out to whatever may be there. If it's God, then let Him answer me for a change. I'm almost afraid to disturb Him. In the past, every time I've asked Him for anything—even to just take away the pain—He's responded by kicking me in the teeth.

Elisha's voice moves closer. "You have a knack for telepathy, for connecting with others. This is the essence of the Breath inside you. But you keep fighting against it."

"Telepathy doesn't seem like it would do much good in battle."

"Don't underestimate the power of authentic connection. The machines seek to isolate us. Why do you think that is?"

The words sink in, and though I know they're true, I don't want to hear them. Psychic connection is fine, but it will do nothing to help me destroy the fire mage or any other war machines. It won't avenge my parents. It won't protect people like Catriona.

"You're afraid," Elisha says.

I keep my eyes closed. "Afraid of what?"

"That you're not in control."

She might be right. I try to let myself go, even the notion of control, and yet nothing comes. My mind wanders back to the village, to the thoughts of what happened with the air mage in the woods. Surely the war machines are hunting me. I'm sitting on the ground trying to connect with nature while they gather their forces. If I'm going to harness the Breath, it needs to happen now.

I reach out further with all that I have, feeling myself sweat again. My muscles shake from the internal strain. *Please. If not now, when?*

My cybernetic heart races, and for a fleeting moment, it almost seems as if an energy might be building. I try to latch onto it, but it slips away.

I open my eyes and discover that I'm gasping for breath. "I can't, Elisha. I don't have the power in me, not the way you think."

"Who said the power comes from you? What if you truly believed that it came from somewhere else, that it wasn't about your strength, your worthiness, your skill? What would you do? How would that change you?"

It's a difficult concept to consider. My whole life has been about trying with all I have to be good enough, strong enough, brave enough, skilled enough. I've spent so many hours on my knees, hoping that if I said the right words in the right way, wondrous things would happen. The key to life, I believed, resided in perfect recitation and behavior, like stumbling through a maze in the dark, trying one path, then another, constantly winding up at a dead end.

But what if I really let go?

So I do. I listen, I breathe, I relax. I let go. I sit still and wait.

The world comes alive. There are Elisha's steps against the ground, but there is more.

What do I feel? *The cool wind on my skin.*

What do I smell? *The spiced scent of the tea olives. They must be in bloom. Those plants were my father's favorite. That's why my mother rubbed them on her wrists.*

Thoughts of the power surface in my mind, but not because I summoned them. Rather, I allow them to come. I remember the brilliance of the moment I unleashed fire on the machine. Yes, anger and rage were present, but even then, I knew it didn't come from those dark places. Those emotions were bystanders, or perhaps symptoms of something more true at the root of it all. It wasn't about destruction.

It was about protecting the child. Protecting *life*.

An energy rushes over my skin when I remember the cry of the baby, how the sound ignited the sense of righteousness inside me. The android had upset the natural balance by taking an infant from its parents. The child knew this was wrong. The parents knew. I knew. But the machine was only a machine. Did it know what it was doing, or perhaps, why it was doing it? Could it ever understand the essence of life?

The question makes me consider their magic. AI discovered long ago the proper words, gestures, and countless other factors to produce elemental miracles. The machines know how it works, but can they know *why* it works? Can they know the source, or perhaps why the power was placed here to begin with?

And I realize I have made that mistake so many times in my life. Like the machines, I was focused entirely on the how. How could I bend magic and power to my will? I never stopped to ask myself why. Why did I want to hold fire in my hands? Was it to destroy one machine, to wreak revenge? Was it to make myself like the powerful steel gods? Maybe the reason the magic worked is because it was the first time I used it not for myself, but for somebody else.

"Open your eyes."

I had almost forgotten Elisha was here. Her words are an invitation, not an order, and so I take my time. I want to hold on to this serenity a little longer. I try to etch the feeling in my mind. This is a truth I must not forget.

I draw in another deep breath—feeling gratitude for the clean air again—then let it go. I open my eyes.

A thin layer of white flame covers my arms. My breath catches. Pure joy surges through my body and soul, a wild thrill that could never be captured by mortal words. It is all the colors and none of them. It is hot but does not burn. It is power. It is mercy.

As it fades, I don't try to stop it. I don't try to cling to the moment.

"Good," Elisha says, and again I hear deeper truth in her voice. She's not praising me for conjuring magic. She's congratulating me for not trying to wield it as if it's my own.

When it's gone, I stay sitting, dwelling on the sensation.

"How do you feel?" she asks.

Before I can answer, Otis's voice echoes through the trees. "Elisha!"

We turn and see the cyborg running toward us.

"Machine transmission," he says, out of breath. "One of the villages has been scheduled for termination."

I already know the rest. "Mine."

Otis confirms my suspicion with a quick look. "The decision came after analysis of a recent attack. They're going to be wiped out."

"How long?" Elisha asks.

"Few days," Otis says. "Maybe less."

The joy dissipates, replaced by a feeling like rocks in my gut. "This is my fault."

Elisha grabs my hand, as if pulling me from the abyss into which I'm sinking. "Nothing has happened yet. There's still time to intervene."

I pull away, not because I don't appreciate the gesture, but because I don't deserve it. "Even if we win the battle, they'll just send more."

Elisha's eyes snap to Otis. "No, they won't."

They look at each other and I remember their conversation about hacking the machine communication channel.

"There's an old server farm in Reddington, part of a machine production facility," Otis says in a low, serious voice that I've only heard him use with Elisha. "About a day's ride from here."

"C'mon," I say. "The signal thing? Will that actually work?"

"You got a better idea?" Otis asks.

I sigh and already know what I have to do. I still don't have my powers in check—not even close—but I can't let the people in that village be killed because of me. "I'm going with you."

I spot Catriona on the way to the dining area and jog to catch up with her. Elisha has invited both of us to join the Scions for dinner, a meal together before we leave tomorrow morning on a mission to obtain the access code for the war machine communications channel. We've only been here a couple days, and I've spent most of that time training. It makes sense that I haven't seen her.

But for some reason, I feel like she's avoiding me.

The dining area is a room that is much like the others in the temple—small, barely enough space for a simple wooden table surrounded by chairs. The other Scions are already sitting down, the food spread out on a mismatched set of dishes. It's all fruit, vegetables, and beans, I assume from Rowan's garden. It looks like Thanksgiving dinner with a huge loaf of bread occupying the place where a turkey would be.

As Catriona and I enter the room, Elisha acknowledges us with a welcoming smile. The rest of them are engaged in a heated conversation, almost like they're bickering siblings.

"I'm just saying," Lark says, enunciating every word in exasperation, "that it *might* be possible. That's it!"

Otis shakes his head. He has a full plate in front of him, despite the fact that he doesn't eat. "It's not possible, at least not by a human. By a water mage, maybe. Rowan, for crying out loud, talk some sense into your sister."

"Well, it is a manipulation of living things," Rowan responds.

Otis throws up his hands in disbelief as Catriona and I take the empty seats at the end of the table.

My chair scrapes the rock floor as I pull it in beneath me. "What are we talking about?"

"Don't get involved." Taron pulls a chunk of bread off the loaf. Sometimes I think that—other than Elisha—he's the most mature person here. He might be a kid, but he has an old soul.

"Involved in what?" Catriona asks.

Lark gestures to us. "Let's ask them what they think. New opinions. Unbiased."

"Fine by me." Otis turns to face us. "My friends Flora and Fauna over here think that—"

"Don't call us that," Rowan warns through a mouthful of spinach.

Otis ignores him. "They think it might be possible for a life mage to walk on water despite the fact that water is clearly in the realm of elemental magic which, to my knowledge, humans cannot control."

"It's not about the water," Lark says. "It's about—"

"Wait!" Otis raises a hand to stop her. "Don't contaminate them with your nonsense. Let's hear what the newbies think about it."

Catriona speaks first. "I could see it."

I look at her in surprise. "Really? How?"

"It's manipulation of living tissue." She reaches for a bowl of mashed sweet potatoes. "Determining whether the body will sink."

"Sure," I say, wanting to keep her talking, "but mass is mass. Can that just . . . go away? You'd have to manipulate either the water or gravity, both of which should be out of your control."

"Thank you!" Otis exclaims, and suddenly I feel like I'm on the wrong side of this argument.

But at least we're part of the conversation. "Lark," I ask, "does your body mass change when you shift?"

She laughs. "Never bothered to step on a scale after I transformed into a squirrel, but I have to think it does. How could it not?"

"Even so," I say, realizing I haven't had such an enjoyably pointless conversation in a very long time, "even if you were much lighter, you would still sink. It's about density."

"No, I'm a pretty good swimmer." Lark gestures at Otis with her thumb. "Unlike this guy over here."

Otis points his unused fork at Lark. "I'll have you know I'm a great swimmer, despite all this metal I'm sporting."

Rowan snickers. "You got a propeller in there somewhere?"

"How much of you is cybernetic?" I ask, gambling at whether Otis will be offended by the question.

"Plenty of what you can see," Otis says, "and most of what you can't. But it isn't flesh that makes you human."

"Agreed." Elisha lifts a glass of water in a toast to Otis's words.

Catriona does the same, then looks to everyone seated around the table. "We appreciate the hospitality that you've shown us." I realize she's speaking on my behalf too. I don't mind at all.

"There are no strangers at this table," Elisha says. "What's ours is yours."

"And you better eat plenty of it." Rowan speaks without looking up from his plate. "We've got quite a ride ahead of us tomorrow. We'll pack what we can and I know the places to harvest wild stuff, but this is the best meal you'll eat for a while."

I take the spoon that's buried in the mashed sweet potatoes and serve myself a generous portion. The first bite makes me realize that I forgot what natural food tastes like. It's sweet and pure and delicious. I nearly fall back into my chair.

"Good?" Lark asks.

The food is so good I almost hate to swallow it. "Incredible."

The compliment seems to catch Rowan's attention. There's a quick glimmer of pride in his eyes. "Better than the settlement camps?"

I nod vigorously. "Everything there was pumped full of vitamins and compounds and who knows what else. Guess I got used to it—I didn't even think about how different it tasted from actual real food. But this . . ." I take another huge bite.

Otis looks away from me and I feel a twinge of regret.

But I don't stop eating, either.

09

IF ANY HUMANS RESISTED, PREDETERMINED
THRESHOLDS WERE SET WITH QUANTIFIABLE
METRICS TO GAUGE THE LEVEL OF DEFIANCE
IN COMPARISON TO THE VALUE OF EACH LIFE.
WHEN SOME POOR FOOL—OR, AS IT TURNS OUT,
LARGE GROUPS OF POOR FOOLS—CROSSED THAT
THRESHOLD, THE SYSTEM CLASSIFIED THEM
LIKE THEY WERE IRREPARABLY CORRUPTED
APPLICATIONS.
THE ONLY OPTION WAS DELETION.
— DR. KIERON RICH

THE MORNING FOG LIES THICK

over the woods. The heavy mist has an eerie effect, like I woke up this
cold morning and stepped into a world that was just created. The fog is
part of that newness, like the steam off food right out of an oven. *A new
world*. Can't say I'd be too disappointed if that were true. The old world
wasn't great to me. Maybe I'll find better fortune here.

The other Scions are here as well, all except Elisha and Taron. Both
stayed back at the temple, though I don't think Taron likes being left
behind. I felt bad to see the disappointment in the kid's eyes, but I can't
pretend like I didn't agree with Elisha's decision. His powers won't do
us any good, not on this trip, and we can't afford to look after him.

We've been quiet most of the morning. Rowan led us out of the
temple using a different path than the lake. Instead, we went through
a narrow, winding tunnel before climbing a mountain of rocks up to a
trap door covered by a thick patch of vegetation. I'm not sure why he
didn't bring us that way the first time we came to the temple. Maybe
they wanted us to experience the wonder of the glowing cave. I decide
not to ask.

We fill the saddlebags with weapons and supplies. The Scions have
a modest armory, but it's enough to equip our small group, especially
since Lark and Rowan fight with magic alone. Otis carries an assault
rifle that he had before the war. Catriona was given a shotgun and
seems comfortable with it. I probably should have chosen the same,

but instead, I'm packing two pistols in holsters attached to my belt. They remind me of the guns I trained with for countless hours during my time in the Human Alliance. Those guns were like extensions of my arms. They used to make me feel like a holy warrior, a weapon of God. I carved angels' wings along the barrels and had them blessed by a priest. Didn't do me much good when the fire mage rolled in, but I'd like to have them back.

These will do, though.

A nervous energy surges through me as I run my hand over the horse's neck, admiring the muscles beneath its fur. The temple has been a safe place, an oasis, even if it was only a short time. Heading back out into a land controlled by war machines has me on edge.

Catriona stands nearby. For the first time since we met the Scions, she's wearing something other than her machine-assigned clothing. Instead, she has on dark jeans, a zip-up leather jacket, and boots. She rubs the soft velvet of her horse's nose, then feeds it a piece of fruit. On this damp morning, her hair pulled back in a ponytail, she's almost captivating. I have to pull my eyes away.

Otis sits atop the largest horse of the group, the assault rifle slung across his back. He's been watching me all morning. "Not sure it's the best idea to bring these two along. He ain't got the hocus pocus figured out yet, plus he's war machine bait. No offense, buddy."

I hold up both hands to tell him I don't mind his comment, but it won't stop me from coming. I saddle up. My horse dances back and forth on its hooves, its body full of energy waiting to be unleashed. I grip the reins, ready to run.

"You don't have to come, Otis," Lark tells him as she and Rowan hoist themselves into their saddles.

"Actually, I *do*," Otis says. His horse shakes its head from side to side and lets out a huff. Otis tries to settle the animal with a quick pat. "Until one of y'all figures out how to intercept war machine transmissions with your brain, I'm the only person who has the internal tech required to connect to the system." Otis gives me a quick look. "Unless somebody isn't telling me something."

My body tenses. Does he know about my implant?

"Thank you for gathering the horses," Catriona says to Lark. I can tell the Scions like her. I don't blame them. She knows how to read the room and shift the focus before things get tense. It makes her easy to be around.

"Well," I say after we're all saddled. "What's the plan?"

"We ride to the facility," Rowan says. "Otis gains access to the machine signal, and we get back here as fast as possible."

Lark regards Otis. "If you can actually pull it off, that is."

"No guarantees," Otis says.

Fantastic. We're about to ride headlong into the unknown with machine drones probably scouring the skies for us, and, even if we get where we're supposed to be going, it might not work.

"Are you sure you can't access the signal . . . say, remotely?" I ask.

Otis gives an exaggerated gasp. "What a great idea! Why didn't I think of that? I'll just do it all from right here." He puts his pointer fingers on his temples and closes his eyes. "Hacking transmission signal," Otis says in a mocking robotic voice. "Access granted. Hostilities terminated. Initiate global peace protocol. All hail the brilliant Gunnar Graves."

"He actually *can* access the signal remotely," Rowan intervenes. "But without the code, he can't receive or transmit any useful commands. If our intel is correct, one of the old server farms may have enough data for us to figure it out."

"It seems a place like that would be heavily guarded," Catriona says.

"The rust buckets don't think it needs to be," Otis says, decidedly more polite to Catriona than me. I guess that beer we shared didn't form such a strong bond after all. "They don't know what I can do," he says, casting a sideways glance at me. "Kind of like how we don't know what you can do, except *my* potential has a better chance of actually panning out."

I want to argue with him, but he's probably right. I look to Lark and Rowan. "Lead the way."

Otis steers his horse to the front of the pack. "Better follow me."

Lark and Rowan fall in behind Otis, riding side by side. Catriona and I take up position behind them. I catch her eye and she smiles. Maybe we'll discover some type of magic with her, also. It seems strange that none of the mages have mentioned it; maybe not everybody can access the power. I'm not about to say anything. I don't want to cause offense or sound arrogant. Especially if it turns out that I'm a one-hit wonder when it comes to magic.

Don't think that way, Gunnar. I return Catriona's smile with one of my own as my horse trots along. I've never ridden one before, but I suspect Lark is connecting with the animals to make sure they don't take off running or start bucking until I fly off.

At least, I hope so.

"You two are twins, right?" I say, raising my voice a little to be heard.

We've been riding for hours. The sun is high in the sky, the light cascading through the treetops in intricate patterns, revealing colors in Catriona's hair that I hadn't noticed before.

I'm not sure how far we've gone. Rowan insists on staying in the woods as much as possible to avoid machine detection, which slows our pace. We've crossed streets a few times, but we kept a fast clip and got back to cover whenever possible.

Rowan casts a wary glance at me before returning his attention forward. "Triplets."

I laugh at first, assuming he's making a joke, referring to both Lark and Otis as his siblings.

The look of total disgust I receive from both Lark and Rowan tells me I've made a mistake.

"Seriously? Triplets?" I ask. "There's another one of you somewhere? You're kidding. Boy or girl? Were they at the temple? What kind of magic do they have?"

Rowan shoots me a look that freezes my body from the inside out. I'm such an idiot.

I take my hands off the reins and hold them up in apology. "Sorry. None of my business. I just thought since you mentioned it, it was okay to—"

"She died when we were kids," Rowan says abruptly.

"You? You were a kid?" I'm trying to lighten the mood, but every word I say feels more awkward than the last.

I'm relieved when Lark laughs. "A geeky kid, actually. Awkward. And allergic to *everything*!"

"That can't be true," Catriona says.

"Thank you." Rowan glares at his sister. "You're absolutely right. Not everything."

Lark gets even more animated. Her horse picks up the pace a little, as if feeling her excitement. "Everything. He was constantly on allergy medications. He couldn't be near flowers. He couldn't eat berries or nuts. He could hardly go outside."

Rowan sways from side to side in the saddle. "I think you're exaggerating."

Lark dismisses him with a wave of her hand. "You didn't start to improve until the machines took over and sterilized everything."

Rowan doesn't argue.

"You were in the one of the villages?" Catriona asks.

Lark nods. "It was one of the earliest settlements. Our parents actually thought that machine rule was a good idea. They were environmentalists."

Otis scoffs. "What does that have to do with anything?"

"A lot," Rowan says. "One of the first machine initiatives was environmental protection—reducing waste, restoring important ecosystems. Besides, our parents were logical people."

"Logical how?" I ask.

"They knew we couldn't win," Lark explains. "They had three kids. They didn't want to fight a hopeless war, so we volunteered to go. It was great, at first. We all had our own rooms for the first time, the two of us and our sister."

"What was her name?" Catriona has a warm way of asking the question, a sweet comfort in her voice.

"Zain," Rowan says. His voice drops a little. "She looked just like Lark."

"I'm sure you had fun with that," Catriona says to Lark. "You must miss her very much."

Lark gives Catriona a half smile, gratitude for her kindness accompanied by the joy of memory, but also undeniable pain.

What happened to her? None of us ask the question, but it hangs in the air. I get the feeling Otis doesn't know the story, either. He doesn't seem like the type for fireside chats.

"It seemed like home for a while," Lark says. "The village, I mean. We had everything we needed. We knew there was fighting going on in other parts of the world, but we never saw it, never talked about it. Maybe the adults did, but we were kids, you know? We didn't really think anything was wrong."

"Zain knew." The way Rowan says it, I'm not sure if the two of them have had this discussion before.

We ride in silence for a few minutes, tension thick between us. Maybe learning this story isn't the best idea. I open my mouth to apologize, but Rowan speaks first.

"There was an uprising in the village." Rowan clears his throat, composing himself. "During a town meeting. Don't remember what it was about. The kids were all playing in the corner of the meeting hall, and suddenly everybody was shouting. Then fighting. The machines came in. Then . . ."

Lark swallows down her sadness. "Zain was in the wrong place at the wrong time."

"Lark . . ." I say under my breath.

"I'm so sorry," Catriona says with genuine tenderness.

Otis keeps silent. I get the feeling he's not particularly skilled at showing sympathy, so it's probably for the best.

We ride for what must be a few hours, all of us progressively removing layers of clothes as the afternoon sun pushes away the cool autumn air. This area must have once been popular for hiking; the paths are overgrown, but we occasionally pass wooden benches nestled between the pines. The forest fills the silence, mostly from above—the warbling of blackbirds, the tapping of a woodpecker, and even the honking of geese. After years without seeing birds, it's strange to hear so many in one area. Maybe it's because I haven't been this far from a machine facility since I was captured. Or maybe they're following Lark.

"Anybody else thirsty?" I ask. Not only is my canteen empty, but I'm ready to get out of this saddle. Lark and Rowan look like they could ride all day, but I have a feeling Otis and Catriona are on my side.

Rowan lifts his head a little, staring off into nothing. After a moment, he tugs his reins, directing his horse to turn right. "There's a lake not too far away."

"You can sense that?" Catriona asks, intrigued.

Rowan gestures to the trees. "They tell me things when I ask."

"So the trees can sense the lake?" My question is one of curiosity, not doubt. In fact, I'm already leading my horse to follow him.

"It's more like a chain," Rowan says. "I ask the ones near me, they ask others near them, and so on until those near the water hear my call and respond."

"Pretty useful," I say.

"Do they tell you anything else?" Catriona asks.

Rowan nods. "If the machines are within a few miles, I know about it."

After a few twists and turns, we emerge from the pines and come upon a large lake. On the opposite side of the water is a grove of tall, slender aspen trees capped with yellow leaves that reflect off the lake. A range of mountains looms in the distance behind them. A flock of pelicans floats across the water, hunting for fish.

I don't realize how sore my back is until I'm out of the saddle. I nearly collapse when my feet hit the ground, but I try not to let anybody see how much I'm hurting. Lark snickers at me, though. The horse probably told her. *Traitor.*

Soon, our horses are drinking at the water's edge while we sit along the bank, our canteens filled. We share food that we brought along— dried vegetables and fruits, some bread. I'm so hungry that I can't imagine anything ever tasting better.

For some reason, I can't take my eyes off the aspen grove across the water. There's something alluring about it, powerful. My thoughts drift back to the night I ventured across the river and into the embrace of those trees. For some reason, it was calming, comforting, but also seemed to give me strength. That was also the night I harnessed magic for the first time.

"It's a single organism," Rowan says. He sits beside me, tearing a chunk of bread.

I regard him. "What?"

He nods toward the grove. "The trees. Tens of thousands, all united by a shared root system." He takes a bite.

I look again. *One living thing.* I would have never known from looking at them.

On the other side of Rowan, Lark finishes her food and jumps up. "I'm going to do some scouting." She doesn't wait for anybody to respond before disappearing in the trees behind us.

"Is she okay?" I ask Rowan.

"She's fine," he says through a mouthful of bread. "Lark never seems to sit still for very long."

The pelicans lift out of the lake, taking to the air in unison. One of the horses stops drinking and raises its head, looking out over the water. The others do the same. A couple stamp their hooves; another lets out a low whinny.

"What's got them spooked?" Otis asks.

I stand and approach my horse, being careful to avoid its legs. The last thing I need is to get kicked in the face. If it didn't kill me, Otis would never let me hear the end of it.

"Easy." I lay a hand on the horse.

The animal rears up with a high neigh. I jump back to get clear.

"Gunnar, look!" Catriona says.

I whirl just in time to see white ripples followed by gray flesh appear on the water. At first I think it's a fish breaching the surface, except it's huge and moving slowly.

The horses gallop away from the bank, but I stand frozen as a long, scaly neck emerges from the lake, creating a low arch.

"What is that?" Otis yells behind me.

A creature lifts its head out of the water. It looks like a serpent, although its neck widens near the surface of the lake, suggesting a huge body.

The monster roars, revealing a mouth filled with razor-sharp teeth. It lunges toward me.

I leap sideways to avoid the attack, energy rising in my body.

A quick glance to my left and I see Catriona next to me, her mouth agape. My hands reach for my guns, but they're not there. We're all unarmed, except . . .

"Rowan!" I yell as the monster raises its head high like it's poised to strike again. "Can't you do something?"

"Like what?" Rowan yells back. "It's not a tree!"

"I got some backwoods magic for him," Otis says, snatching his rifle off the ground.

The creature bellows again. Otis keeps his distance, but takes aim.

"Stop!" Lark charges out of the woods behind us. Rowan dives and grabs the barrel of Otis's gun as he fires, knocking it off target. A burst of bullets rips through the air, but none hit the beast.

Otis shouts curses as Rowan wrenches the weapon away.

Lark dashes toward the creature, her hands up. The beast moves its head in her direction, then locks its gaze onto her.

"Lark!" Rowan screams, the fear cracking in his voice.

Lark keeps her focus on the beast but dismisses Rowan with her off hand. "It's fine, Rowan."

Lark and the creature approach each other. The beast glides through the water, teeth still bared. A low groan escapes its mouth, but it's no longer a roar.

Lark lowers her head a bit, still holding her hands up.

"Incredible," Catriona whispers.

My fear transforms into wonder as the beast touches its nose to Lark's hand.

"There." Lark strokes the monster's face. Suddenly, she looks like a child who found a puppy.

I take a step forward, watching the beast closely. "What is it?"

Lark shakes her head like even she can't believe what is happening. "I have absolutely no idea." She pets it a few more times before pressing her forehead against its nose. The beast leans into her, letting out another sound, slightly higher pitched this time. It almost sounds like a cooing child.

"Okay." Lark pats its cheek. "Go on. I'll see you later."

The beast drifts away and sinks into the water, sending small waves washing over the shore.

I shuffle back so the cold water doesn't soak my boots. Lark watches as the beast—now a dark shape beneath the surface of the river—swims away, much faster than should be possible for a creature so large.

Rowan joins her on the riverbank. "That thing was enormous."

Lark gives a little laugh. "Actually, it was a baby."

We ride close to the river for the rest of the afternoon. I keep my eyes on the water, hoping to catch another glimpse of the beast. A hundred questions burn in my mind, but I wait until we stop for the night on a small cliff overlooking the water.

Our exhaustion is minimized only by our hunger, so we make quick work of building a fire—I don't even try to conjure any magic flames, though I wish I could—and soon we're sitting in a circle, feasting on bread and beans.

When the rumble in my stomach is gone, I set down the metal bowl and lean back against a fallen log next to Catriona. "Lark, did you know that thing was in the river?"

Lark sits across the fire from me, Rowan to her right. She picks at the last of her beans with a small spoon. "I felt something when we first approached the lake, but it was so unfamiliar that I didn't think it was an animal. My powers aren't fully developed, so I wasn't sure."

"Are there more of those things out there?" Otis sits farther away from the fire than the rest of us, clutching an empty bowl. He doesn't eat, but brought dishes anyway, I guess to make it a little less obvious how different his body is from the rest of ours.

Lark watches the fire. "I don't know. It reminds me of what Elisha said when she first found us. It was after Zain . . . well, it was afterward. Our parents were in denial about everything."

"What she's trying to say is, they went bonkers." Rowan takes a drink from his canteen.

Lark admonishes him with a glance before returning to her story. "Anyway, we escaped. We didn't know where we could go, but I think we were already using our powers without knowing it. It felt like nature was guiding us to Elisha. She recognized our potential immediately and started training us."

I wonder if it took them as long to develop their powers as it's taking me. Did Lark and Rowan spend years staring at a pile of wood trying to light a spark? Did they put in the hours, or were they just two kids wandering through the woods who happened to stumble into magic?

Lark takes in a deep breath and releases it slowly. "It was so strange. We had never seen anything like magic, but it was right there in front of us. Elisha helped us recognize that, not only in ourselves, but also in the world. She said that when the Breath awakened, it was like . . . I can't remember exactly how she put it . . ." Lark bites her lip and looks up, as if searching.

Rowan takes another drink. "Wonder has been reborn."

All our heads snap to him. Talking about the rebirth of wonder is the last thing I'd expect Rowan to say.

"Yes." Recognition lights Lark's face. "That's right. She said wonder had been reborn in the world. Maybe that means certain types of things are . . . back."

"Back?" Catriona leans forward. "You mean things that once existed but were . . . gone? Like monsters?"

"Maybe," Lark says. "I mean, would you still think what we saw today was a monster if there were a lot of them? Things are only monsters or supernatural . . . impossible, even . . . if we can't see them. That's pretty arrogant if you ask me, as if humans get to define reality."

Catriona nods, though her head is down. She plays with a stick, drawing designs in the dirt. "Yes, things aren't always what we think they are."

I watch her, questions forming in my mind. I don't know why Catriona was designated as an outcast, and it's not my place to ask.

But we're not captives of the machines anymore. Whatever reason they had for marking her, would it still bother her even now? After all that's happened?

Otis regards me from across the fire. "What about you, Sparky?"

The heat that rushes over my body isn't from the fire. I blink in confusion. "What *about* me?"

"We don't know anything about who you are," he says. I'm not sure if it's a question or a challenge.

I shrug. "Not much to know, I guess. Spent most of my teen years fighting with my parents in the Alliance."

"Where were you before that?" Lark asks in a decidedly less aggressive tone than Otis.

"Grew up in Atlanta."

They all pause, just like Michael in the cafeteria. I don't need the ability to read minds to know what they're thinking, so I answer the unspoken question. "I was there for the attack. I saw Stone Mountain rise and fall."

Saying it brings the memories back to mind. It was one of the machines' first major displays of elemental magic—using a company of earth and air mages to lift a large section of the granite mountain from the earth and heave it toward a major Alliance stronghold outside the city. I can still feel the rumble of the ground, see the cloud of dirt and debris that lingered in the air for days after. They could have deployed bombs. They could have stormed our facilities using androids with assault rifles; they had the numbers.

Instead, they chose a show of dominance. They displayed extraordinary powers that humanity hadn't even thought possible, let alone harnessed. This glory was uniquely machine.

Many in the Alliance doubted the war machines would ever be able to do something like that again. Even then, we knew their ability to use magic required massive amounts of power.

But once was enough. After that, many surrendered. My unit fled.

Rowan mutters a curse under his breath. Lark looks away. Catriona reaches out and briefly touches my arm. Her hand is warm. Otis keeps his eyes on me.

Silence lingers for a few moments before Rowan stands. "We should get some sleep. Who wants to take first watch?"

"Oh," I say, somewhat surprised. "We're taking turns?"

Rowan furrows his brow at me. "Why wouldn't we?"

"I just kinda figured that Otis, I mean . . ." I trail off.

Otis contorts his face in a sour expression. "Figured that I what?"

I'm not sure how to say it. "I guess I thought, since you don't have to eat or drink, you didn't have to sleep, either."

Otis rolls his one human eye. "Typical."

"Otis, you *don't* sleep," Lark scoffs.

Otis is looking at Lark but he's pointing a finger at me. "True, but this idiot doesn't know that. And I do like to close my eyes."

Catriona rises to her feet. "I'll do it. I'm not tired anyway."

Although I feel a little ashamed, none of us argue. We unload our bedrolls and soon I'm watching the stars between the branches. Every so often, I sneak a glance at Catriona. She sits on the ground, her arms crossed over her knees. She seems different tonight. I wonder if something Lark said over the campfire bothered her.

Then again, maybe not. By the time I hit adolescence, all my time and attention was focused on training to fight war machines.

I don't know anything about women. Outcast or otherwise.

10

THAT KIND OF CHAOS DOES STRANGE THINGS
TO PEOPLE. OR MAYBE IT'S CIVILIZATION AND
ORDER THAT DO STRANGE THINGS TO PEOPLE.
WHEN THOSE SAFEGUARDS ARE STRIPPED AWAY,
WE RETURN TO OUR NATURAL STATE. VICIOUS
AND BROKEN.

— DAVID ASHLEY, SOCIOLOGIST

"GUNNAR!"

Catriona's voice jolts me awake. I jump to my feet, my eyes trying to adjust to the darkness. "What's going on?"

I hear Rowan and Lark rousing as well. Otis turns in slow circles, rifle in hand as he searches the area. I draw both pistols and disengage the safeties. The woods are silent, but the air is pregnant with a sinister element. I can feel it in my bones.

"There's something," Catriona says, her shotgun ready. "I don't know what it is, but it's out here somewhere."

"War machines?" My muscles tense. I've never had this experience before. It's like I can feel the cold presence of danger.

"I'm scanning for machine frequencies," Otis says. "Not picking up anything."

"I feel it, too," Rowan says, then thrusts his finger into the air. "In the trees . . . there!"

I whirl around as a dark figure falls from one of the surrounding branches. It lands on Rowan and drives an object into his neck.

"No!" Lark cries out. She morphs into a panther and lunges.

Before she reaches the attacker, another appears behind her and, despite her panther state, tackles her to the ground. Before she can regroup, she is pierced in the neck with a syringe.

"Don't y'all move now!" a voice calls out. It's high, whiny, but human. "Bring 'em in, boys!"

The pine trees shake and the ground trembles with the rumble of engines. Headlights appear at a distance, closing fast from all sides.

Figures surround us, silhouettes in the growing light. They have the shapes of men, though their bodies are contorted in odd places—a jagged rib, an elongated arm. The headlamps are so bright that I can't get a clear look.

But I can see that most of them hold shotguns.

I raise my pistols and glance at Catriona. She watches our enemies directly down the barrel of her own shotgun.

The man in front of us wears camouflage coveralls, though the top half of his clothes hangs from his waist, revealing a tattooed, muscular chest. A patchwork of metal covers portions of his torso, poorly stitched to his skin, leaving grotesque scars. He has a shaved head and wears a hockey mask that is painted to look like a demon, complete with horns and fangs. "Ain't this our lucky day? Two cyborgs for the price of one."

How did this thing know what I am on the inside?

My heart races, both from the realization that my secret may be out and the notion that it might not matter if this maniac decides to splatter my guts all over the ground.

Another man approaches. He stands a bit shorter and also wears a mask, along with a beer company T-shirt and ripped jeans. One arm has been completely replaced with an android limb that hangs at his side. "The wizards are both down. What do you want with the rest of them, Quinn?"

"Blindfold 'em and throw 'em in the trucks," Quinn says.

The enormous tattooed arms of a third attacker appear out of the darkness behind Catriona and grab her, pinning her arms to her waist. The man in the beer T-shirt seizes Catriona's shotgun with his metallic arm and wrenches it from her grasp.

"Let her go!" I take aim, but a huge body slams into me, knocking me to the ground and pressing all its weight on me. It's so heavy that I feel like my bones will be crushed. I manage to look up and see Catriona struggling with her captor.

He laughs as he wrestles with her. "This one's stronger than she looks. Got any machine in you, darling?"

Catriona snaps her head back, connecting with his nose and choking his words away. He stumbles away, grasping his face. Catriona hits him with a quick jab that sends him back farther. Blood pours out of his nose and stains his gritted teeth. "I'll kill you!"

Catriona stands ready, her feet set and fists clenched.

I try to break free, but whoever is on my back isn't letting up.

Quinn saunters over, shotgun in hand. He presses the barrel of his weapon to my head. "That's enough of that."

Catriona's eyes flicker as she looks at me.

"Run," I manage to say with what little breath I can gather.

"Sure. You run, little rabbit," Quinn urges. "Go right ahead. Won't stop ya. Don't need ya. But your boyfriend here will be dead before you break a sweat."

Catriona says nothing.

Quinn kneels down. He smells like blood and bug spray. "Didn't run. Maybe she cares about you after all? Or maybe she thinks I'm lying. She's probably right."

"No," I say. "She's just not afraid of cowards."

He responds with a devil's laugh, then hammers me with the butt of his shotgun.

I think I hear Catriona cry out before everything goes dark.

When I come to, I'm being dragged by my feet through what appears to be some type of camp deep in the woods. Ramshackle cabins surround me, some with walls of sheet metal that look like a slight breeze would blow them away. We pass an open garage filled with motorcycles, dirt bikes, and ATVs. The vehicles appear better maintained than most of the homes.

My back scratches against the leaves and dirt. My head throbs with pain. I think I hear rushing water nearby, but that may be the sound of blood in my ears.

People watch from doorways and windows, but in my blurred, foggy vision, they seem strange. Maybe I'm not seeing clearly because that jerk slammed his gun into my face. Maybe I'm dreaming. Most of them look malnourished, sick, and diseased. As sad as that is, it's not what makes my gut churn.

They're all cyborgs.

Men, women, small children—all of them have some type of metal implant. A few have faces with steel plates. Others have at least one robotic eye, though only about half of them are glowing. Thick, bloody stitches attach the steel parts to their skin. Strange dark lines are visible beneath their flesh, much of which appears to have been stretched too thin. None of the onlookers say a word or move a muscle. It looks as though they're afraid.

The man dragging me seems to be the size of a mountain and clutches my ankle with a cybernetic hand. He doesn't wear a shirt, probably to show off his physique, but his pants are a patchwork of materials. They're too short for his massive body. The way the ground thumps with his every step, I'm guessing he has steel in his legs. Atop that mound of metal and muscle is a shaved, scarred head. Otis's rifle is slung across his back.

Catriona and Otis are on either side of me, both with black hoods pulled over their heads, hands bound with rope, and guns pressed into their backs. The men escorting them wear masks painted to look like insane clowns. Each carries one of my pistols.

Quinn—still wearing his demon mask—strolls along behind us, carrying Catriona's shotgun on his shoulder like a lumberjack's axe, whistling some cheerful melody. I guess they prefer our weapons to their own. It makes me wonder whether their shotguns were even loaded.

My head is swimming and my back hurts so much that I'm not sure I can move. This guy might have paralyzed me for all I know. I try to summon the magic, reaching deep inside myself for a spark. Nothing comes.

They take us into the biggest cabin, though that isn't saying much in this dilapidated community. If the machines did an aerial scan of the place, they would probably think it was uninhabited. Hard to believe anybody would call this home. It doesn't seem like a great place to live.

And it's probably a worse place to die.

As soon as I'm dragged through the door, I'm blinded by bright lights. My hand moves to shield my eyes as dirt gives way to wooden planks beneath my back.

When my eyes adjust, I survey my surroundings. I'm in a log cabin that looks much sturdier than the homes I saw outside. Mismatched wooden planks are nailed to walls in makeshift repairs. The windows are boarded up, which makes my blood run cold. They don't want anybody seeing what happens in here.

The room is hot and a strong scent of chemicals lies heavy on the air. Equipment fills the space, though I can't tell exactly what it's for. Scrap metal and android parts cover the metal tables and shelves that litter the floor. Are these people disassembling war machines and bringing them here?

A thin, wiry man in a lab coat slouches over one of the tables, inspecting tools spread out on a tray. He pauses to study us through smudged eyeglasses. His white lab coat is stained with old blood. The man presses his lips together in a sort of grimace, almost like he's disappointed to see us.

Rowan and Lark sit unconscious and slumped over in chairs on the other side of the room, an area that might have once been used for dining. Their hands and feet are bound tight with rope. Two other chairs are empty, facing what appears to be an operating table. The clowns remove Otis's and Catriona's hoods.

"What is all this?" Otis says, scanning the room. "Y'all building your own pet androids?"

Quinn watches us through his demon mask. "Not exactly. Put him on the table."

The big one lifts me off the floor like he's picking up a child's toy. For a second, I get a better look at the room. It's almost entirely machines or medical equipment, but against one wall I see a shelf crammed with books. Along the spines of some are arcane symbols. I can make out the title of the biggest one.

Elemental Incantations.

"You can't be serious," Catriona says.

She breaks away from the man guarding her and confronts the leader, staring boldly right into Quinn's demon mask. "This is all a delusion. You can't actually believe that you can access magic this way."

Quinn cocks his head to the side, as if sizing her up. "Well, not yet, but fortune favors the bold, little rabbit. Got some strange readings off your boyfriend over there. Whatever he's got inside him might be just what we've been looking for."

The big guy plops me down on the table so hard it sends a new rush of pain shooting up my back.

"Ha!" Otis's face lights up with understanding. "You've been doing your *own* cybernetic implants to gain magical powers? That's crazy, even for me."

Quinn lays Catriona's shotgun on a table, grabs a rusty scalpel, and examines it. "Maybe it is. Maybe it ain't. As you can see from my family, we've been doing alright with the cybernetics so far. The good doctor here had some experience in the area before the world fell into the abyss."

He taps on his skull. "He even saved my life with a little tech upgrade. Now, we've given him the opportunity to use his skills for the betterment of mankind. And we're doing just dandy, if you ask me. Got the drop on you, didn't we?"

The big guy rips open my shirt with steel hands, exposing my chest. Quinn approaches, wielding the knife. He grabs a lamp and shines it into my face. "Nice thing about you is that we don't have to worry about keeping you alive."

"No!" Catriona darts to me. But the behemoth grabs her and holds her in a giant bear hug. She kicks at his knees, but her foot thuds against what must be more machine than bone. She gasps, but then kicks again, searching for a weak point.

I try to will the magic out of myself, struggling to remember what it felt like in the village when the android seized the baby. It was the rage inside me that sparked the power, the same rage I feel now. I focus on that anger, that intensity, trying with all I can to force it forward, screaming out with my mind and soul for the fire to return so I can blast these hillbillies to kingdom come. *C'mon! If there is a God or Breath or whatever, now is definitely the time to show up!*

Nothing comes. No spark. No tingle up my spine or glow in the corner of my vision. Nothing to save me from the demon looming over me with a rusty blade.

"The doctor will handle most of the procedure, but I like to make the first few cuts myself. Don't worry. I'm getting pretty good at it. Gotta keep learning new things, friend. That's how you stop the aging process."

"Don't do this," I say, trying to buy myself some time. "You want to learn more about the tech that's inside me? Keep me alive. Study me. Seriously, how much do you really know about what you're doing here?"

Quinn straightens himself, grabs his mask, and removes it. A half-human face looks back at me. The flesh on the right side of his face appears to have deteriorated, revealing a mess of steel and wires. His right eyeball is held in place by metallic prongs. It looks as if his skin has been eaten away by the machine.

"You really are quite the monster," Otis says.

Quinn gives Otis a sinister look over his shoulder. "Well, you're one to talk, aren't you? We're not so different, you and I."

Across the room, Lark moans a little in her chair. She stirs and tugs against her bonds.

One of the men points at her. "She's waking up!"

Quinn looks over his shoulder. The human side of his face twists as his voice screeches. "Then dose her again!"

The man produces a syringe from a pouch on his waist. He goes over to Lark and prepares to jam it into her neck.

Otis breaks into a full spasm, struggling violently against his bonds. He jumps up and down, thrashing like he's losing control. "This is all insane! Look at you."

The man with the syringe pauses and looks to Quinn for orders. Lark is muttering under her breath, trying to break free of the drug-induced sleep.

Quinn gives Otis an evil grin. "He's trying to stall. Give her the dose *right now!*"

The man does as he's told, shoving the needle straight into Lark's neck. Seconds later, her head slumps over.

Otis doesn't stop. "Do you have any idea how much data it takes to successfully perform elemental magic? I do. It's way more information than any android could store on its own, let alone your stupid hillbilly brain. Not to mention the insane amounts of power it takes to cast a single spell. So unless you're planning to connect your head to the machine data cloud and happen to have a metric ton of spare batteries in this dump, none of this is going to work!"

The other cyborgs cast glances at each other. I can't see their faces through the masks, but they're looking to each other as if for affirmation. Is this working? Is Otis actually causing them to doubt each other?

Still holding the scalpel, Quinn pushes away from the table and marches toward Otis. The doctor watches from the side of the room. For the first time, I notice a scar on the doctor's left cheek. I don't need telepathy to know he's not one of them; he's as much of a prisoner as I am.

As Quinn approaches him, a single bead of sweat forms on Otis's brow and trickles down the human side of his face. The two of them are a stark contrast. Otis's implants are the handiwork of the war machines. The lines between metal and flesh are clean, seamless. His steel shimmers as if new.

But Quinn is a twisted thing, like sin given form, corruption animated. The metal in his face is various shades of black and dull silver, probably pieced together from scrap and spare parts. Judging from my surroundings, I wouldn't be surprised if the rough workmanship wasn't the doctor's fault. This facility doesn't exude a sense of quality.

Quinn holds the scalpel to Otis's face, the edge of the blade a twitch away from carving into his eye. "What's your alternative, friend? Living in their prison camps or hiding out here in the woods"—Quinn swats at something near his head with his free hand—"with all these cursed bugs! No. This is our chance, and we will take it. *Men at some time are masters of their fates.*"

"*Death will come when it will come,*" Otis responds.

Quinn draws back. He seems surprised.

Otis spits on the floor. "I've read a few books too."

"You missed a few words," Quinn says with a smirk.

"I didn't miss anything," Otis says. "I just like it better my way."

That garners a knowing chuckle from the mad cyborg. He turns back to me, ready to get to work, but waves a hand in the direction of Otis and Catriona. "Kill them both. She's worthless and I'll pull what I need off his corpse later."

"No!" I shout louder, struggling against my bonds, trying with everything I have to break free.

As Quinn leans over me and readies his blade, two of his men place guns to the heads of Otis and Catriona.

Suddenly a loud roar shakes the cabin. The sound is deafening, like the engine of a war machine bomber jet. Dust falls from the ceiling. Metal instruments rattle and tumble to the floor. Have the machines found us? Did they track us to the camp? I might rather die here than go back with Andy.

But there's no explosion, no crackle of gunfire that accompanies war machine attacks.

Outside the cabin, somebody screams. I remember the brief moment when Lark was trying to wake up, the low mumbling, and I realize what she was doing. I never thought I'd be so glad to hear this word shouted in terror by one of the cyborg flunkies.

"Monster!"

The wall of the cabin bursts apart, the wood splintering to millions of pieces. The river beast rams its head through the wall, water dripping off its scales.

The largest cyborg is closest to the wall, but before he can react, the monster chomps down on his body with massive jaws. It lifts the hulking man into the air, then flings his bloody body across the sky. Otis's rifle falls to the floor.

Otis and Catriona move at the same time, both throwing their shoulders into the stunned cyborgs, causing them to drop my pistols. The weapons slide across the floor and under a table.

The beast crashes its way in through the broken wall, its huge feet like those of a hippo, though much larger and bearing claws. Its eyes lock on Quinn, and it pauses as if savoring the moment.

Quinn hurls his scalpel at the monster in desperation. The beast rears back for an instant.

"Hold it off!" Quinn dashes toward the door, pushing through his clown-faced henchman as they come to their feet. Both men step forward, putting themselves between the beast and their fleeing leader.

The monster strikes like a prehistoric viper, clamping down on the first cyborg clown. When it pulls away, the lower half of the cyborg's body falls over. A pool of blood spreads across the floor.

The other cyborg bursts out of the room, leaving us with the monster. Only the doctor remains. He stands frozen against the wall, his mouth agape.

Catriona runs over with a bone saw from the table. She uses it to cut my straps. There's a question in her eyes and I know what it is.

But I keep watching the beast. It's nudging Lark with its nose, trying to rouse her.

I jump off the table and rush to Lark and Rowan. Amazingly, the monster pulls back to give me room as I cut their ropes.

When their bonds are severed, Otis and I lift Rowan out of the chair and carry him between us.

Catriona moves to grab Lark, but the monster pushes her out of the way with its nose. The beast gingerly lifts Lark with its jaws.

We collect our weapons and head outside. The other cyborgs in the village watch us, but none make a move. The ones who held the guns to our heads are nowhere to be seen. All that's left are those who appear sick and weak. They watch us with wary eyes, the children hiding behind the legs of their parents.

It's strange; they don't seem threatening anymore. I'm surprised at the sudden compassion I feel for them, even after their leader tried to cut out my heart. These people are hungry, deformed, and desperate, trying to make their way in the world. For all I know, they were unwilling captives of that maniac.

But that doesn't mean I trust them, either.

I can hardly imagine what we must look like—a giant river monster with a mage in its jaws, surrounded by two more people and a cyborg carrying another mage.

As we leave, they follow us, moving slowly. When we're at the edge of their camp, I let Catriona take my place under Rowan's arm. I face the cyborgs, making eye contact with each of them.

The doctor steps to the front of the crowd. He starts to speak five different times before finally settling on, "Thank you."

I'm not sure what to say, but before I know it, words are coming out of my mouth. "Do you think he'll come back?"

The doctor shakes his head. "I don't know. Quinn is persistent, but I have a feeling he's more likely to come after you. He's drawn to power."

The last thing I need is another enemy, but there's nothing I can do about that now. "Then you're all free now. What you do with that freedom is up to you."

"If you need our help, you know where to find us," the doctor says.

I don't want anybody cutting me open and shoving more tech in my body. I don't say it. Instead, I nod. "Thanks."

The community stares as we leave. It doesn't seem like a threat, but maybe a plea for help. Perhaps if my telepathy was stronger, I'd be able to tell what they're thinking. Maybe the doctor can take over. Hopefully he's smart enough to keep them alive.

The whole scene reminds me of the insanity of the world. Voluntary cyborgs trying to backdoor their way into elemental magic by impersonating their steel warlords. Then again, they're trying to survive in this mad world like the rest of us. For now, I'm just glad they're not attacking.

I'm not in the mood to see anybody else die today.

"So you called out to her?" I ask Lark as we ride through the woods. Lark and Rowan are hunched over in the saddle, their bodies swaying as they fight off the grogginess of the cyborgs' drugs. We probably should have given them more time to recover after the river monster returned home and Lark called back our horses, but we didn't want to wait too long before pressing on. Who knows what else might be lurking in these woods?

"I guess I did," Lark says. "I don't remember much of it, to be honest. I kept having weird dreams that *I* was swimming through the lake, hunting for fish. The next thing I knew, I was smashing through a wall and eating cyborgs."

"Speaking of life connection," Catriona says to Rowan, "how did those cyborgs get to us so easily? Don't the trees warn you if there's danger around?"

"I sent out a last call for signs of androids before I went to sleep." Rowan continues to sag, though I'm not sure it's all from the drugs. His demeanor reminds me of when Lark told us about their sister, the way he nearly broke down in tears. "But those weren't androids. I didn't think to check for . . ." He shakes his head in apparent disgust with himself.

"A bunch of freaks trying to be gods?" Otis says from the rear of our pack. "A bunch of crackpots who thought if they could make themselves look like the machines, jam enough gears and techno-junk into their bodies, they could start doing hocus pocus too?"

What did they want with you, Gunnar? I keep waiting for somebody to ask the question. I'm not sure that Lark and Rowan are thinking clearly enough to realize I had something the cyborgs wanted. Otis knows, but he hasn't brought it up. Maybe he's keeping the information so he can hold it over me later.

That leaves Catriona, but she still hasn't asked the question I know is on her mind.

"Can't blame them," I say, trying to shift the topic. "I've been trying forever to develop whatever type of magic is inside me."

Catriona glances at me. "What type of magic do you want it to be?"

The question catches me off guard. "What do *I* want it to be? Do I get to choose?"

"The Breath chooses you," Rowan says. "And it chooses how it will use you."

"No choice, huh?" There's a hint of jealousy in Otis's voice that I don't think he means to reveal. "Sounds like being a slave."

"Okay." Catriona looks around at everyone, eyes curious. "But if you could choose any power, what would you pick?" Catriona gestures at Lark and Rowan. "And not the power you already have, or each other's powers." She flashes a smile that mesmerizes me for a moment.

Rowan glares at her as if she's a small dog barking at a large bear, both annoyed and confused. Suddenly, the tension disappears from his face. "Flight."

The mental image of Rowan taking to the air is hilarious, but I don't laugh. I wonder whether he would want actual wings.

Catriona smiles again, then shifts her focus. "Lark?"

Lark rocks her head back and forth like she's shaking ideas around to see which one falls out. "Bending light so I could make myself and other people invisible."

I raise my eyebrows at her. "That's really specific. You must have thought about this before."

"Maybe." Larks ruffles the hair along her horse's neck.

I cast a look behind us. "What about you, Otis?"

"I don't play fantasy games," he says. "Got no desire for the Breath or the fire or the blood or whatever people want to use to try to get an edge. Worrying about that is how you end up like those people that tried to skin us alive."

He's not wrong, I guess, but I want to keep the game going. "Catriona?"

She shakes her head, her cheeks flushing. "Oh, no, I didn't mean everybody."

Lark reaches over from her horse and taps Catriona's arm. "It's a fun idea. What would you want to be able to do, if you could do anything?"

"I don't know," Catriona says. Then more slowly, "Actually, I do. But it's a little silly."

"Even better." I offer my most reassuring look. I don't like seeing her uncomfortable.

"Well," she admits, "I'd like to be able to be somewhere else. In a totally new place." She snaps her fingers. "Just like that."

"Teleportation?" Otis raises his eyebrows. "Not sure any of the known magics can do that."

"Known magics?" I ask.

Otis swats at a bug buzzing near his head. "Well, it's not elemental, so the machines can't do it. It does have to do with moving the body, so maybe life-based magic could achieve it, but I've never heard of anything like that."

The paintings on the temple wall come to mind. Didn't one of them show a human body vanishing into thin air? I decide not to bring it up. I'm still the new kid in school.

Lark eyes him. "Now you're the authority on the Breath?"

Otis touches the metal part of his skull. "Got all kinds of information downloaded to the old hard drive, kitty cat."

"Speaking of that," I say, "what was that exchange between you and the cyborg leader back at that camp? All those lofty quotes you were trading back and forth?"

Otis laughs. "Crazy idiot was quoting Shakespeare. Guess he thought that made him clever."

"You recognized it," I remark, "and spit some right back at him. Does that make you clever too?"

"Only drawing attention to his own ridiculousness." Otis gives a mock bow in the saddle as if he has performed a grand service. "Memorizing pieces of great works so you can spout them out is arrogance. Knowing them and keeping them to yourself is called being cultured."

Lark scoffs. "Right, Otis. You're a real scholar."

"What other information are you keeping to yourself?" Rowan asks.

"Don't worry about it." Otis gives him a wink that makes me hold my breath for a second. The comment breaks the conversation and we return to riding in silence. Maybe it's better that way.

11

REDDINGTON IS A SMALL CITY

but appears to have been fairly affluent. A few tall buildings occupy the center of town, surrounded by smaller shops and restaurants bathed in the mid-morning light. I had almost forgotten that an entire civilization existed not long ago—buildings, cars, TVs, smartphones; now they almost seem like things from a storybook, another world. Otis explained on the ride that most of this city existed purely to support the android factory, back when people believed that robots—among many other purposes—would fight wars *for* them, not against them.

It's incredible to consider with the benefit of hindsight—an entire town devoted to sustaining mankind's creation of its own destruction.

Seems like a nice place to live, though.

As best we can tell, the streets are deserted. Our horses' hooves clop on the pavement as we ride past pharmacies, clothing boutiques, and trendy restaurants with exposed ceilings and chalkboard signs. There must not have been any fighting here after the war broke out; everything seems to be weathered, but there isn't much structural damage. It's like everybody decided to leave all at once, taking nothing with them.

Lark and Rowan ride at the front of our group, Otis behind them, followed by Catriona and me. I catch Otis taking an extra long look at a blue linen blazer in the window of a men's shop. "Want to try it on?" I ask him. "I mean, it is going to be your first day at the office. You want to make a good impression on the machines."

Otis scoffs. "Knew a few people who used to dress in suits like that. Drove nice cars, ate fancy food, the whole bit. Most of 'em turned tail early when the machines took over. The ones with the backbone to fight got themselves killed pretty—"

Lark pulls back on her reins and holds up an arm, signaling the rest of us to stop. She faces us and holds a finger to her lips.

"What?" I mouth. If I trusted the Scions more, I would allow them access to my mind so we could speak telepathically, although that wouldn't do Otis any good, and Catriona hasn't shown much knack for the Breath, either.

"Androids." Otis maneuvers his horse to the front, his eyes on something ahead of us.

"Aren't you able to detect them?" Catriona whispers.

Otis doesn't respond.

Far down the street, a few androids amble between the shops. Their steps are rigid, slow. They move as a group, but don't seem to walk in a specific direction.

"They're not transmitting any signals." I'm not sure if Otis is talking to us or himself.

"How's that possible?" Rowan asks. "Aren't they all connected wirelessly to the hive mind?"

"Supposed to be." Otis rides closer.

"What are you doing?" I ask. "This isn't the time to pick a fight."

"Just trying to get a scan." Otis inches toward the machines. The androids keep moving as if they don't realize that we're here.

"You've got to be kidding." Otis is grinning when he turns his horse and trots back to us. "Get a load of this. They're *decommissioned*."

The rest of us exchange confused looks.

"And y'all treat me like the dumb one," Otis says. "They're old models, scrap, discontinued. Machines probably decided it's more efficient to take them offline than destroy them. They must have some juice left in their bodies. I bet the hive mind wipes their programming, disconnects them from the comms signal, and lets them loose to eventually run out of energy and fall over."

"Could we use them?" I wonder. "You know, maybe reprogram them or something?"

Otis shoots me a look. "You got any android traps on you, Sparky? Maybe if you whistle real sweet and pat your thigh, one will come over and you can take it home. It's your responsibility, though. I'm not walking that thing."

I raise my hands in surrender. He's got a point.

Otis steals a quick glance back at the machines. "Interesting idea, though," he says under his breath.

"So they're not going to attack us?" Lark asks.

"I have no idea what they're going to do," Otis replies. "For all I know, they might not be capable of combat anymore."

Down the street, one of the androids turns its head in our direction. A low beeping sound emits from its body and it starts toward us.

I point at it. "We're about to find out."

Lark's horse shuffles back, huffing and twitching. She rubs its neck to calm it down. "Otis, is this a problem or not?"

"I'd rather not find out," Otis says as he trots away.

The other androids start in our direction. None appear to have any weapons, but here in the city, Lark's and Rowan's powers might not be quite as effective. There's very little life to draw energy from here.

The rest of us quickly turn our mounts and ride after Otis. Soon, we're at a decent run, taking the corner at the end of the block and moving down another street. I keep casting glances behind us, but the machines haven't caught up. At least if they're disconnected from the main war machine comms channel, they're not signaling to the hive mind that we're here. That means no mages.

At least, I hope not.

We take an indirect route around the city and onto a side street that leads away from town. The buildings dwindle away behind us, and soon we're in clear country again. It's flat here, few trees, but plenty of lush green grass and low, rolling hills. The factory emerges in the distance, located on a stretch of land not too far away. As soon as I see the parking lot, I mutter a low curse.

More androids.

At least it's not many. Probably fifteen or twenty wander the parking lot and the sides of the building. They're not bumping into each other, but they don't all move in the same direction, either.

"Why are they doing that?" Lark asks Otis.

"Beats me," Otis says.

Catriona has been surveying the area around us. "I think I know," she says. "This is where they were made, right? Where they were born? They lost their way, so they came back home."

"Whatever the reason," Otis points out, "we've got a big problem. My schematics say this building is a fortress. Our one viable entry point is right through the front door, which is currently blocked by those metal deadheads."

"I hate when people stand in doorways," I say.

Nobody laughs at my ill-timed joke, but Catriona does me the courtesy of quirking a smile.

"Seriously, though." I savor the sight of abundant greenery near the facility. "We've got some firepower and a bit of magic. Otis, how much time do you need?"

He pulls off his hat and wipes his brow, despite the fact that it's cold outside. "I need to get to the server farm and hardline in. It's long since disconnected from the grid, of course, but I can probably send enough phantom power to the box to—"

"*How much time?*" Rowan demands.

"Fifteen minutes," Otis says. "Maybe longer."

"Hopefully shorter," I remark. "Not only do we have to deal with a bunch of unpredictable zombie androids, but if this takes too long, the commotion might draw the attention of war machines that haven't been cut from the team yet."

"It's the original source of the signal," Otis goes on. "The juice is worth the squeeze. If I can get the access code, I can hack the primary comms channel and tell the war machines whatever we want."

"We're doing it." From the tone of Rowan's voice, he's not interested in hearing any counter opinions.

I don't deny the twinge of fear creeping into the back of my mind, but there's also exhilaration. The cyborgs got the drop on us in the woods. At least this time, the element of surprise is on our side.

And the truth is—decommissioned or not—I've been itching for a chance to smash some machines.

"Wouldn't be mad if Zara was here right now," Lark mumbles under her breath.

"Who's Zara?" Catriona asks.

"Besides being the focus of Rowan's interests," Otis jabs "Zara can turn herself and those around her invisible, even against thermal imaging. Useful trick."

Lark continues the explanation. "She and a few others ventured out several months ago to look for more like us. We haven't had contact with them since they left. They—"

"Let's move." Rowan cuts the conversation short by heeling his horse forward, his shoulders tense in a posture indicating he's not comfortable with the chatter.

We turn down the small, curving side street that leads up to the facility. I pull one of my guns as we ride toward the door. "Probably shouldn't attack until they do."

"Agreed." Lark nods. "Let's not start anything, but we'll finish it if we have to."

When we reach the parking lot, an android appears to notice us. It halts for a few seconds, then starts walking in our direction.

"Let's make this quick." Otis rides to the door, the rest of us close behind. When we reach the door, we form a defensive semicircle while Otis uses his metal arm to smash through the glass.

"Y'all play nice and wait for Daddy right here," he says, then disappears into the building.

Lark rolls her eyes.

The machines shuffle toward us, gathering like storm clouds. The horses churn their hooves on the pavement and turn in tight circles.

"Let's dismount." I step out of the saddle. "Rather fight these on foot."

The others do the same.

"I'll tell the horses to wait for us at the road," Lark says. The horses take off at a run, moving through the androids. The machines pay no attention to the animals, as if they're not even there.

They continue pressing toward us.

"At what point do we consider this aggression?" Catriona readies her shotgun.

I draw both pistols. "I think we're about there."

As if on cue, one of the androids lunges forward and tries to grab me. I dance back and put a bullet into the weak spot in its neck. The android falls over.

More of them raise their arms. Their eyes flicker like the power inside them is fading. Even for machines, I can tell they're dead inside— disconnected from the power that once animated them, that gave them purpose. I know the feeling.

Lark shifts her hands into paws and jumps at an android. She latches onto its metallic frame and uses her powerful claws to rip out its wires, disabling it.

More approach. I take one down with my pistols. Catriona blasts the head off another with her shotgun. Rowan turns the flesh on his arms to bark and punches a few androids, causing them to falter back.

When another comes close enough, I gun it down. It's satisfying to watch the glow disappear from their eyes as they fall, but the experience is odd. "This seems kinda . . ."

"Easier than it should be?" Lark prepares to attack the next machine that approaches. Despite our counterattacks, the androids don't move any faster or slower. They keep coming at the exact same pace.

"Not for long." Catriona says as another group moves in from the other side of the parking lot.

I turn and shout through the broken glass door. "Otis! Hurry up!" I wheel back around and take aim with both pistols.

The wave of machines grows thicker in front of us. Rowan knocks a few more back. Lark swipes at a couple, severing more wires, but she's more defensive now, striking quickly and backing away. Catriona blasts an android, then slips behind us to reload.

I drop two more, but they're immediately replaced by reinforcements. A quick glance to my left and I see that Lark and Rowan have their hands full too.

Before I can turn back, an android hammers me with its arm, dropping me to the ground. Catriona fires, blasting the android back.

"There's too many!" Lark yells as I come to a knee, firing at two more.

"We can't let them through!" I shout. Otis is still inside getting the access code that might be our most powerful weapon against the machines. We have to buy him more time.

Catriona and I fight side by side, shooting as fast as we can. Rowan and Lark use their powers to keep the others at bay. It feels like we're holding them off, but I notice that we're also backing a little closer to the door every second. The machines are surrounding us, flooding us, their eyes cold and lifeless as they reach for us.

My guns click empty. Catriona's does the same, so she flips the shotgun in her hands and swings it like a bat. *She's about to be overwhelmed.*

The fire comes to me without thought, starting as a sharp stab in my chest. The sensation is more intense than before, but the pain doesn't bother me, not this time. A feeling like hot, carbonated liquid surges down my arms. Every hair on my body stands on end. The air crackles as the energy builds, as if anticipating what is to come.

The power explodes out of my hands, obliterating three androids in front of us.

"Yeah!" I jump to my feet and blast again, taking out two more androids that apparently didn't get the message.

But just as quickly as it came, the fire dwindles. I can feel the flow of it diminishing in my veins.

I strain, trying to spark it again, but I can't. The power is gone, and Andy is coming on stronger than ever.

My heart races. I shove an android away with my bare hands, but another hits me in the back of the head. I stumble into Catriona, knocking both of us to the ground.

Panic wracks my body. If they swarm us while we're down, we might never get up.

The android is looming over me, reaching with metal fingers.

Something behind the android grabs its shoulder and pulls it back, giving me enough time to get to my feet and help Catriona to hers.

Once up, we see that another machine has grabbed the one that attacked me and thrown it to the ground. My savior android grips its brother's metal skull and wrenches it off.

"Are you seeing this?" I look around. More androids are seizing the attacking war machines, pulling them away from us. It's only a few in the crowd, but it's enough. The attacking androids turn on the traitors in their midst, wrestling against them.

"They're fighting each other!" Lark shouts and slashes at an android that's being held by its brethren. The androids devolve into chaos—the attackers trying to break free, the defenders pulling them away and destroying them.

"Got it!" Otis appears in the lobby of the building, running toward us at full speed. He hurtles through the broken glass door. "Let's go!"

Rowan charges into the crowd of warring machines, clearing them with huge wooden arms.

We dash through the cacophony of androids fighting amongst themselves. When we reach the other side of the horde, we sprint to the road where the horses are waiting for us.

I grab onto the saddle and prepare to pull myself up. Before I can, something grabs hold of my mind. The sensation is jarring, like a tuning fork in my head. I stagger back. I hear my horse snort and buck, but my vision clouds as the feeling travels down my spine and into my chest, tugging at my heart, beckoning me.

"Gunnar?"

At the sound of Catriona's voice, the sensation dissipates. My vision returns. I collect myself, trying to determine what's just happened. *Must have been an aftereffect of the magic.*

CORONARY IMPLANT POWER LEVEL: 35%.

The rest of them watch me from their mounts. My horse is twitching, but Lark holds an open hand toward it and the animal settles down.

"What's wrong with you?" Otis asks.

I shake my head and pull myself into the saddle. "I'm fine. Let's go."

From their faces I know they want to ask more, but we can't linger. Otis takes the lead without further questions.

We ride away as fast as we can.

"So they were protecting us?" I kneel to drink from the river, then splash some cool water on my face, thankful for the cover of the trees that arch over my head. Catriona and Rowan do the same, while Lark tends to the horses. The cold water is refreshing, reassuring—pure, abundant life washing over me. The strange sensation hasn't returned. My heart stopped pounding a few minutes after we were back in the safety of the forest, but none of us have spoken until now. I kept expecting to see another android hiding behind every tree.

"Seems pretty obvious to me." Otis lounges at the base of a pine, watching the rest of us. I can tell by this posture that he loves being the expert on the war machines. Maybe it's his insecurity about being the one Scion who doesn't use magic, but talking about the machines gives him an excuse to look down on the rest of us. "The original prime directive of the AI was to protect human beings. All the other garbage got heaped on top of that code—the best way to protect most of us would be to destroy some of us, the well-being of many outweighs the needs of few, all that . . . logic." He laughs to himself.

Rowan fills his canteen. "Then why did some of them attack us?"

Otis shrugs. "I don't really know. I couldn't see inside their heads. My guess—their programming is screwed up, but maybe not screwed up in the same way for each one. Some still operate on the attack protocol, others have the protect command."

Lark feeds the horses by hand. "Is there any way to tell the difference between the friendly androids and the murdery ones?"

"Nope." Otis pushes away from the tree and stretches. "Not that I can tell."

I take another drink and stand up, reliving the attack in my head. At least the magic showed up, if only for a few seconds. I guess that means I'm getting closer, but closer isn't good enough in a world that's constantly trying to destroy us, one way or another. If those androids hadn't turned on each other, they would have torn us apart.

No use dwelling on a bad thing that didn't happen. I regard Otis. "You got what you needed though, right?"

Otis grins. "Sure did. Access codes for the machines' primary communication signal."

"Have you already hacked into it?" Catriona asks him.

Otis shakes his head. "The signal's not strong enough here. I need to get back to the bunker. I've got amplifiers there."

"Then let's go," Rowan says shortly, returning to his horse.

I start to respond, but out of nowhere, the strange vibration returns. I feel the pull on my heart again, stronger this time, urging me toward the west, the opposite direction of the temple. The sensation almost makes me nauseous. Catriona's eyes are on me, and it makes me wonder if she feels it too.

"I'm not going with you," I say. "There's . . . something out there that's calling to me. Maybe it's connected to my powers. I don't know, but I have to go find out."

"Alone?" Lark raises an eyebrow. "You think you can survive out here by yourself? Your powers are growing, but you have a long way to go."

I appreciate what Lark is saying. She's not being unkind, but I can't stop thinking about the androids. They almost had us back at the facility. It was worth the risk, but now that we have the access codes for the machine comms signals, the stakes have changed.

"Lark's right," Rowan says. "You're literally walking through a landscape made of things that my magic turns into allies. You don't think you need this kind of backup as you venture off into the unknown?"

Rowan's right, but this is bigger than me. "The truth is, I'm sick of looking at all of you."

That gets a snicker out of Otis, but the others don't bite. They have learned that I hide behind sarcasm.

"All right." I try a different approach. "Think about it this way. The access code is way too valuable to risk losing. This time we were up against zombie-bots. Before that, it was freaking cyborg psychos and river monsters—"

"Hey!" Lark interrupts. "That river monster saved your life."

"True," I agree. "I only meant to say we don't know what we're going to run into out here. And what if next time, Otis doesn't make it out and we lose our ability to hack the machine frequency? It's not worth it."

They exchange glances, but don't say anything.

I take a breath. This is the moment where I make myself clear. Besides, maybe what I need is some solitude. Maybe the power will continue to develop if I don't have magic trees and monsters to bail me out. "This isn't up for discussion. If you stick with me, I'll make a break for it the first chance I get and leave you all behind."

"You think we can't find you, hot shot?" Lark gestures to the trees and nature and everything else that speaks to her and her brother. "Out *here*?"

"Sparky's right," Otis answers as he pulls himself into the saddle.

Rowan shoots him a glance. "You would say that."

"Fine, I'm a real jerk," Otis retorts. "I like the kid as much as any of you. He's right, though. What I've got in my head is too valuable."

"Look," I say, stepping toward them. "I'll be surrounded by nature, right? If things go wrong, I promise to tell the nearest sapling. Maybe you'll be able to feel it or whatever. You can come back and help me out. I'll be fine. Maybe I'll attract less attention on my own."

"You shouldn't go alone," Catriona says.

I open my mouth, but she lifts up a hand. "I'm coming with you."

The others stare at her and I start to protest before realizing how much I would like her company.

I nod and give her a smile. "Let's go."

"Fine," Lark huffs. "But you both be careful."

The sensation grows stronger as Catriona and I ride for what seems like hours in the direction of the pull. The experience is so all-encompassing that I don't notice the passage of time until the sky is filled with stars. On another night, I might have suggested that we make camp, but the mystery keeps me going. Stopping is not an option.

The ground gets steeper every moment. Soon, the trees clear

away and I see a mountain shrouded in darkness in front of us, looming like a giant.

"Do you think that's it?" Catriona asks. "That's where it's coming from?"

"Seems as likely a place as any."

"It's not what I thought it would be like."

"Really? What would you have preferred?"

She smiles. "I don't know. Maybe a place to train, but . . . quietly. Leisurely."

"I can't have too much leisure. I'll be too busy getting all magical."

She laughs. It wasn't *that* funny, but in a few seconds, I'm laughing too. It's because of her, I think, but suddenly the whole exchange seems absolutely hysterical.

Catriona stops laughing long enough to take her hands off the reins and wiggle her fingers, casting a fake spell. "Abracadabra!" The horse shakes and Catriona nearly loses her balance. She grabs the saddle, barely avoiding falling off.

It's the most hilarious thing I've ever seen. I can't breathe I'm laughing so hard. Tears well in my eyes. I've never been drunk before, but I imagine the experience is similar.

What is happening? A small piece of awareness inside my mind starts to speak, but it's buried beneath layers of clouds. It's like I'm watching myself become intoxicated with laughter, but I can't do anything about it.

"Why . . ." I almost can't get the words out. "Why . . . are . . . we . . . laughing so hard?"

"I have no idea!" Catriona almost snorts.

The laughter becomes uncontrollable, my body at war with itself. The horses whinny; something is wrong. Really wrong.

My hands start to move on their own, directing the horse toward the base of the mountain. I'm watching it happen from the inside, trapped in my own skin.

"Gunnar!" Catriona has tears in her eyes, but I can't tell if it's from the laughter or the fear. "We have to get away from here." But her body follows me.

The laughter grows so strong that I can hardly breathe. The horse follows my lead. Trees clear again and we're at the base of the mountain. In front of us, a large fissure opens into a dark cave.

Catriona manages to climb out of the saddle, but when I try, I lose my balance and hit the ground.

"It's some kind of drug," Catriona gasps, barely managing the words.

I try to pull myself up, but I can't. The laughter tapers off, pushed away by a thick fog in my brain. The vibration returns, but now I feel as if it will make me vomit. The sounds around me grow distant and distorted. My vision blurs as the clouds spread over my eyes. Catriona and the horses become vague, wavy shapes.

A dark figure glides out of the mouth of the cave.

"Look . . ." I try to raise my hand, try to piece the words together, but they evade me. I can't grab hold of any of them, no matter how hard I try. "Look . . . Cat . . ."

More figures emerge. Some appear to envelope Catriona.

The incantation of the fire mage spills out of my mouth. *"Ignis sacer terrae. Mandata mea."* Somehow it's the only thing I can say.

The power flickers in my body, but the fog moves over it, dousing the flames.

My arms lift, but not because I told them to. No, not just my arms. My entire body is lifted and moved into the cave. It's like I'm flying; my entire body numb.

The shadows claim me, just as they did on the day my parents were killed. I try to cry out with my mind to Lark, Rowan, Taron, even to the trees, but I can't push anything out of my head. The darkness won't let me. The nightmare overtakes me, but that isn't the most terrifying part.

What scares me more than anything is the warmth of it, the comfort, the happiness. There is something here for me, I know it. Whatever this is could kill me, destroy both of us, but it doesn't.

So what does it want?

12

I CAN'T SEE ANYTHING. I CAN'T

hear anything. My body won't respond to my commands. I have a vague sense of my surroundings, but it's muffled and murky, like swimming through dark water. It makes me wish that I would pass out. That would be better than this terror.

After a while, the haze that clouds my mind dissipates, as if drawn away by invisible hands. It happens so fast that it's unsettling. I almost try to cling to it, like a child yanking back their covers to hide from the morning light. I didn't want to go to sleep, but now I don't want to wake up.

The light approaches from a distance, but closes in fast. The world rushes in—a cavernous room, a chair against my back, a stone table beneath my outstretched hands, the warm smell of roasted meat. My mouth waters. Maybe this is a dream after all, but it's a realistic one.

Strange statues line the surrounding walls. A stone dragon perches atop a jagged rock, wings outstretched, with long, curved horns that come to a point and appear to hold a human mask between them. A bird's head is cocked at an impossible angle on a woman's body. A man rips himself in half and doesn't seem to mind. Serpents, mermaids, monsters, angels—all of the statues watching as Catriona and I sit surrounded by hooded figures. The table is adorned with dripping meats, fruits, vegetables, and breads. A goblet of red wine waits in front of me.

Don't show them your fear. I try not to let my voice shake. "What's with the hoods? Does the chanting start soon?"

The figure across from me shifts in his seat. His voice is low, definitely male, though I can't discern his age. "*You* were chanting, Gunnar Graves, just moments ago. Attempting to conjure the war machine fire spell, yes?"

I glare at him, trying to think of a witty comeback. Nothing comes.

"It won't work," the hooded figure goes on. "You can't perform magic their way."

I lean forward. "And you're the authority on that?"

The hooded figure lifts a hand. An invisible force presses against my chest and pushes me back into my chair.

Next to me, Catriona takes in a sharp breath, but says nothing.

My eyes widen a little. "The Breath? Is this life magic?"

"In a way," says another of the figures, but I can't tell which one. "You should try your food. You must be famished."

I reach for a chicken leg on my plate, but pause before I touch it.

The figure across from me laughs. "Eat, Gunnar. If we wanted to kill you . . ." He flitters his hand like he can't be bothered to finish the sentence.

I pick up the chicken. "Since you're so generous, why don't you tell me how you did that? If it wasn't magic, what was it?" I take a bite. The chicken is juicy and spicy and so amazingly good I have to stop myself from melting in the chair.

The figure nods. "It was magic, but not the Breath. Don't buy into the false dichotomy, Gunnar. '*Our magic versus their magic.*' It's not that clean. It's not that limited."

"There's more?" I say through a mouthful of food.

Catriona hasn't touched her plate. Her face is ghostly white.

"Indeed," the hooded figure says. "And we would be happy to show you, to teach you."

I chuckle. "Well, you may regret that. Turns out I'm a pretty terrible magic student. Couldn't teach myself. Couldn't be taught by the Sci—" I stop before I reveal the name of the group. Is that a secret? Should it be? I need to be more careful.

"The Scions," the figure says. "Yes, we're aware. We would know even if we hadn't been inside your head. The name of Elisha has traveled well among the Underground."

"The Underground?"

The figure casually cracks his knuckles. For someone shrouded in darkness and mystery, he conducts himself like he's at a Sunday picnic. "It's what we call people who study the supernatural. Our order in particular dates back thousands of years."

I survey the room. The statues are giving me the creeps. They remind me of Lark's river monster. Did some of these other weird things once exist in the world as well? Are they back? And if so, are they lurking here somewhere as part of this order? "Thousands of years, huh? Your homecoming parties must be pretty awesome." I take another bite, watching the figures closely, looking for signs that maybe I'm dancing too close to the edge.

If they're offended or rattled, they don't show it. "There is immense power in what we do," the man says. "That's why we brought you here. We see great potential in you."

I sip the wine. It's smoother than I expected, tingly on my tongue. "This is a recruiting visit? You could have just sent a brochure."

I look into the dark figure's eyes, or at least, the place where I think his eyes ought to be underneath the hood. "If the Scions were here"—my tone changes—"they would tell you that I'm not a big fan of uninvited guests in my head."

"A necessary trespass," the figure says. "I would offer an apology, but it wouldn't be sincere. In the end, you'll thank me for bringing you to this place. After all, we're ready to offer what you've always wanted."

I'm suddenly aware that Catriona is breathing so hard beside me I think she might hyperventilate. Are they hurting her? Is this some type of magic? A cold sweat breaks across my forehead.

Enough games. Time to figure out what is going on. "And what have I always wanted?"

"Power." The figure raises his wine glass. White fingers grip the goblet, so pale that I wonder whether these people have been underground for years. Not a bad place to hide from the war machines.

"Revenge," he goes on, swirling his wine. "And more. Godhood."

"Godhood?" Now I know they're messing with me. I make a show of snatching a grape off a fruit plate in front of me to toss it into the air. I catch it in my mouth. "That's a pretty bold promise."

"We've never felt raw power like yours," the figure says.

"Is that so? Well, I've heard that one before."

He laughs. "Yes, I'm sure Elisha told you the same. We're not so different from the Scions, not when considered from a distance. To the war machines, we're all humans. Like the Scions, we're a greater threat because we wield a greater power, but the AI likely classifies us the same."

My body tenses. "Then how *are* you different?"

The figure reclines in his chair. He knows he has my full attention. "Call it a manner of perspective. To follow the Breath is to be enslaved to a higher being, your power totally dependent upon its whims. But our magic . . ." He lets the word ring out in the cavern, and it seems to echo for longer than is natural, as if the statues chant it back. "With our magic, we are the masters."

Next to me, Catriona trembles. I want to find out if she's okay, but her expression stops me from asking.

"What type of magic?" I ask instead.

"I'm surprised you don't know." The figure levels a finger at Catriona. "After all, you've been riding with a blood mage for quite some time."

My heart stops. A blood mage? That can't be true. My mind flashes back to the woods, to the first night in which we fled from the air mage and the other androids. Her lips moving with no sounds. Her bloodstained fingers.

She can't be . . .

But when I look for denial in her eyes, all I see is fear.

I don't have to ask.

"How did you know?" I realize that the question goes two directions. Did Catriona know she would bring me here, even when we were back in the village? How did these people know she was a blood mage?

Catriona says nothing, and across the table, the man uses his pale hands to grasp the sides of his hood. He pulls it back, allowing the dim firelight to fall on his face. Without his cover, I can see his bald head, his skin covered with splotches. One eye appears to be glazed over.

A glowing red gem hangs from his neck. "I know quite a lot about Catriona. We used to be very close, my daughter and I."

I feel like somebody has ripped the metal heart out of my chest. *His daughter?* It's too much to process at once. I consider taking another bite of food to buy myself some time, but my appetite is gone. In fact, I feel like I'm about to throw up all over this table.

Keep it together, Gunnar. I set my face. It's time to be strong, now more than ever. They're watching me, waiting to see what I'll do. I look him in the eyes and shrug. "So you're her father. Not sure what that has to do with anything."

"I guess it doesn't." He stands. "My name is Kedrick. I thought you might want to be introduced to your girlfriend's father. You know, meet the family and all."

I begin to correct him but Catriona speaks first.

"I'm not his girlfriend." It's the first thing she's said since we got here.

Kedrick raises his brow. "Well, listen, Gunnar. I'll put in a good word for you. Nothing beats the approval of a father in the eyes of a little girl, I think. Catriona used to do *everything* that I told her. She was a very fast learner."

He steps behind me as he talks. The invisible force that pushed me back into my chair is gone. At least, I think it is. If I try to stand up and it's still there, holding me back, it's going to make me look weak.

But I'm not a big fan of this guy lurking over me. It's a manipulation tactic and I'm sick of people trying to pull my strings.

When I stand, I find that there's nothing holding me in place. I shove the plate aside and take a seat on the table, putting my feet up in the chair, showing my back to the rest of them. It's probably an insult. I don't particularly care. "This has been great and everything. I should really be going. Stuff to do. Maybe when this is all over, we can grab a beer and you can play big man, toss out a few threats about what you'll do if I break her heart."

Kedrick shakes his head. "This isn't about threats. It's about opportunities."

"For you?"

"For all of us." He frowns thoughtfully. "I want what's best for my daughter."

I narrow my eyes. "You're not letting us leave, are you?"

"No, I'm afraid not. Not yet, at least."

I kick the chair over and jump to my feet. In a second, I'm face-to-face with Kedrick. The power stirs inside me. I wonder if now, of all times, it will *finally* answer my call. If I try and fail, I have no idea what these people will do to me or Catriona.

But I want to try.

"I don't like people telling me where I can and can't go." I stand a little taller than Kedrick. I make sure he knows it by looking down at him.

"You think I can't stop you?" he asks. "We've mastered our magic, Gunnar Graves. Have you? Can you call it forth at will? And if so, can you keep it from killing you along with everybody else?"

I keep my eyes on him. He's right to call my bluff, and I've never considered that summoning the fire might get out of my control and hurt me or anyone I care about. I try not to let him know he's rattled me as I nod back toward the table. "How about you leave the rest of your pajama party out of this? Just me and you, huh? No magic . . . blood or Breath or otherwise."

Kedrick steps close, his face nearly pressed against mine. "You have no idea who you're challenging, boy."

I clench my fists and consider my first move. If he's had any combat training, he'll expect the overhand right. It's hardwired into human DNA, the first move thrown by any irate moron who doesn't know better. So what does he think of me? If I fake it, will he go for the block and open himself up to a different strike?

"You want to test yourself against me?" Kedrick asks, stoking the flames of my anger.

My hands start to rise.

"Stop!" Catriona shoots out of her chair and moves between us. She places a firm hand against each of our chests. If I ever doubted that Kedrick was her father, his response to her touch proves it. There's a familiarity in the way his body loses tension, a momentary lapse in the story he's acting out with his words and actions. He won't risk hurting her.

"Let me talk to him," she says to her father. "Somewhere private."

Kedrick bestows her a smile. "Of course, my daughter. I have a room prepared for you. I even brought your things from home. You can talk there, take some time, then we'll reconvene."

Her things?

Catriona touches my arm and I follow her toward an opening between two of the statues, leading into a hallway lit by torches.

"Don't take too long, though!" Kedrick calls after us. "I'll be waiting."

Catriona and I are led down a dark corridor by a hooded figure. We pass several closed doors. How many of these people are here with Kedrick?

Eventually we stop at a door that appears no different than any of the others. The figure quickly rushes away, disappearing into the dark hallway, leaving us alone. I watch Catriona brace herself before she pushes the door open to reveal a small room. There's a single bed against the far wall, a candle burning on a nightstand, and a wooden trunk. A threadbare rug lies in the center of the floor.

Catriona pauses, then crosses the room and sits on the edge of the bed. She looks at me, her face taut. "I'm sorry, Gunnar." She takes a breath. "This is going to be hard to explain."

"Oh, you think?"

Her eyes are somber. "Don't pretend we don't both have secrets. I know those cyborgs saw something in you."

My first instinct is to deny it. I've spent years hiding what I am.

But I don't want to hide from her. "You're right," I say. "I haven't been totally honest with you."

Her expression softens. "I know, Gunnar. It seemed like something you couldn't talk about until the time was right. Maybe that will help you understand why I haven't told anyone about this until now."

Her logic makes sense, even if I'm not crazy about the overall scenario. There are better times to find out your travel companion is a blood mage than right after her father and his order of dark sorcerers have kidnapped you and are holding you prisoner in their underground temple.

But I'm in no position to point fingers. If it wasn't for me, Catriona would still be living her quiet, simple life outside the village. I'm beginning to understand why she enjoyed it so much. I have to give her the benefit of the doubt.

"All right, Catriona," I say. "Talk to me. I really mean it. I'm listening." I sit down beside her.

She fidgets a little, then gives a slight nod. "I don't know about my mother, but my father practiced potion magic for as long as I can remember. It was nothing at first, almost like a hobby. But when the war started, it became our way of life, not just his. We started meeting with others, studying all sorts of ancient books, casting spells for protection and concealment. At first it was all herbs, roots, holy waters, that sort of thing. Some of us never went any further than that. But my father and I . . . we . . ."

I nod to let her know I understand. "What kind of blood did you use?"

She bites her lip. "It depended on what we needed to do to survive. Certain types are more powerful than others. Sometimes we tried to cast spells against the machines, as if we could actually help humanity turn the tide. But those spells didn't seem to be as effective, so eventually, it just became about survival."

I stand and wander to the wall. *Blood magic.* My thoughts are filled with images of dark rooms, blades, candles, chalices, strange incantations. The truth is that I have no idea if that's how it works, but it's unsettling.

When I turn to face her, a single tear slips from the corner of her eye. "There's more," she says.

I brace myself. "Okay . . ."

She looks down. "We were captured by the machines. Some of us were killed, but my father was given a choice. The machines wanted to know how blood magic worked, specifically for tracking."

"Tracking?"

"Location is one of the simpler blood magic spells. If you have a sample of a person's blood, you can find them pretty easily."

"So if the machines had my blood . . ."

"They would be able to find you at all times. But even a close genetic match can be useful. Your blood would be required to know your exact location, but if they have the blood of a sibling, a child, a parent . . . there are spells that would give them a close approximation of where you are."

I freeze. That can't be possible.

Catriona looks up at me. "Was anyone in your unit ever captured? Anybody that would've been related to anyone that was still with you?"

Several. I don't say it. She already knows.

"My father . . ." She falters. There's a long silence before Catriona draws a shaky breath. "My entire group, really"—her voice cracks—"we were responsible for the death of your parents."

A new kind of pain pierces my heart at the memory of what I've lost. Anger starts to rise.

But as I look at her, as quickly as the anger and pain appears, so does my sympathy. I know how it feels to carry something inside that you have to keep hidden from the entire world. Neither of us had much of a choice, but it doesn't matter. The shame remains. "You were a child. I'm sure *you* didn't give the machines anything, and even if you did, I can't blame you. You didn't know how they would use it. Like you said, you were trying to survive."

Her head drops again. "Thank you." Her voice is almost inaudible.

But I'm still wondering one thing. "Is this why you didn't participate in any of the Breath training?"

She offers a melancholy smile. "It won't work for me because of what I've done. Forces like that don't use people like me. The blood magic did things to my soul that can't be undone."

I go to her side. "We don't have to stay with the Scions," I say, and despite everything that's happened, I mean it with all my heart. "Maybe you and I can go somewhere else. We'll find a—"

She stops me. "I don't want to leave that group. I believe in what the Scions are doing and I'll play whatever role they ask me to play."

"Why would you believe in a power that you can't use?"

When Catriona looks at me, I realize she's much wiser than I could ever hope to be. "My belief in something has nothing to do with my ability to use it or control it," she says. "I made my choices and I'm okay with them."

I place my hand on hers. "Then we'll stay with the group."
She nods, eyes glistening with tears of relief.

Kedrick sends two of his mages to fetch us about an hour later. They appear at the door, their skin totally hidden by dark robes. At this point, I'm pretty certain the cloaks are more about intimidation than magic or tradition.

They lead Catriona and me down a series of hallways lit by torches. Again, we pass several wooden doors built into the rock walls. The doors are thick and reinforced with metal slabs. It makes me wonder what else the blood mages are hiding down here.

We come to another room, large like the dining area, but with an altar built into the far wall. Kedrick stands atop a stone platform, still in his robes, but with his hood pulled back, and flanked on either side by blood mages. Dozens of candles cast him in firelight. In front of him is a small stone table, upon which sits an oversized chalice. Behind him, a massive tree is carved into the rock. The flickering candlelight gives the illusion that the tree is burning.

Catriona and I are ushered to stand in front of the table, looking up the steps at Kedrick and the other mages.

I gesture toward our hooded escorts as they slink away. "Your people here are pretty chatty, Kedrick. Told us all your secret spells and everything."

He snorts. "I doubt that. These are initiates, new to our order, still proving themselves."

"They said they were here for the free food." I can't help myself. "They're going to take off in another day or so."

Kedrick ignores me and addresses the hooded figures. "Show them."

The mages who led us here stand along the far wall. They remove their hoods in perfect unison. It's a man and a woman, both roughly my age. The man has dark hair, shaved short. The woman's is a bit longer, though not much. They're attractive, except for the fact that neither has a mouth. The skin is smoothed over where lips should be.

I clear my throat. "Nice trick. Makeup?"

Kedrick spreads his hands. "There are lots of powers available to us that the Scions and the machines either can't or are afraid to achieve. Facial manipulation, teleportation, mind control . . ."

"Tracking," I add. "That's the trick you used to save your own skin, isn't it?"

Kedrick turns to Catriona. "So you told him."

"He knows everything," Catriona replies, a bit louder than she usually speaks.

Kedrick merely waves a hand. "Good. That should save us some time. Yes, we showed the machines how to use blood magic to track humans. It's a simple process, really. And it's one of the first spells you'll learn."

I point a finger to my chest. "That *I'll* learn? Did I sign up for something?"

"We did you a favor," Kedrick says. "You have to abandon childish notions of God and of good and evil. Right and wrong is an illusion. There is only power and those who are willing to take it and wield it. Don't let preconceived notions cloud your judgment. You use blood once and people call you a blood mage forever. I'm not apologizing for that, but there is so much more to our order. We are the true students of magic. You want to make a difference, Gunnar Graves? You want to destroy the machines that killed your parents? I can give you that opportunity. I can teach you. There is great power in you, anyone can see that. I would wager that many people already have."

My stomach tightens. "What's that supposed to mean?"

Kedrick looks at me, bemused. "Found it difficult to hide, have you? When you were in your settlement camp, I bet you wanted nothing to do with anybody else, yet the people were drawn to you, weren't they?"

This is getting weird. How could he know that?

"Despite your best efforts," Kedrick goes on, "they wouldn't leave you alone, right? Do you know why? It's the power, Gunnar. People— even those who don't know the first thing about magic, even the morons with no idea about the real world—are drawn to it. They're attracted to your strength. They can't help it."

"Meaning what?" I ask. "Is this the part where you tell me I'm the chosen one?"

Kedrick shakes his head. "That's not how it works. Prophecies take away the free will to choose your own path, much like the machines. We fight against such ideologies. You are not the chosen one, but you may be the one who chooses. That's what this is all about."

He's stealing Elisha's lines. I don't mention it.

"What about the Scions?" I ask. "I suppose aligning with you means that I'm against them? I can't do that. They saved my life. They saved your daughter's life."

"I have no war with the Scions." Kedrick shrugs. "They are free to practice their religion however they like. I would prefer that they join our fight against the machines, but I will not punish them for abstaining, either."

He tilts his head as if considering something. "But if they get in the way . . ." He doesn't finish the sentence.

I turn the idea over in my mind. Other than the magic they used to bring me here, the blood mages haven't hurt me, and I definitely believe they have power. It's dark, of course, but maybe that's what I need to defeat the machines.

But Kedrick is playing games with me. Elisha may have thus far failed to unlock the magic within me, but she's given me no reason not to trust her.

I give Kedrick an oversized smile. "Guess I'm pretty lucky to be friends with the boss's daughter."

"I'm only in charge of this cell," Kedrick says. "There are more in our order. Many more."

Catriona remains beside me, listening. She knows all of this already, I'm certain of it. She's being quiet so that I can make a decision on my own. She's long since chosen her path.

"And if I refuse?" I direct my question to all of the mages, not just Kedrick.

He tenses. "Don't be foolish, Gunnar. We have you at our mercy. Refusal isn't a wise choice."

The instant he says it, I'm sizing up the room. On instinct, my hands move slightly toward the guns I know aren't there. "Not so different from the machines after all, huh?"

"Your blood has power," Kedrick states. The friendliness is gone from his voice. "And it is in our possession. If you will not join us willingly, we will make good use of you, nonetheless."

"Then you'd better be ready to kill both of us." Catriona lifts her chin.

I like to think of myself as courageous, but if I had half her strength combined with whatever magic everybody thinks is inside me, I could tear this temple apart.

Kedrick's gaze moves back and forth between us and the other mages. He mouths a single word to his daughter. It's fast, but I catch it. *Please.*

Catriona shakes her head. I can't imagine how difficult it must be to turn your back on your parents, no matter who they are, if they show even a hint of caring about you. I gave up my parents' belief in God a long time ago, but they were dead when it happened. In a way, that was probably easier. I never had to look them in their eyes and tell them I was taking a different path, never had to see their disappointment or anger. Catriona faces it now with fearlessness.

Kedrick says nothing. Is he communicating with the other blood mages telepathically?

My answer comes in the form of invisible hands pulling on my body. I fight for a moment, but they're too strong. They bring me to my knees, immobilizing me.

"Take them to the cells," Kedrick says. "We need time to prepare the ritual."

13

"DO YOU REALLY WANT TO KNOW

how it happens?" Catriona is a voice in the darkness. The blood mages left no torches burning after depositing us in adjacent cells. I spent a few minutes running my hands along the rough rock wall, trying to find a crack or an opening, cursing myself for not having the power to destroy this cage and free us both.

After a while, I relented and sat with my back against the rock, trying to put myself as close to her as possible.

"No, don't tell me." I bring my hands up to my face, chewing on the knuckle of my index finger. I'm not afraid to hear *how* they're going to harvest my blood, but I don't want to imagine anything bad happening to Catriona. *That,* I can't bear. "I'm sorry I brought you here. You would've been better off with the machines. This is all my fault."

I know what comes next. She's going to say that it isn't my fault and that she would make the same choices all over again. It'll be a valiant attempt to assuage my guilt, to lend me some comfort before I die.

"Yes, in a way, it is," she says.

My mouth drops open. I huff in disbelief.

"Not what you were expecting?" she asks.

"No, not exactly."

"I'm sorry, Gunnar. It's true. But not for the reasons you think. We're not here because you accidentally used magic to save a baby. We're not here because you couldn't master the Breath. We're not here because you sent Lark and Rowan back with Otis."

The silence is heavy in the damp air of the dungeon. "Then why are we here?" I ask.

"We're here because you don't have faith in anything or anybody."

Despite the fact that we're in total darkness and there's a stone wall between us, I shoot a perplexed look in her direction. "What does that have to do with anything?"

"The Scions saved your life," she says. "They gave us food and shelter. They demonstrated real power and offered to share it with you, but you wouldn't open your mind to them. If you had allowed that psychic connection, you know what would be happening right now? You'd be reaching out to Taron and Elisha. You'd raise the alarm and trees and lake monsters would be storming the gates."

"I trusted *you*," I shoot back. "And you turned out to be a blood mage."

A few seconds of agonizing silence. *Why did I have to say something so stupid?*

When Catriona speaks again, her voice is softer. "Just because I didn't tell you doesn't mean you can't trust me. Trust doesn't mean you get to find out absolutely everything right at the beginning."

"Then what does it mean?"

"It means you believe in someone enough to know that you don't have to understand everything about them, what they're doing, what they've done. It's about knowing that they'll be there for you when you need them, that they will do the things they say, and that they have your best interest at heart, even when some things are hidden from you. Demanding to know and understand everything at all times is another way of demanding control, Gunnar."

She sounds like my parents, telling me to trust God, that understanding isn't necessary for belief. That faith didn't work out so well for them, and it didn't work out so well for me. We did everything we were supposed to do. We followed the rules. We were honest, good, courageous, and loving people.

And for all our trouble, they got incinerated and I became a prisoner. If God and people are so good, then why am I here, trapped and broken? Elisha would say He's preparing me, but it feels more like He's kicking me in the teeth every time I dare to lift my head.

Catriona's voice breaks the painful thoughts. "Gunnar?"

She's looking for a response to what she just said. This is the part where I'm supposed to apologize and tell her she's right. I know that I should. It's been a long time since I've let anybody get close enough for me to hurt them. I draw in a breath to speak.

But instead, Catriona says, "Thank you."

I pause, confused. "For what?"

"In the village, you saw me as a person, not just an outcast. When you spoke to me . . ." Her voice trails off, then she continues. "It meant more than you could know."

There's something about her words that makes my pulse rate increase. The power indicator flashes on my visual display.

CORONARY IMPLANT POWER LEVEL: 25%.

I have secrets too.

I go to the cell door and say her name.

I reach a hand through the iron bars, stretching as far as I can toward her voice. I don't tell her what I'm doing, but when I can't possibly reach any farther, her fingertips brush against mine. She's reaching for me too. Maybe she has been all along.

We touch.

"This wasn't much of a pep talk," I say, hoping she can tell that I'm smiling. "Not the kindest thing to say to me before I die, how this is all my fault."

"We're *not* dying here." Catriona's voice is firm. "I'm not going to let it happen."

"I'm not sure what we can do about that. Do you have some power I don't know about?" I hesitate to say what I'm really thinking. "Forgive me for asking, but is there some hidden blood magic thing you can do to get us out of here?"

For the first time, I hear a tone of absolute defeat in her voice. "No. Teleportation is possible. I studied it for years, but I was never strong enough to come close."

Teleportation?

Catriona's words when we were riding in the woods come to my mind. "So that's why you said you would've chosen . . ."

"Teleportation, yes. My whole life, I wanted the power to be somewhere else. It's tied to the tracking spells, or it can be. If you have somebody's blood, there are spells that can transport you to wherever they are, but it takes a lot of power. The larger the object, the more blood you need. It can get . . . messy."

A chill runs through my body. *I can't begin to imagine the things she must have seen and experienced in her life.* "Well, for what it's worth, I'd give you all my blood right now if it would get you out of here."

"I'd look pretty silly dragging a bloodless corpse around with me," she says.

She'd take me with her. I don't say it. Instead, I let the kind joke hang in the air a few moments, savoring what I hope is hidden between the words. "Yes, you would."

She laughs. I laugh. If the blood mages can hear us, they must think that we've lost our minds. Maybe we have.

Because I believe her. We're not dying here, not like this. I have absolutely no idea how we can escape.

But we're not dying today.

I don't realize that I fell asleep until I hear the creak of my cell door opening, the rusty hinges heralding that my time has come. I can't see the mages in the pitch black, but I feel their hands on me. Maybe they have night vision powers.

I don't fight back as they lift me off the floor, but I don't help them, either. Instead, I go limp. I'm going to make them use every last ounce of strength to finish me off.

The hooded figures stay silent as they pull both of us from the cells. A torch ignites between them, casting light over their robes, but refusing to penetrate the darkness of their hoods. Part of me wants to rip the fabric back and look my captors in their faces, but this is about Catriona. Maybe Kedrick will at least let her live. There's no need to start a fight I can't win and get us both killed.

They lead us down the corridor back into the main room. I expect to find some type of torture equipment waiting for us—sacred blades, fire pits, or maybe just a big bucket to hold all of my blood.

But the room looks the same as it did when we left. Kedrick had said that he needed to prepare for the ritual, but it doesn't look like they've done anything. He's the only blood mage with his hood removed. The others line the walls.

"Not that I know anything about blood magic," I remark as I'm pulled to the center of the room, "but I expected a little more fanfare than this, if my blood is so powerful and all."

A bead of sweat drips down Kedrick's brow. "Your blood will not be liberated here."

"You're taking us somewhere else?" Catriona asks.

"*You* are staying right here," Kedrick says pointedly. "And *I'm* not taking your friend anywhere. *They* are." He gestures toward the entrance of another hallway.

The heavy stomping of metal feet thunders down the stone corridor.

I try to charge him, fighting against the grip of the mage. "You told me we were going to fight the machines."

Kedrick is no longer playing the part of the confident, charismatic leader trying to lure me to his side. Now, his nostrils flare; his face is red. "And maybe we could have, if you weren't so stubborn. I tried to save you, but you wouldn't let me. Now, I'm saving her."

"And what about your followers here?" I ask, waving one hand at the other blood mages. "They're fine with all this too?"

At once, the blood mages—including the one holding me—appear to crumble into the ground, as if their bodies have been instantly removed from the robes. Only piles of clothes remain where they once stood.

I blink. The machines' steps grow louder, closer.

Catriona stands, stunned. She looks at her father. "How did this happen? We saw their faces, the ones with no mouths."

Kedrick doesn't look at her. "Illusions. All of it. The war machines gave me everything I needed to find him, including a lot of very powerful blood."

Catriona goes rigid.

Ten androids file into the cavern, each carrying an assault rifle. A mage walks in the middle of them, its silver flesh shining in the torchlight. The thick brown circle carved on its forehead denotes its status as an earth mage. In the Human Alliance, we called those Dusty.

Two of the androids seize my arms with their cold metal hands and tear me away from Catriona. I try to fight back, but they're too strong. I try to summon the magic, but the power won't come. I curse it all—my weakness and the Breath. If this isn't a good enough moment for the power to come, then what could ever be?

"Stop!" Catriona tries to get to me, but her father grabs her around the waist and holds her back. It's the first thing he's done that I appreciate.

Catriona struggles, then suddenly stops and rakes her fingernails across the skin of her left forearm. Blood ribbons appear. She smears her fingers over it, then wipes the blood onto both hands as she chants an incantation, her voice shaky, but determined. She pushes both arms forward.

A gust of air whooshes by my body, but it doesn't harm me. Instead, the two androids lose their grip on me as they're knocked to the ground.

"Run, Gunnar!" Catriona yells.

I don't make it two steps before the androids seize me again. The earth mage steps forward, eyes on Catriona. At the same moment, the blood gem around Kedrick's neck glows brighter than ever. He mutters a few words and Catriona's arms pin to their sides. She fights against the invisible binds, but she can't break free.

Kedrick addresses the earth mage. "She's a child. She doesn't know what she's doing. Leave her be."

The earth mage stands still, but I feel a tremble in the rock beneath my feet. Dust sprinkles from the ceiling as the walls begin to shake.

The chant is low, almost imperceptible, but I hear the words of the mage. "*Sacri pulvis terrae. Mandata mea.*"

Kedrick's voice pitches as he pleads. "Don't do this! I beg you!"

The earth mage turns and starts back toward the corridor. The androids follow, dragging me along the ground as the shaking increases.

A renewed strength surges through my body as I try to free myself, but their hands are iron vices on my arms. Sweat pours over my body. Fear clouds my mind.

I manage to turn my head for an instant. When I do, I see Kedrick quickly remove the blood gem from his neck and place it on Catriona.

"Father, what are you doing?" she asks.

The shaking of the temple grows to a deafening roar. Kedrick doesn't speak, only grabs Catriona's arm and pulls her toward me. Before the machines can react, he places her hand on my shoulder and grasps the blood gem. He cites a loud incantation.

Chunks of rock fall from the ceiling. The machines halt. We're all going to be crushed.

Then, some type of power takes hold of me. It doesn't start inside my body like the magic before, but rather like hot steam moving over my feet.

"Father!" Catriona's cry is filled with emotion. "No!"

I look down. My boots are gone, then my legs. What is happening?

The temple crumbles as the warmth moves up my body. Catriona's lower half disappears as well, though all of Kedrick remains.

The warmth reaches my waist, then my chest.

Catriona is a floating head when the ceiling caves in. "Father!"

Then, darkness.

14

CATRIONA BREATHES IN THE

darkness. The blood gem glows faintly on her neck, flickering like a candle fighting the wind. I touch her. The air is cold, damp, and the floor feels like solid rock, but her skin is warm.

She speaks. "Gunnar, my father—" Her voice catches.

"Kedrick," I say out loud. Moments ago, I was ready to kill him. Now, I half hope that wherever he sent us, he's here, as well. Despite everything, he couldn't let his daughter die. I know I can't trust him with my life, but at least he's proven that he'll protect her. For now, that's good enough.

But somehow I know he isn't here.

"What happened?"

She takes a moment to compose herself. "Teleportation. He actually did it."

"Where do you think we are?"

"I don't know." She's quiet a moment. "But I'm sure that it's somewhere safe." I notice the glow of the blood gem has faded away.

"Do you think you could use the gem to figure out where we are?" I ask. "Or at least give us some type of light?"

"No." I sense her shaking her head. "My father must have used up its power with the spell. It needs to be . . . recharged, basically. There are rituals, but the truth is, I'm not sure what they are."

"We're on our own, then," I say. "Let's start walking. Take my hand so we can stay together."

She does so and we begin to walk. Her hand feels comfortable in mine. I don't think either of us have any idea in what direction we're heading. We take slow, careful steps. For all we know, the ground could suddenly disappear from beneath us and send us falling into an endless chasm.

Wherever this is, at least we seem to be safe for the time being. The good news is that there are no signs of machines. The bad news is, there are no signs of anything else.

The echo of our steps changes a few seconds before we walk into a wall. We're moving slowly enough that it doesn't hurt, and I'm glad to encounter *something,* at least. I run my free hand along the surface as we change directions. The worst-case scenario would be that we're in a large, round room, that we'll keep walking in circles without ever being aware of it.

But it feels like we're going somewhere, like a force is pulling us forward. I've felt that way before, of course, and it led us directly into a trap.

Neither of us speaks as we continue, probably because there isn't anything to say. I can only imagine what she must be going through. And I *assume* she's lost her father. I didn't see him die, and his survival would not be the strangest thing that has happened. Wherever he is, he's not here, and it must be affecting her.

I don't ask her about it. If she needs to talk, she'll tell me. There's a lot for her to process. Kedrick nearly got us killed and saved our lives all in the span of a few minutes. My mind kicks into overdrive. Before today, she might not have known he was alive. How long have they been separated? Where has he been all this time? Or maybe she did know, but she didn't want to see him. She couldn't be blamed for feeling that way.

A faint light appears far ahead of us—a dim, golden orb against the black, like a single star in space. Catriona tightens her hold on my hand. We quicken our pace.

And with each step, the pull on my heart grows stronger.

When I reach the light, the energy is so strong that I think the vibration in my chest is going to explode. The light itself comes from a small hole, no bigger than my fingertip. The sound changes—I can no longer hear my steps echoing in front of me. The air is still and neither warm nor cold, almost as if I have stepped out of the world and into another place where temperature does not exist.

I reach out my hand. My fingers graze the wood of a door—textured, but smooth. If I had to guess, it hasn't been touched in a very long time, but I don't feel any dust. It reminds me of Taron speaking into my mind, except it isn't a human voice. It's something older, more subtle, but far more powerful.

"Do you want me to come with you?" Catriona asks quietly.

"No," I say. "I think I need to do this alone."

I push open the door.

Light seeps around the edges of the wood the moment I press on it. The door is misshapen, its lines cracked and curved, almost like it's not a door at all, but a jagged section of wall opening up.

When I step inside, what I see before me nearly stops my cybernetic heart.

I'm in a small room, but there is an opening in the rock ceiling through which a ray of light streams down into a fountain. Ripples run from the place where the light touches the water to the edge of the pool, as if the light is powerful enough to disturb it. The water glows with the golden light, but the ripples make it impossible to see what's below the surface.

The sight steals my breath. My parents used to talk about a sunset being so marvelous—painted with impossible pinks and purples—that they couldn't help but think that God created it just for them. Gazing at the beautiful water, I finally understand what they meant. Is it possible that this was made for me? And if so, what am I supposed to do here?

I explore the rest of the room. There are only a few feet of rock between the wall and the water. The cave glistens with lines of mineral or quartz, but there seems to be nothing in here that was made by the hands of man.

I kneel at the edge of the pool and dip my fingers into the golden ripples. The water is cool and refreshing, but I'm disappointed that it doesn't feel in any way remarkable beyond that. I'm not sure what I expected, but I expected *something*.

I submerge my entire hand, quickly losing sight of my fingers. My palm touches the bottom before I'm elbow deep in the water.

I consider trying the door again, returning to Catriona with the disappointing news that—while this room is beautiful—there's nothing special about it beyond the pretty water. But I won't give up. There's a reason this room is here. There's a reason I'm here.

Maybe it's deeper in the middle. I step into the pool, placing my foot in the same place where my hand was seconds earlier.

The bottom isn't there.

The realization comes an instant too late. My body lurches forward, feeling nothing underfoot. I throw out my hands, trying to grab onto the edge as I go under, but I grasp nothing.

The water pulls me down. Panic hits. I try to swim to the surface but it's no use. I'm sinking so fast that it feels like I'm falling.

Too fast.

Impossibly fast.

The gold above me dims and disappears, and again I'm wrapped in darkness.

I fight against it, but my body begins to turn, and even if I could swim, I wouldn't know which way to go. I want to scream for help, for Elisha, for the Scions.

For Catriona.

The cybernetic heart thunders in my chest. I can hardly think. *I'm going to die here. I'm going to die.*

I hold my breath as long as I can until my lungs burn, more fiercely than any pain I've ever experienced. On instinct, my mouth opens and tries to inhale.

And somehow, I breathe.

I take a deep breath and my lungs are filled with . . . *I don't know what.* It can't be oxygen, but it sustains me. The panic dissolves, replaced by relief and surprise. I exhale and breathe again. *How is this possible?*

My body stops turning. I don't feel as if I'm falling anymore, but I never landed, either.

I am simply here.

Breathing. Waiting.

But right now—and maybe for the first time in my life—that is enough.

It's peaceful, and my mind drifts. I wonder how I got here. Falling into the pool is a distant memory. It takes effort to recall the war machines, the Scions, even Catriona. I try to grasp onto the memories, the thoughts of my unit and my parents, but they keep slipping away, no matter how hard I try to hold onto them. It's disconcerting. Without those memories, without the pain and the mission that has grown from it, why am I here at all?

It feels as if all my thoughts are being taken away from me, pulled gently but by a force with great strength.

"Let go."

The voice speaks in my mind like Taron's, but it's not him. It's familiar, resonating, almost like a sound that has been with me all along, but I didn't hear it until I turned up the volume.

Or maybe until I turned the volume down on everything else.

A light above me catches my eye, a faint glimmer that grows fast. I realize that I'm moving toward it. Maybe it's the surface of the pool, but I doubt it. I thought I was still going down, but now it feels like I'm ascending, and I'm not sure when I changed directions.

The light reaches me and engulfs my body. I haven't returned to the surface of the pool, but the light is similar, though stronger. What I saw on the surface was merely a piece of this energy. This is the source of the power; it must be. This is what Elisha was talking about, except I'm not thinking about magic anymore. I'm not thinking about how I can harness it, not even to do the things I know are right and good.

Right now, I only want to be in its presence.

The light pours over me like sparkling water covering my skin, then moves inside my flesh, in my blood, my bones, all the way to my soul. The shimmer sets me on fire in the best way and I am connected to the source, the creating energy that formed the stars and the cosmos, that breathed life into existence. It is unending and unrelenting. It is love and power.

I have not taken hold of it. It has taken hold of me.

The feeling pauses. I remain in the light, but there's a tug on my soul, a question, a request. It asks if I would stay here, never to leave, never to return to the people in the world above and below.

I remember Catriona, and I hesitate.

It's not my time to die, not yet. As beautiful and wondrous as this is, I haven't earned my rest, haven't yet done what I'm supposed to do. It would be easier to die, but there is so much for which I need to live.

The light diminishes. The energy releases me gently. My decision made, I sink away, slowly at first, then gaining speed.

The water rushes by my body again. It accelerates so fast that I can't tell in which direction I'm heading until I see the light above me.

This time, I swim for it, the energy pushing me up, helping me to the surface.

I gasp for air when my head breaches the top of the pool. I swim to the edge and lift myself out. I should be exhausted, but I feel strong.

I notice the power reading in my optics.

CORONARY IMPLANT POWER LEVEL: 50%.

50%? My power level has never increased without the recharging station in my quarters. I didn't think it was possible.

Despite my soaking-wet clothes, a smile spreads across my face. I push wet hair back and turn for the door.

When I push it open, Catriona is waiting there for me. I allow the door to close behind me, wrapping us in darkness again, but hopefully for the last time.

The energy ignites around my hand at my slightest thought, setting her face aglow, more beautiful than ever before. It's as if I'm seeing her with new eyes.

She smiles.

The light of my power makes finding our way out of the cavern much easier. In the darkness, this place seemed like such a maze; I would've been certain it was nothing but twists and turns all leading to dead ends. With the slightest bit of light, everything becomes so clear, including the way back home.

As soon as Catriona and I step out of the cavern and into the afternoon light, we find two horses waiting for us. These aren't the same horses we rode when we left the Scion temple, but I have a feeling Lark sent them, especially because they're already saddled. Perhaps she sensed what happened to me in the fountain. Maybe the experience sent out another psychic signal.

The animals are beautiful—one black with a white star pattern on its forehead, the other a reddish shade of brown. Both bristle and stomp the moment they see us, but they don't seem to be afraid. In fact, they look like they can't wait to run.

Soon Catriona and I are mounted and riding. The animals seem to know which way to go. And they move really, really fast.

The ride takes us away from the mountains and the trees into an area of rolling hills as far as I can see. As soon as we reach open ground, the horses break into a full sprint. I don't have much riding experience, but I know they aren't supposed to maintain an all-out run for very long. I wonder if we should slow down, but then I feel the energy. The animals are drawing power from the grass, brilliant glows of lights emanating from the vegetation and into their bodies as they move, fueling them forward. It reminds me of the lake monster and Lark's words about the supernatural reemerging in nature. *What an incredible world this could be.*

Should be.

My sense of self becomes lost amid the constant rhythm of their hooves against the earth and the rush of the wind by my ears. On instinct, I raise up a little in the saddle, bending my knees to help absorb the shock of the run. The energy comes alive inside me, but the power doesn't ignite. Instead, it keeps me strong. It's been a while since

I slept, but I'm not tired. I can't remember the last time I ate, but I'm not hungry. The power sustains me. It whispers that it is enough.

Every few minutes, I look to my left to see Catriona keeping pace alongside me. She looks so free on the back of her horse. She is beauty and power as the wind blows her brown hair and the light of day shines on her skin. The blood gem bounces against her neck and I could almost swear that it has grown brighter. Maybe this experience has recharged its energy, or maybe it's only the light.

I have no idea where we are, but the horses run. I'm not sure they would follow my lead if I tried. We must be taking a different path back to the Scions. The road out was all trees and wilderness; the way back is wide-open grass and so much speed that it's like flying.

And despite how much I enjoy it, I know our time is running out. How many days has it been since we left? In everything that's happened, I'm not sure. Otis said the machines would attack the village soon. For all I know, we're already too late.

As if it knows my thoughts, my horse picks up speed, as does Catriona's, both creatures thundering us back into the battle. It's a strange sensation, the anticipation of what is to come, of what we're riding toward. Thinking of Catriona brings what has been buried to the surface, and part of me wishes that Catriona and I could turn back and ride into the country. We could find a remote place, maybe reach the coast and take a boat to some forgotten island. The machines would never bother to come looking, not for two mere humans lost in an entire world. We could build a modest shelter, forage for food, and spend our evenings dancing on the beach. Maybe we could be happy, living in blissful, willful ignorance.

A nice thought, but it could never be. Strange that—not long ago—the one thing I wanted in the world was to destroy things. Now, all I want is to be near her and build upon life from there.

But the memory of the fire mage draws me forward. It's always been there, the fire mage, burning in the back of my mind, promising to forever haunt my nightmares, no matter how fast this horse runs, no matter how far away I get. It will be out there.

Until I destroy it. And now, I might have the power.

The thought stokes the flames of my courage, sustaining me for the hours we ride.

The horses stop once at a small river to drink water, again acting on their own accord. It seems our entire path home has been plotted for us, even the breaks, not that we mind.

The water is invigorating. After Catriona and I have each taken long drinks from the river, I splash my face a few times before looking again at the blood gem hanging from her neck. "Is that recharging? It looks brighter than before."

Catriona holds it between her finger and thumb. She furrows her brow. "Probably. It should be drawing trace amounts of blood through my skin."

"Like bleeding you dry?"

"Oh, no. Such a little amount that you wouldn't notice, almost like soaking up moisture from your skin, except it's blood."

"And when it's recharged, you'll be able to . . . ?"

"No." She tucks the blood gem under her shirt. "Won't be doing that anymore. Never again." She stands and heads into the woods. For personal business, I assume.

Then, it's just me and the horses. I regard the one I've been riding. "I guess I said something wrong."

The horse neighs at me a little, then returns to drinking from the river.

I sit and wait for Catriona to come back, scolding myself for suggesting that she might use blood magic again. But if not, why has she kept the gem? Maybe because it's the last thing she has of her father. Probably his greatest gift. Their relationship seemed strained, to put it lightly, but he was her father. I know what it's like to feel betrayed by your parents' religion, like you've been lied to your whole life, but at the same time, knowing that they didn't do it to hurt you.

At least, hoping they didn't.

I'm still mulling it over when she returns. She seems to have been gone way longer than necessary. Maybe she needed some time to herself.

"I'm sorry about earlier," she says.

"You don't need to apologize for anything. It's none of my business."

"No, you're just curious about me. It's only natural. I'm curious about you too."

We're interrupted by the snort of a horse. I glance over my shoulder at them. Both are bristling.

"We'd better go," Catriona says. "I think our rides might leave without us."

A cool dusk has settled over the sky by the time we reach the lake entrance to the Scion temple. Rowan isn't here to clear the alternate entrance, so we dismount and dive into the cold water. Adrenaline urges me to swim faster. I feel as if I'm being chased, like there are hands reaching out to grab me, but I'm not sure from where.

When we swim up into the cavern, Taron stands waiting at the edge of the pool. I guess I shouldn't be surprised.

"How did you know we were here?" I ask, pulling myself up out of the water. "You force your way into my head again?"

Lark's huff comes from behind us. I didn't know she was there. "The horses told us you were coming."

I whirl around. She's perched on a rock, her body curled in on itself like a cat.

"You can speak with the horses that far away?" Catriona marvels.

Taron beams with pride. "A new idea we've been trying, combining powers. Her ability to speak with animals at a range that's amplified by my telepathy."

"Interesting," I say. There are plenty of follow-up questions I'd like to ask, but a more pressing issue is on my mind. "What about—"

"The village?" Taron asks. "Still there."

I hadn't realized how much tension I was carrying until I hear those words and my whole body relaxes. The last few hours of riding had been difficult. The joy I found earlier eroded with each passing hoofbeat back to camp, replaced by a sense of foreboding, of rushed panic. Maybe it was because we were running toward danger, simultaneously concerned about what would happen in the battle, but even more afraid of what would happen if I didn't make it back in time to join the fight.

"But maybe not much longer." Lark springs off the rock and starts down the tunnel. "Let's go. We have a village to save."

We find Elisha and the others in the main area of the temple. Otis holds a long-range rifle with both hands, barrel pointed down as he gazes through the scope. "Just in time."

"Did you find what you were looking for out there?" Elisha asks.

It's the question I've been asking myself since we left the river. Several times, I've wanted to test my powers, to determine whether what happened to me in the fountain was real. But I didn't. I kept telling myself it was because I didn't want to waste the energy, or risk hurting the horses or Catriona. The truth is, I was afraid the whole thing was me fooling myself. Again.

But there's no reason to show fear and doubt to the Scions, not when we're heading into battle. "I did."

Then another thought hits me, the fear creeping back in, enough for me to hedge my bets. "But if you've got any more guns, I won't say no."

"You'll need this too." Taron turns and runs down a hallway, disappearing into the dark. A moment later, he reappears holding a green bundle in his arms. His face goes from beaming to an almost sheepish expression. "Sorry, I wasn't prying, but I saw this in your head. I thought you might want it."

The magic doesn't ignite, but the same energy surges through my body as Taron hands over my Alliance jacket.

15

BY THE END OF IT, WE WEREN'T FIGHTING BECAUSE WE THOUGHT WE COULD WIN. THE MACHINE NUMBERS WERE OVERWHELMING AND THEIR COMMAND OVER THE ELEMENTS MADE IT HOPELESS. WE USED TO TALK ABOUT IT, THOSE OF US WHO FOUGHT. WE ENVIED PEOPLE WHO COULD ABIDE MACHINE RULE, COULD LIVE WITH HAVING THEIR FREEDOM TAKEN AWAY. BUT WE HAD NO CHOICE. WE COULDN'T ACCEPT IT. WE JOKED THAT IT WAS AGAINST OUR FUNDAMENTAL PROGRAMMING.
— AMY ROBBINS, SOLDIER

I STAND AMONG THE OTHER

Scions at the edge of a cliff, overlooking the lights of the village that for two years was my home. The ground in front of me slopes down into a thicket of pines that covers most of the land between here and the village. It's all that stands between me and my former prison.

Catriona is beside me, peering through the night and into the distance. I haven't told her the truth, not all of it. It used to seem so terrifying, the idea of sharing the knowledge about my cybernetic heart. Now, talking about it seems almost like a formality. I'm pretty sure she already knows, but it's a source of regret as I prepare for battle. I don't want to die before she knows who I really am.

Guess I'll have to survive.

Rowan clears his throat, breaking the silence among us. "When's the termination scheduled to begin?"

Otis grips a scoped rifle with both hands. "Less than an hour. I'll give them this, they're dependable."

Lark raises her eyebrows at him. "*You're* mostly machine, Otis. Why aren't you more efficient?" But she smiles.

Otis responds with a dirty look, but I can tell he's suppressing a grin. Maybe he's more fond of this group than he lets on. "Little birdy, just wait until I start shooting at some can-heads. I'll show you efficient."

Lark chuckles.

Otis, Catriona, and I are the only ones carrying physical weapons.

Catriona again wields a shotgun. I have my sidearms. My connection to the Breath has increased, but I'm not completely confident in my ability to use it. When I pull these triggers, I know they'll fire. I can't yet say the same about my magic.

"Focus." Elisha stands poised, her face calm, almost serene. It makes me wonder if she somehow knows the outcome, but I doubt it. There's nothing about life magic that makes me think it's possible to see the future.

Regardless, Elisha moves and speaks like a person unafraid of what may come. "Our advantage is the element of surprise. The attack must be coordinated and precise. Taron will stay here to amplify the psychic link between us. Between *all* of us."

Her last sentence sends a small charge of electricity through my body. Despite everything that's happened, the idea of opening my mind is uncomfortable.

Elisha appraises me. "It's the only way, Gunnar."

I shake my head. "Not happening," I say, then glance at Taron. "No offense, kid."

Rowan crosses his mighty arms. "If Gunnar wants to get himself killed, let him." His words ride atop an aggressive tone, clearly meant to rile me.

I touch one of my sidearms. "I can handle myself."

Lark bursts out with a laugh. "Oh really? Did Otis load some magic bullets in those for you?"

"Nothing magic about those beauties," Otis says, beaming. "Just pure, steel-piercing ingenuity. Two clips filled with get-off-my-planet. I made them myself with—"

He stops himself abruptly, head snapping to the side. His expression shifts.

"What?" Lark asks.

Otis stares forward into the air, concentrating on something that none of us can see. "Just intercepted a transmission. They're pushing up the schedule."

Elisha turns to face the village. "Then the time is now."

Our group scatters as we make our way down the cliff. Taron and

Rowan stay behind. Taron crouches low, but Rowan spreads out his arms, preparing to use his power.

Catriona moves alongside me as we sidestep down the cliff. The ground levels off a little once we're under the cover of the trees. Catriona breaks into a run, her shotgun at the ready, her eyes glancing at me every so often. *She's as worried about me as I am about her.*

When we reach the bottom of the hill, a small group of war machines emerges out of the forest to our left. As the androids move toward the village, the trees near them begin to sway as if pushed by a mighty breeze.

But I don't feel any wind.

The movement of the trees grows stronger, more dramatic, until their branches reach out and wrap the war machines' bodies. The androids try to counter, but long limbs tear the rifles from their hands, then rip off the androids' heads.

I smile to myself, picturing Rowan on the hill, standing proud, with his arms outstretched and eyes glowing with power. Commanding trees to dismember a platoon of war machines is pretty impressive. The guy can be a bit of a pain sometimes, but I'm glad he's on my side.

My attention shifts to the village. Between the huts, people go about their business, unaware of what's coming for them. I almost envy their blissful ignorance. A lot of them have accepted their fate and found some semblance of happiness in their life under the steel fist. They didn't ask for what's about to happen. It's not their fault they're all about to die.

The screams start when the eyes of the mage—standing motionless on the platform in the center of town—begin to glow. I knew the machines would waste no time replacing the magical unit I destroyed; I had assumed it would be another air mage. But instead of three curved lines, this one has a circle carved in the center of its head.

Earth mage.

The ground shakes. The shouting grows louder.

"Not good," I declare. "Even if we stop the gunners, that thing will open a chasm and drop the entire village into the ground."

Catriona pumps her shotgun, face grim. "Not if we stop it."

We race toward the village, Otis and Lark running on our right.

The village has dissolved into chaos—people shout and run in every direction as the ground breaks beneath them. Some flee into their homes, as if that will protect them. Others scream out alerts of the attack. A few grab tools to wield as weapons.

As we draw near to the village, I see a second contingent of war machines appear on the other side of the huts. A few are caught in the trees, but there are far more than Rowan is able to stop. They open fire.

The earth mage lifts its hands, gathering power.

When we reach the border of the village, courageous men and women charge the machines, some armed only with the valor in their hearts. Shouting fills the small spaces between the rat-a-tat of automatic gunfire. More humans fall every second, but they continue the attack.

When I'm in range, I raise my pistols and take aim at the nearest android. I pull the trigger and manage to hit the android in the side of its head. Not where I was aiming, but Otis's ammunition performs as promised. The machine falls, dropping an automatic rifle that is immediately claimed by a villager.

A nearby android collapses as well, though I hadn't fired another shot. A quick glance over my shoulder and I see Otis kneeling, peering down the length of his scope. The barrel of his rifle moves slightly and he fires again. Another android falls.

The rumble in the ground snaps my attention forward. The earth in front of me tilts upward, as if lifted by an underground giant.

Catriona stays in step with me as we run up the growing hill. We reach the crest, a place in which the earth has broken, and jump.

We fire as we descend. I miss both shots, but Catriona blasts an android in its back. The machine falters forward as we land. She pumps and fires at its head. The android falls.

A streak of blond fur flashes across the village to my left. It's Lark in the shape of a wolf, bounding through the battle, dodging incoming fire as she engages another android. She leaps and shifts into a massive bird. Swooping, she seizes the head of an android between her talons, tearing it from its body.

I clench my fist in triumph as Lark lands behind another machine. She shifts into a bear as the android turns. I fire a shot to distract it, my bullet glancing off its shoulder, slowing it for a moment.

It's all Lark needs. Her massive bear form lunges at the machine, mauling its circuitry with powerful jaws. She rips the wires from the machine's neck and lets out a roar that rivals the quaking earth as her opponent drops.

"Gunnar!" It's Taron's voice, trying to press into my mind.

I fight to keep him out, trying to keep my focus on the battle without allowing him in my head. *Not now. I'm fine.*

The flow of the battle consumes me. I dash through the fray, firing at war machines, jumping from one side to the other to avoid the shifting ground. I manage to hit a few androids, my bullets tearing holes in their steel exteriors.

The energy surges inside me, though my skin does not burn or glow. It doesn't matter. Every android destroyed feels like revenge for what was taken from me. I could die happy like this—fighting without fear of being killed. This would be a good death.

Ahead, the glow increases in the eyes of the earth mage. Huts collapse as the ground rips and tears apart, creating large chasms. Villagers and androids alike fall into the gaps, some trying to cling to the sides before the ground gives way, sending them to their doom.

"Gunnar!" Taron's voice again, but outside of my head this time. I freeze. *He's here.*

The kid ran onto the battlefield to reach me.

I fight my way through the chaos, trying to reach Taron as he runs toward me. A mess of steel and flesh and shifting ground separates us and I lose sight of him, though I still hear his voice through it all. "Gunnar!"

The ground lifts again, larger this time, like a towering wave of dirt that appears out of nowhere, so large it casts a shadow over me. The wave breaks apart like a bomb exploded inside it. The force sends me hurtling back through the air and I crash at the base of the platform.

Forget this. I face the earth mage on its platform, leveling both of my sidearms at its head. I pull the triggers.

Both guns click empty.

I swear as the android looks at me, the same deadly glow in its eyes that destroyed my family on the night when fire rained from the sky.

Two towers of dirt and rock rise on either side of the mage, great arms reaching up from the planet, preparing to crush me.

"Gunnar!"

My head snaps around at the sound of Taron's voice. The boy runs in my direction, his eyes filled with fear, but also courage.

Panic sparks inside me. I deserve to die, not him.

"Taron!" I clamor to my feet and dash toward him. The earth mage will bring literal tons of dirt and rock crashing down on me any second. Maybe I can protect him from the worst of it, shield him from the blow. Maybe he'll even survive.

The ground falters and I dive forward, knowing that the hammer is falling, thinking only of covering his body with mine.

Please God, me, not him.

The instant I reach Taron, the energy sparks to life and a bright light flashes in my eyes.

I throw myself over Taron as a corona of white fire envelops us. It burns without pain, without harm. I'm aware of the earth crashing on top of us, but we do not break.

We do not break.

The pillars of dirt and rock dissolve upon touching my body. The white light fades to a haze, allowing me to see again, though everything seems much brighter.

Taron looks up at me, his fear replaced by wonder. "The Angel Sword," he breathes.

I release Taron and face the earth mage. With a thought, the star fire surges down my legs and propels me off the ground. I hover, remembering the moment in the forest when I stood face-to-face with the air mage.

"Hi, Dusty." I thrust both hands forward. Energy erupts from my fists and hits the earth mage in its chest. The fire strikes with a power and speed far beyond my expectations. It is terrifying. It is exhilarating.

The mage's torso is ripped from its waist. Steel legs crumple as the top half of the machine flies back through the air and crashes into a tree.

The star fire carries me forward through the air. The legless earth mage raises a hand, lifting a large clump of earth from the ground and hurling it at me.

I blast the mound of dirt into millions of pieces. The few scattered chunks that hit me disintegrate in the surrounding field of fire.

The earth mage watches as I close in, mounting no other attack. I wonder if it knows that any further attempt is futile. It's studying me, perhaps transferring data back to its central database, learning about my power. This is not my true enemy, I realize, but a mere extension of it.

I garner the energy inside me, letting it build until I believe my body can no longer withstand it. The resulting burst of star fire is more powerful than before, a massive boom of power that obliterates the earth mage's body.

I allow myself to descend, the power dissolving at my command as soon as my feet touch the ground. I glance over my shoulder to find Taron watching me from a few paces away.

"You okay?" I ask him.

The boy doesn't respond, but only stares at me. There are no signs of damage on him beyond a few nicks and scratches. My power reading level catches my attention.

CORONARY IMPLANT POWER LEVEL: 100%.

My breath stops. My cybernetic heart is fully recharged.

I scan the village. Rowan and Lark, as well as several villagers, approach me. Android bodies litter the ground, a few twitching, clinging to their last moments of functionality.

Soon, I'm surrounded by Scions and villagers, most of them covered with dust, oil, and blood. Even Otis looks like he got into the thick of battle. He shakes his head at me. "I don't believe it."

One villager steps forward. It's Michael, the father whose baby was almost taken the night I destroyed the android.

"It's . . . you," Michael says. "The machines told us you were dead." I can't decide whether I'm reading relief or disbelief in his eyes, but I see the same look in the other villagers. They knew me for years, or at least, I'm sure they *thought* they knew me. Then one night I used magic to start a war with the machines, to save the life of a child, probably dooming everyone else. Judging from their faces, they don't know what to think of me anymore. *The machines told us you were dead.* For so many years, it felt like I was.

Now, I feel alive.

Elisha eases through the crowd, her calming presence almost palpable, as if she can reach out a healing touch to my soul, to the souls of everyone close to her. Despite the incredible display of power I've shown, she doesn't seem the least bit surprised. When she speaks, it's not just to me or just the Scions.

She addresses everyone. "Come, friends. We have a lot to discuss."

The villagers crowd into the meeting hall, all talking over each other. Tension and confusion spread throughout the room, increased every so often by raised voices.

The Scions and I stand off to the side, keeping quiet as the villagers cast wary eyes at us.

I lean over to Elisha. "How long do we let this go on?" It feels as if they're deciding our fate, which strikes me as ridiculous. We're here to defend them, not fight them, but we could easily overwhelm them if we had to.

Despite the magic, it's Otis that they're watching the most. From the scowl on his face, he's well aware of it. In fact, the only one of us who shows no sign of tension is Elisha. "They will decide when they're ready to hear from us," she tells me.

Michael steps onto a table, raising his hands as a way to gain the attention of the room.

A few of the people turn their attention to him. The room quiets down.

"This is madness," Michael announces. "All of it. The machines won't let this stand. They will be here soon. They'll send more to destroy us."

A woman speaks up. "They were going to destroy us anyway."

"Why do you believe that?" Michael points a finger in our direction. "Because *they* said so?"

I hold still, remembering the power that burned during the battle and how it protected Taron and me. I wonder if I could spread it wide enough to cover all of us. Maybe if they attack, I can defend us so we don't have to fight back.

Rowan crosses his arms in a way that seems to say, *"Try me."* Beside him, Lark stands ready, a stony expression on her face.

Michael continues. "Why should we believe anything they say? They have an outcast and a cyborg with them."

Otis takes an aggressive step forward. "You want to say that to my face?" Rowan places a hand on Otis's chest to stop him.

I move forward as well, but to talk, not to fight. I gesture at Otis. "This cyborg saved your lives. In fact, he's still saving all of you right now."

That gets Michael to look at me. "Is that right? How's he doing that?"

Somebody else should probably explain this, but at least I'm a familiar face. I hope they're slightly more likely to believe what I say because I was once one of them. "There's a signal. The machines are blinded by it. It's our one advantage. As long as Otis keeps sending the signal that everything here has been destroyed—including all of you—the machines won't return. We'll be safe."

Michael jumps down from the table to face me. "And what if you're wrong? Even if we can trust the cyborg, why should we trust that you know how the machines work?"

Elisha is a few feet behind me, but it sounds like she's whispering in my ear. "The truth might not be enough. You have to give them a hope they can understand. And you might have to give them a part to play."

She's right. As I look across the room, I see nothing but faces that have lost any illusion of control. They're caught in a war between powerful machines and people who can summon the fire of the stars and bend trees to their will. They need to believe they have some agency over their destinies.

"We'll be ready to fight," I say. "All of us."

Michael comes right up to me, those between us making way for him. "Fight? How can we fight? Even with your magic, there are too many of them."

Without hesitation, I summon my power in response. A white glow surrounds my body. I raise the volume of my voice but try not to sound threatening. "The power of the machines can never match our own, if we reach our potential. I'm telling you all—this energy, this Breath, flows through all of us."

A woman in the crowd calls out from behind Michael. "Are you saying you'll give us magic?"

I quickly shake my head. "It's not mine to give, but we can show you the way to find it."

"What if it doesn't work?" someone else asks.

I address the room. "What would you rather do? Wait for them to come back and finish you off?"

That raises another round of commotion among the people, but it's lower this time. I'm getting through to them; I can feel it. But I can't let up yet. "If we're going to die, wouldn't we all rather die fighting?"

That gets another response from the crowd, a rise that sounds like an agreement.

I push harder, speaking as if they have already committed to following me. "Then we prepare to fight. We develop strategies and build fortifications. We defend our homes. We protect our children."

Some of them shout "Yes!" All eyes are locked on me.

"And when the machines return . . ." A surge of power washes over me as if a divine spirit is pouring gasoline on the flames of energy. "We show them power unlike anything they've ever seen."

The woman raises her arms. "The Immortal Gunnar Graves!"

The rest of the crowd responds in unison. "The Immortal Gunnar Graves!"

The chant continues, catching me off guard, but I don't let my face show it. I can sense the other Scions behind me and I wonder how they feel about my newfound fame among the villagers. But I can't afford to doubt myself, not when I've created a bridge between the people and the Scions.

I look out over my people, standing strong, and raise my fist of fire.

16

AMIDST THE DEATH AND DESTRUCTION, THERE
WAS BEAUTY TO BE FOUND. PEOPLE SET ASIDE
PETTY DIFFERENCES AND CAME TOGETHER. THEY
COMFORTED EACH OTHER, SHARED STORIES,
TOLD JOKES, FELL IN LOVE.

IN A WAY, WE BECAME MORE HUMAN THAN
EVER BEFORE.

— AMANDA GRAHAM, MINISTER

AFTER THE VILLAGERS DISPERSE,

I duck away into the woods without a word. So much has happened so
quickly; I need time to escape into the embrace of the trees.

As soon as I'm out of sight, I hear a familiar scurrying in the
branches.

"Niko!"

My friend glides through the air, lands on my shoulder, and starts
running circles across my body. His tiny claws grip my clothes as he
moves over my shirt, the legs of my pants, almost as if checking me for
damage, making sure I'm not hurt. I wonder how much he knows about
what's happened, if he can somehow sense it.

"I'm fine, Niko," I say, hardly able to contain a laugh of joy and relief.

Apparently satisfied, the animal scampers up my chest and takes his
place on my shoulder. Niko rubs his warm fur against my neck.

"I missed you too, buddy. Where have you been?" Niko's presence
makes me wonder if Lark is keeping tabs on me, but I'm not sure her
magic works that way. If Niko has any control over it, he won't give
away our location.

Besides, there's something I need to do.

We trek back to the site of my Human Alliance camp, the long walk
giving my mind time to settle. Here, it's like nothing has changed. The
sound of my boots on the ground is the same as it ever was. The air
has grown a bit colder, but not much, and the cool wind is soothing.
For two years, this was how I found peace, maintained sanity, fought

off the ever-approaching depression that threatened to end my life one way or another.

By the time I'm standing in front of my parents' memorial, my body feels at ease, but my thoughts have not slowed down. Maybe Mom and Dad will have some answers for me.

"The people," I say, "we saved them. Otis is certain that the signal will work, but we're preparing our defenses anyway. Elisha says she'll start testing people right away to see if any show signs of the Breath working through them."

My voice catches against a lump in my throat. They would have loved this, my parents. They would have called it a miracle, a work of God's hands.

"Elisha says that . . ." I manage to choke out, then take a deep breath and release. "She says that children are more likely to be open to the Breath than adults."

A breeze pushes over me, scattering the dust of the graves. My emotions well up.

"I've never really cried, not about anything. Not when I got hurt as a kid. Not after you were both . . ." I stop, then start again. "Sometimes I think I would feel better if I could. Like maybe I could release all the emotion. But crying . . . God didn't put that inside me."

I pause, thinking about it.

"But the pain is always there."

I kneel in front of the graves and run my fingers through the dust, wishing I could touch my parents' hands again. "I'm sorry I didn't figure all this out sooner. Maybe I could have protected us. I'm so sorry."

"It's not your fault, Gunnar."

I look over my shoulder and my heart skips a beat. Catriona stands about twenty feet away from me, her brown hair pushed to the side by the breeze. "I hope you don't mind me following you. I was worried about you."

I quickly rise and approach her. Her presence is warmth. She knows who I am, and now that she's seen this place, she knows everything she needs to know about me.

Almost everything.

I prepare to share my deepest secret. "Catriona, I . . ." I take in a breath. "I have to tell you—"

"You're a cyborg."

I almost ask how she knew, but immediately I realize . . . how could she not? She's been with me through so much. She's heard the words of the cyborgs in the camp. She's known for a long time, but waited for me to tell her.

"I'm sorry I didn't tell you sooner," I say. "I tried."

"I know, Gunnar."

"After my parents were killed, the machines . . ." I begin, then consider my words. *Saved me?* No, I'll never give them credit for that. "They kept me alive. I have a cybernetic heart, and there's probably more tech inside me that I don't even know about."

She regards me for a moment, her eyes holding neither pity nor dismay. For that, I am grateful.

"Thank you for being willing to tell me," she says. "But Gunnar, I've only known you as the man you are now. To me, there is nothing about you that is cybernetic, especially your heart."

There is a genuineness and familiarity about her that brings true comfort. I draw her into my arms and hold her close.

Niko accepts her too. He tells me so by moving onto her shoulder, a gesture that makes Catriona and I laugh. We ease apart.

"There's something I want you to have." I reach into my inner jacket pocket and pull out a small pocketknife. I flip it open. "I want you to know how much I trust you. I have no idea what this war might bring. We may have to run. We may not be able to stay together."

She places her hand on mine. "Gunnar, please don't say that."

I use the tip of the blade to prick my finger. A drop of blood arises, a deep red rose meant for her.

"Are you sure?" she asks, and I know she's thinking about her father, about the secrets of blood magic that he shared with the machines, about the way it likely led to the end of my family. She's thinking about the darkness of her past, the guilt, and the shame. It's a feeling with which I'm familiar.

I just hope that with this gesture, we can get past it. Together.

"How much do you need?" I ask. "To ensure you'll always know where I am?"

"Gunnar, are you really sure—"

"How much?" I repeat.

"A trace will be enough."

I hold my bleeding finger up while closing the pocketknife with my other hand and returning it to my pocket.

When I pull my hand back out of the pocket, I'm holding the silver locket ring that I've carried in my jacket since Niko gave it to me. I open the clasp and allow a single drop of blood to fall inside the locket. I close the ring and offer it to her.

Her eyes go wide.

I rush to explain. "Carry this however you choose. You can even wear it around your neck. But whatever happens, I want you to be able to find me."

After a moment that seems like an hour, she holds out her hand and I place the ring in her palm. She curls her fist around it and holds it tight.

"Thank you, Gunnar."

"Gunnar!" It's Taron's voice in my head, shattering the moment. There's a desperation to it. A pain.

Catriona can see the sudden fear on my face. "What is it?"

"Something's wrong," I tell her. "We need to get back."

When we get there, the Scions and several of the villagers are gathered in the meeting hall, sitting at a wooden table. We walk into the middle of a flurried conversation, unable to make out anything that is being said. Nobody looks in our direction.

In the corner of the room, Taron sits on the floor, his knees pulled up to his chest. His head is down. His body is covered with sweat and he's shaking. Elisha sits next to him, her hand on the boy's shoulder. She gives me a solemn look.

Michael stands by the table, chair pushed back. He gestures in

Taron's direction. He's so different than he was the time I ate breakfast with him in the cafeteria. His wife sits next to him, clutching the infant in her arms. *The machines never returned for their baby, then.* Nonetheless, it seems that night changed Michael. I guess it changed all of us.

Michael's voice is raised. "How do we know we can trust whatever this boy claims to have seen?"

Rowan looks like he's trying to stop himself from ripping the man limb from limb. He doesn't stand for outsiders insulting the Scions, least of all Taron. "If he says he saw it, he saw it."

Otis leans over the table, holding out his hands empathically. "Why would anybody lie about that?"

Another man—somebody I don't recognize—chimes in. "Your group marches in here and we're supposed to trust everything you say?"

Catriona and I draw nearer.

"What did he see?" I ask. Catriona goes over to Taron.

Every head at the table turns to us. They all quiet down. The tension eases. They're afraid of me and what they've seen me do. I'm not sure that's a good thing, but I'll use it to my advantage. "Will somebody tell us what's going on?"

Rowan looks at Taron. "You should hear it from him."

I regard the boy, trying to soften my expression. "What is it?"

Taron looks up at me, breathing heavily. He takes a moment to compose himself. "I saw something. Something bad."

I go to Taron and kneel in front of him as Catriona steps aside to give me room. With a glance, I ask Elisha's permission to push a little. I hate the idea of making the kid do this, but I need to know.

Elisha nods gravely.

"Taron," I whisper. "These people will listen to me, but I need to know what's happening."

Taron bites his lip. "It was a vision."

"A vision of what?"

Elisha lays a hand on Taron's back. "It might be more useful if you show him."

Taron gives her a reluctant nod before addressing me. He looks straight into my eyes. "If you want to see, you'll have to let me in."

I pull back on instinct. *Why does everybody in this group want to get inside my head so much?* But when I look at the kid, I know this is the last thing he wants. Whatever this is, he's asking because it's important.

"Okay," I say. "Don't break anything in there. There are things I'd like to remember." I give Taron a reassuring smile.

The power stirs inside me, but I don't ignite. Instead, I let it disintegrate the walls of my mind. As I feel them fall away, I realize those walls have been there for years, so long I wasn't even aware they were up. I never realized how closed off I had been until I opened my mind.

Taron keeps his eyes on mine, and it begins.

In my mind's eye, I see an android in a village, carrying another child away from screaming parents. At first, I think it's my own memory, but the village looks different. The huts are the same, but there are fewer of them and not as many trees. I don't recognize the parents, and in this vision, I don't run in to stop the machine. The android simply walks away with the child in its arms.

The vision changes. The child is placed inside a glass tube and loaded onto a rack in the back of a truck. Other tubes surround it, all filled with infants. They look like they're asleep.

Suddenly, I'm in a facility, staring at the child, still in his glass tube, which has been installed upright in a wall. Machine arms extend from the sides of the tube and insert syringes into his arm. Blood seeps out of him and flows through the tubes.

My perspective widens as if I'm backing away and I realize that I'm in a large circular room filled with technology. Tubes of children line the wall, all with blood being extracted from their bodies. The blood tubes feed into a large vat in the center of the room.

A war machine mage stands on a platform over the vat, chanting spells. The symbol on the machine's forehead is one I've never seen before—a deep red circle.

A blood mage.

The mage's chant increases in speed and volume. Below, the vat of blood begins to boil.

I gasp, leaping back. I'm in the meeting hall again, surrounded by the villagers. Somebody nearby is breathing so loudly they sound like they're going to explode.

Then I realize that's me.

Catriona kneels at my side. She puts her hand on my arm.

"What was that?" I ask, still reeling from what I saw.

Michael speaks up from the table behind me. "You saw it, too?"

I ignore him. "Elisha, what were they doing?"

Elisha usually appears so serene, joyful even during the darkest times. This is the first time I've seen her look despondent, truly defeated. "We believe the war machines are using the children to harness blood magic."

Rowan walks over, takes Taron by the hand, and brings him to his feet. His voice is unusually gentle. "Let's go get some food. They don't need us right now."

After they leave the meeting hall, Catriona, Elisha, and I take places at the table. All attention is on me as I tell the villagers what I saw. There are several loud gasps.

"Why are they using blood magic?" Michael asks.

Elisha answers carefully. "The Breath is the secret that the machines have been attempting to unlock since they first discovered elemental magic. They read the legends. They knew there was deeper, more powerful magic in the world, but they couldn't determine how to harness it."

"Because they're not alive," I insert.

Elisha nods. "The Breath is different. The war machines cannot manipulate it like the elements, at least not directly. They must believe that blood might be a back door."

"But why children?" a villager asks.

"Their blood is more powerful," Catriona says to the table. I can't imagine how hard this must be for her. "It's more innocent."

The room is silent. Our own children in the clutches of the machines, their blood being drained so the androids can gain more power. Even for the most reluctant fighters among us, it has to be difficult to stomach. Living under strict machine rule is one thing. If nothing else, the people are at least clothed, fed, and sheltered. Though they have no freedom, at least they have life.

But this is a much darker truth.

Michael's expression has shifted, and he addresses me. "We're all grateful for what you did. You didn't just save us, you ensured that no more of *our* children will be taken." He eyes his infant son. "It's a terrible thing to have lost so many, but there's nothing we can do about that."

What?

"Cowards." Lark nearly spits the words.

That comment causes an eruption of arguing at the table. I lean over to Elisha. "Can't you stop this madness? Can't you tell them what to do?"

Her focus is steady on me. "That's your role now. They see you as one of their own, but also as a more powerful being. They will follow you, Gunnar. You must decide where you'll lead them."

The arguing continues around us. Maybe the naysayers are right. Saving children seems obvious, but what if we don't stand a chance? Defending a village is one thing. I'm certain the machines sent only what they believed would be required to destroy the target, a small fraction of their available forces. Attacking an important facility will be a much bigger task.

Even with my new powers, I don't see any way we can win. Trying to take a machine facility would cost us every able-bodied fighter we just risked our lives to rescue. What would happen to their children with no one to take care of them? The loss would be too great.

"Stop," I say, loudly enough to be heard. The room gradually quiets.

"You're right," I say, measuring my words. "This is a tragedy, but we have to be smart. An assault on a war machine facility is suicide. That won't save the children, and we'll all be killed. Our job now—all we can hope for—is to protect ourselves."

This next part hurts the most, but if I'm going to be a leader, I must be willing to make hard, painful decisions. I'll ask forgiveness later. "There's nothing else we can do."

The place erupts again. Lark shoots me a look of disgust and storms out of the room. It hurts to see her so angry with me, but not as much as the look of shock on Catriona's face.

There was nothing else I could do.

17

THE CHILDREN WILL SUFFER THE CURSED
WORLD WE HAVE CREATED.
THE INNOCENT CHILDREN.

— UNKNOWN

I RETREAT TO THE RIVER AFTER

the meeting, desperately wanting to be alone, tormenting myself for the decision I've made. The vision that Taron shared lingers with me—the children's faces stricken with terror as blood is stolen from their bodies, their lives exploited so that their rulers can gain more power.

But the decision is made. No noble intentions can change reality—we can't beat the machines. We might as well try to blot out the sun by throwing our bodies at it. All that will happen is we burn to death.

The song returns to me on a gentle breeze. I sit in the grass and sing, hoping it will ease my guilt. "The gravedigger's spade is a friend to me . . ." The tone fades until I'm mouthing the words. "'Cause I carry the water that washed me clean . . ."

"A beautiful song."

I'm grateful to hear the sound of Elisha's voice, but I don't turn. "My parents loved it. That's actually where I got my name."

Elisha sits next to me. "Gunnar?"

I shake my head. "Graves."

"Your family name?"

"My dad told me it was safer to use a fake surname. 'Too much data attached to our real name.'"

She nods and is quiet for a moment. "They were killed in the war?"

"A platoon led by a fire mage. Destroyed everything . . . except me, I guess."

"Is that why you joined us? For revenge?"

Her voice isn't accusing, but I don't answer. Instead, I gather a pebble in my hands and skim it across the river. It bounces three times before sinking. I'd much rather not talk about the past.

"You're not at peace with the decision you made today," Elisha observes.

I skim another rock. "It doesn't matter if I'm at peace with it. It was the only way to protect the people."

"Was it?" Elisha's smile is that of a teacher in gentle disbelief over their student's ignorance. "Where is your faith? You touched glory in that pool, Gunnar. For a moment, you released all the anger and resentment you held on to for so long. And when you did, what you experienced was nothing short of a miracle. You will never be the same after something like that. Look at the power you now wield. Could you have ever imagined you'd be able to do the things you can do? Is that not evidence enough?"

"Evidence of what? Of God?"

"Perhaps."

"I don't believe in God. Haven't for a long time."

She regards me. "I don't think that's true. Everyone believes in a god, Gunnar. They just may not know it. Most often, they're hoping that their god will be turn out to be themselves."

That gets me to look at her. "You think I'm trying to be God, Elisha?"

"For years, you've been striving to harness supernatural powers to use as you saw fit," she replies.

"I'm trying to correct things that never should have happened."

"So were they," Elisha says.

"Who?"

"The machines. They took it upon themselves to correct the mistakes of humanity. By any means necessary."

That gets a derisive laugh from me as I turn my attention back to the water. I throw another stone, a little harder this time. It bounces once. "You're saying that I'm like the war machines."

Her tone remains calm. "I'm saying they're like us. All of us. The sin of the machines was the same as the sin of man. We're all trying to be God."

I snort.

Elisha stands, her robes billowing in the wind. "But you are not God, Gunnar Graves. And you will never find peace until you accept that."

Before I can respond, Elisha walks away.

I spend the afternoon sitting by the water and return to the village at dusk to find the Scions and the villagers building fortifications. They construct walls from scrap metal, wood, and even rubble from the attack. A watchtower is being built on top of the platform where once stood a mage. Makeshift gunner positions are erected at different points in the village. Rowan and Lark carry looks of dissatisfaction, but they're helping.

Michael has taken the lead and directs people from his position on the platform in the center of the village. "Keep moving!" he shouts. "We don't know how long we have until they return."

Otis emerges from one of the huts near the platform and starts walking in the opposite direction.

Michael spots him. "Oh, the cyborg has decided to unplug himself long enough to walk among us. Do you plan to help, or are you still busy sending out your magic signal?"

Otis wheels around, fury on his face. "You got a lot of courage standing up there on your pedestal. Why don't you come down here and we—"

"Stop!" My voice thunders as I ignite my star fire and take flight. Every head turns as I hover into the center of the village. I pulsate my energy in a full display of power. I don't want them to be afraid, but I need them to know that I'm serious.

I lower myself onto the platform, taking a position between Michael and Otis.

Michael tries to look relaxed, but fails. "We've started building fortifications and stationing fighters in defensive and lookout positions on the outer perimeter." I can tell by the tone of his voice that he expects me to be proud of his progress. In other circumstances, I might be. At least he's doing something.

But it's not what I want right now. "Call back as many people as you can."

Michael looks at me in confusion.

I speak loud so that everybody can hear. "We're attacking the blood facility." My tone is firm. I won't force anyone to follow me. But I'm going, and I know I'm not going alone. "Otis, can you locate it?"

Otis looks as if he doesn't want to answer. But after a few moments, he nods sharply.

Michael's disbelief breaks his facade of respect for me. "You're insane. We can't risk a direct attack on the machines. It'll ruin the cover your friend has provided."

Otis gives him a mocking grin. "Happy with the signal now, are ya?"

I quiet him with a look.

I turn so that I'm facing the villagers, who are gathering near the platform. The fear is evident on their faces. But they're listening.

"The machines have divided us for too long," I announce. "They split us into small groups so we can't unite into a force large enough to fight back. That ends now."

"You're talking about attacking what is most likely a heavily guarded facility," Michael counters. "We won't make it to the front door."

I notice Taron in the crowd, standing near Rowan. "There are more of us out there, right?" I ask him. "More who have the Breath inside them?"

Taron nods.

"Send out a signal," I say. "Tell them we're fighting."

Taron shakes his head. "It won't work. If any other mages were close enough to contact, I would've connected with them by now."

"I'm not asking you to connect with them. I want you to be a beacon. Throw a signal out as far as you can. Maybe nobody who receives it will be powerful enough to send one back to you. But if they hear you, they might come."

He pauses. "I don't know if I can."

"I believe in you." I feel terrible about placing such a burden on a kid. Chances are, nobody will show up and it won't be his fault. But we have to try.

Taron draws in a deep breath, and by the time he lets it back out, he seems like a different person. He stands up straight, confidence in his eyes.

"I'll do it."

At dawn the next morning, the Scions, Catriona, and several villagers load into the supply trucks previously used by the machines. Some of us are armed with rifles, others with tools, and a few—but not nearly enough—with magic.

Men and women hug their children and elders before they leave. I watch a mother embrace her son. The boy looks barely old enough to walk, but he stands and raises his arms, calling to his mama. She lifts him up and holds him tight against her chest, a rifle slung across her back. It's almost too much to watch.

"You're having second thoughts," Elisha says beside me.

"Is that a question?"

"No," Elisha says. "It isn't."

I look at the ground, then shake the words away. I can't afford to doubt myself, not when so many people are charging into danger because they're willing to follow me. "Time to go."

As the trucks pull away from the village, a few children chase after the convoy, trying to keep up. I watch them in the rearview mirror. One by one, they fall hopelessly behind until we see nothing but the dirt road.

Otis drives our truck. I ride shotgun. Rowan, Lark, and Catriona sit in the back, Lark resting her head on her brother's shoulder. Rowan's eyes are straight ahead, cold and determined.

"Might as well get some sleep," Otis says, gripping the wheel. "Gonna be a while."

I glance back and reach behind my seat to find Catriona's hand. She holds tight for a moment, then slowly lets go. I lean back in my seat, trying not to think about what lies at the end of the road.

I don't realize I've drifted off to sleep until Rowan's coughing rouses me awake. It's a relief. I had been dreaming dark dreams about the battle ahead, and it didn't go well.

I glance over my shoulder. Rowan is covered in sweat and coughing like he has gravel in his lungs. Catriona looks on in concern.

Lark holds a hand on her brother's back. "Rowan, what is it? What's going on?"

Rowan tries to respond, but he's struggling to breathe. He grunts with intense pain that appears to increase every second.

I lean over the seat. "Hey, are you okay?"

Before he can respond, Rowan doubles over and growls in agony.

Lark's face goes white. "Rowan!"

Otis drives like he's oblivious to what's happening. I lean further over the seat but there's nothing I can do. I anxiously wonder if Elisha can help.

Rowan raises his head with great effort. His entire body trembles. He coughs, then looks past me toward the front of the truck.

When I turn, a thick cloud of smoke appears in front of us. It's so dense that I can hardly see the road. *What is going on?*

"They burned it," Lark says, her voice weaker than I've ever heard it. "They burned it all."

The road dips and the smoke clears enough to reveal the landscape. Far in front of us, I see the blood facility—a massive dome in the middle of a canyon valley, though from this distance, the building is a tiny dot.

But it looks as if a major battle has already taken place. The trees, the grass—everything has been burned. Where a lush valley should be, there is a scorched desert as far as I can see.

Everything is dead.

18

BUT SOME WERE TOO AFRAID TO FIGHT. THOSE
PEOPLE WERE OFTEN MORE DANGEROUS THAN
THE MACHINES.

— AIDEN RYLAN, JOURNALIST

OUR CONVOY PULLS OFF THE

road into a small gravel lot with an old sign that reads 'Scenic viewpoint.'
Far below and in the distance, we can see the canyon that protects the
facility. According to the maps, the canyon opens on one side, through
which runs a heavy line of trees that we had planned to use for cover
while moving up to the facility itself.

But the trees are gone. The grass is scorched. Smoke billows out of
the canyon like it's a chimney.

The gravel crunches beneath our tires as we come to a stop. When
we step out, the villagers look on in silence.

"I don't understand," I say to Elisha, who looks as if she's mourning
the loss of a loved one. "Why do this?"

"To choke away our supply of life energy," she responds. "So that we
have no power to draw upon during the battle."

"They knew we were coming?"

Elisha nods.

Rowan sits on the ground, his back against the side of a parked
truck. He seems to have stabilized, but still looks terrible.

Lark kneels next to him, giving him sips of water. "How could they
possibly know that we were coming?"

Otis leans against the truck, his arms crossed, his expression blank.
"Because I told them."

"You what?" Rage floods my body. In a second, I lunge at him and
grip his jacket with both hands.

Elisha reaches for me. "Gunnar . . ."

I jerk away from her. I don't need her peace and guidance, not right now.

Instead, I ignite my power. "Otis, you better start talking."

Despite the fact that his life is being threatened by an angry mage whose body is literally on fire, Otis is almost stoic. "Kill me."

I grit my teeth. "Is that a dare?"

The cyborg shrugs. "Take it however you want, hero. The machines have an upgraded body waiting to receive my consciousness as soon as the lights go out on this one. I would have done the job myself hours ago . . ." He smirks, points a finger gun at his temple, and pretends to fire. "But I just *had* to be here when y'all saw this."

I tighten my grip on him, my power flaring everywhere except my hands.

"Go ahead," he says. "I'm good and ready."

My body feels as if it wants to explode and incinerate every fiber of his being.

But that's what he wants, too. So instead, I hurl him backward.

Otis tumbles over the hood of the truck, crashes onto the pavement, and rolls like a tumbleweed. When he stops, blood seeps from the skin that remains on his body.

He laughs like a devil. "Typical. You should be thanking me."

Taron runs forward, as if ready to take on Otis himself, but Catriona puts a strong arm on the boy, keeping him away.

"How could you do this to us?" Taron asks, fighting the tears in his eyes.

Otis's sarcastic sneer disappears as if his one regret is Taron's disappointment. "We can't win this, kid. And maybe we don't deserve to win, anyway. Maybe it's best that the machines are running the show. I risked my life to save these people and they still treat me like scrap metal. I didn't choose the sides here. *They* did. Those people will never look at me and not see an enemy."

Otis's face hardens again. Any sadness, any empathy he might have experienced even seconds ago, is gone. "Well, so be it. They want to challenge me, they're going to get what's coming. If they knew the whole truth, I wouldn't be the only one they cast out into the wilderness."

The words hit me like a knife. *Don't tell them. Not now.* The last thing I need is an already overmatched army starting to doubt whether they can follow me into battle because of the tech inside me.

Otis stands and locks eyes with me. "That's right, Sparky. Picked up the energy signature radiating off your metal heart the moment I saw you. You're a cyborg. Just like me."

Satisfied, Otis surveys the gathering villagers behind us and raises his voice. "So what do you think? Y'all going to throw in with this one now that you know he's got oil in his blood? Still going to bow down and sing praises to the Immortal Gunnar Graves?"

Nobody says a word.

Otis dusts himself off. "Lucky for y'all, Uncle Otis came to the rescue again."

"You doomed us," Lark snaps.

"Only if you attack, little kitty cat. I told you, the machines are better gods than we ever had. Give them what they want . . . what they *need* in order to keep us from making a mess of everything again . . . and they'll let you run on back home." He sneers. "You'll return to your quiet little village like good boys and girls and live out your lives like nothing happened."

I try to control my anger. "And what is it that they want?"

"The secret of the life energy," Otis says. "They get that, they'll stop taking your snot-nosed kids. Won't need them anymore."

The other Scions wear solemn looks on their faces, including Elisha. Rowan has managed to stand, though he's hunched over in obvious pain. I have to put an end to this.

I walk to Otis, ready to stamp out his life. Before I reach him, he points a finger behind me, indicating the canyon.

"It's waiting for your decision," Otis taunts. "All these lives are in your hands."

I pause. If they knew we were coming, the machines definitely outnumber us by a huge amount. We might have stood a chance with the element of surprise, but Otis's betrayal has ruined that.

His betrayal.

A darkness pours over me.

Otis doesn't flinch when I place my hand on his shoulder and ignite the star fire. The energy transfers to his body. His metallic eye glows brighter as he melts from the inside.

Within seconds, his body crumbles to ash. The wind carries him away.

We're still on the side of the road as dusk yawns over the sky. Someone had the good sense to bring food along, so we sit and eat, mostly to distract ourselves.

In the distance, the smoke clears and the machines wait.

There isn't much sound beyond chewing, the occasional grunt and cough, and small conversations about nothing. A few times, I try to rally my own emotions, but fail. Am I really going to lead these people into the jaws of death?

Taron keeps vigil at the edge of the cliff, staring at the machines in the distance. "They all look exactly the same." The way he says it, I'm not sure if he's asking a question or making an observation.

But I nod. "Andy found the most efficient way to make itself, and kept on doing that exact same thing—churning out one identical unit after another."

"Not very creative," Taron says under his breath, turning away.

"Creative?" a nearby man from the village says with disgust. "That's what you're thinking about? Son, we're all gonna die. If this wasn't a suicide mission before, it sure is now. The signal is gone. We can't go back, and if we run, they'll hunt us down."

A few others nod in agreement.

Rowan grunts. "Cowards."

The man shoots up and takes an aggressive step toward Rowan. "Big words for a mage who just lost his source of magic."

Green veins appear beneath the surface of Rowan's skin. His flesh begins to harden into tree bark. "I can spare a little for you, if you like."

"That's enough," Elisha says, standing and facing Rowan. She hasn't eaten anything. Instead, she's been sitting in silence, her eyes closed until this moment. I assumed she was praying, meditating, something. Who knows anymore?

Rowan's face is red with anger, but Elisha continues to gaze at him. I've never seen her challenge anyone before. After a moment, Rowan looks away in surrender.

"We gain nothing by fighting each other," Elisha says. "The machines won't have to destroy us. We'll do it ourselves."

"It doesn't matter." The words come out of my mouth on their own.

"Have you lost hope, too, Gunnar Graves?" Elisha asks.

"I haven't *lost* anything. Our hope has been taken from us. Do you see what I see down there? You had me believing we might be able to pull this off. I tried to have faith, Elisha. You know that. But if we can't replenish our power, we don't stand a chance."

"And your faith is limited to that, is it?" she challenges. "To what you can see in front of you?"

I roll my eyes. "I'm not in the mood for your preaching. No more catchy little sayings from the wise old master. It's over."

On the other side of the circle, Taron's head perks up. He looks as if he's heard an unfamiliar sound and he's trying to locate it.

"No." A smile of joyous disbelief appears on the boy's face. "It's not over."

I scan the area, trying to see what he's looking for. The other Scions and some of the villagers do the same, but Elisha's eyes stay on me.

"They're here!" Taron exclaims.

I ignite my power and jump up. "The machines?"

He shakes his head. "The others!"

What 'others'?

A rustling from the woods on the other side of the road catches my attention. I clench my fists, preparing to fight. If the machines are flanking us, I'll take a few of them down before I die.

A woman appears in the trees, materializing out of thin air where before there had been nothing, as if she just allowed the light to touch her. She stands in front of the wood line, wielding two swords. The blades are double-sided, thin and light. She wears some type of padded battle armor that looks strong but flexible. The woman has black hair and olive skin. A scar stretches across her cheek.

"Taron?" the woman asks. "I thought that was your voice in my head."

"Zara!" Taron runs to her. He wraps his arms around her.

Zara returns his embrace, then glances over her shoulder and shouts into the woods. "They're here!"

A group emerges from the cover of the trees. Some are dressed in the same light earth tones as the people from my village, but others wear robes of dark colors, ragtag armor, and camouflage. Some carry the Alliance symbol either stitched or painted on their clothes. A few glow with various shades of energy emanating from their eyes and hands. No two of them look alike.

The sight is beautiful.

"Taron," I breathe, "how did they find us here? I thought your signal told them to meet us at the facility."

"When I first sent it out, it did." Taron grins at me. "But I never stopped sending it."

It's remarkable. Even I didn't think he was *that* powerful. I almost tussle the boy's hair, but it doesn't seem appropriate. That's the type of thing you do to a kid. Instead, I grip his shoulder as I would a brother-in-arms.

"Are you the Immortal Gunnar Graves?" Zara asks.

I nod, bemused that Taron decided to tell others about me. "More or less."

The mage crosses her swords in front of her chest and gives me a short bow. "I'm Zara. We're here to fight with you."

I look across her people, those with magic and those who seem to have brought nothing but their courage to the fight. I'm honored to have every single one of them. If they are brave enough to follow me to the gates of death, they deserve everything I can give.

"Taron, can you connect us?" I ask, then realize I should clarify. "All of us?"

Taron watches me intently. In his eyes, I see that he understands what I'm saying.

"I can," Taron says, though the look on his face speaks much more. He is half my age, but he is proud of me.

I nod. "We attack at first light."

At dusk, we take five vehicles and drive toward the facility. We don't try to quiet our engines. Instead, we rev them as loudly as we can, maybe to remind ourselves to be courageous, maybe to herald to the machines that destruction is coming to claim whatever excuses for souls reside in their tin skeletons.

The element of surprise is gone. The machines know we're on our way. The sky tells us as much. Storm clouds gather unnaturally fast, but there is no rain. The android mages are stirring up a dust storm. Pillars of swirling dirt and debris fill the canyon as lightning crackles overhead. Flames streak through the sky. The thunder is so loud that I can hear the rumble over the sound of our engines. We have drawn the attention of the gods, and they are angry.

So be it.

My window is rolled down, so I pull myself out and sit on the door as we ride, the rough terrain jarring my body. Nothing living lies ahead. Every tree is ash. Every blade of grass is scorched. Even the air feels cold and empty.

The unnatural dust storm taints the sky a sinister shade of red. Our vehicle is in the lead, heading for the gap between the canyon walls. Tall spires of rock reach up to the sky along the walls, like arms welcoming us into our doom.

When we cross the threshold and enter the canyon, I see the machines—thousands of glowing red eyes, steel bodies reflecting the fires, marching through the swirling dust over scorched desert. Maybe we're not bringing destruction with us after all.

It's already here.

"Zara!" I say out loud, but also with my brain, our minds telepathically linked and amplified by Taron. "Now!"

The mage lifts the effect of her powers, revealing the forces running alongside our vehicles as we charge the battlefield. A contingent of men and women wield rifles and melee weapons. They shout battle cries as they charge. Among them I hear prayers to God, curses, and names that

I assume belong to loved ones lost to the steel enemy. Their courage is a mighty wind, pushing me forward. I will not fail them today.

I jump out the window and ignite my powers, the star fire enveloping my body as I take flight.

My fellow Scions join me in leading the attack, a collective of supernatural individuals forming the tip of our collective sword.

Lark becomes a swarm of insects overhead. Rowan growls as he runs, becoming like a living tree, his legs and arms powerful limbs, his skin covered with bark. I spot other mages as well, some covered in fur or bark. A few fly or flex muscles the size of small boulders. Some slip in and out of visibility, while others move like shadows given life.

The machines open fire. Through the swirling dust, I spot the mages behind them, standing on scattered rocks and holding silver-fleshed hands up to the sky, summoning our demise in dramatic fashion.

The sandstorm intensifies, slinging chunks of earth and rock through the air. The debris disintegrates when it hits my star fire, but the others will have to fight through it.

Lightning clouds churn overhead, then release a powerful strike of electricity. The ground in front of me erupts, sending more rock into the air.

"Taron!" I say out loud, but also with my mind as I unleash blasts of energy at the machines before me. I'm not sure how his power works, but I want to make sure he gets the message. "Am I connected with the others?"

"Our group," he says in my head. "Yes."

"Good. Lark, can you find that storm mage?"

Overhead, her swarm moves like a living black cloud soaring over the chaos of the battle. The machines fire at her, but the bullets pass between the insects, doing no harm. The swarm descends toward the machines.

I continue my attack but keep my focus on Lark's trajectory, following it down until I see her target.

The storm mage is atop one of the canyon walls. I can see the glow of its eyes as the storm intensifies.

When Lark reaches the mage, her swarm pours over its body like a plague. The black cloud holds on top of the mage for a few seconds, then blows past it. The mage's synthetic flesh is gone, leaving only the metal exoskeleton that topples over.

Lark descends to the battlefield and shifts into a mountain lion an instant before she touches the ground. She doesn't break momentum as she attacks another war machine. "Storm mage down."

I use my power to propel myself higher into the sky and fire energy bolts at other androids. "Can you do that again?"

"Not without more power," she says. "We better hope there aren't too many more mages out here."

Then I see it. At first, I think it's another flash of lightning through the dust, but it endures for too long, a streak of red across the sky, a tail of flames trailing behind it.

A fire mage.

"Incoming!" Rowan yells.

I target the approaching fireball—a hunk of flames and earth. My energy blast bursts it into pieces, but more are coming.

"Gunnar!" Lark shouts. "Behind you!"

I glance over my shoulder to see an air mage carrying a contingent of androids through the sky behind us, just like it did in the woods. Except this one is shooting down at our army.

I turn my attention toward the air mage and its platoon, propelling myself higher into the air, dodging between dust cyclones as I approach my enemy.

The machine platoon spots me and fires in my direction. The first wave of bullets disintegrates against my flames as I fly toward them.

Suddenly my shoulder erupts in pain. A red streak appears, oozing through my shirt. How did a bullet break through my energy barrier?

My powers are failing. I can feel it inside. The energy is running thin. I continue to fly, releasing energy bursts as fast as I can, knocking androids out of the sky, fighting my way toward the air mage.

My muscles are sore. The strain of magic increases rapidly as my power fades. I can't keep this up much longer.

"Gunnar!" Taron says in my head. "The other mages are running out of power."

I land quickly but continue blasting toward the sky. "Then we hit them right now with everything we've got!"

My energy falters with every blast, each attack weaker than the one before, but I manage to thin out the air mage's group until only the mage itself remains. It flies over me before I can get a clear shot, landing near the facility.

To my right, I notice Lark still fighting in her mountain lion form, bounding between enemy units and ripping into them with powerful claws. Her skin shifts back to human flesh for a second before returning to fur.

Moments later, it happens again, lasting a little longer.

"Lark!" I call out. "Fall back!"

She either doesn't hear me or doesn't care. Lark tries to jump, but her leg shifts and falters, causing her to stumble. A bullet rips into her side.

"Lark!" Rowan rumbles to her. He's still in towering tree form, but his body shrinks as he runs. War machine bullets bombard him, chipping away his bark, sending splinters into the air. When he reaches Lark, he throws himself over her as he struggles to maintain his armor.

The next voice I hear in my head belongs to Elisha. "It's time."

"Time?" I ask, looking back and finding her on the battlefield behind me. "Time for what?"

Elisha doesn't answer. Instead, she spreads out her arms and her feet lift off the ground. She closes her eyes, raises her head toward the sky, and drifts to the center of the canyon as if unaffected by the conflict. A glow emits from her torso.

"What is she doing?" I shout.

Taron's voice shakes as he responds in my mind.

"Resurrection."

The glow spreads across Elisha's body until I can no longer see her human form. She becomes an orb of light so bright I almost can't look at it. A faint music drifts through the chaos, the same that I heard in the temple.

The battle ceases. The dust settles and the storm clouds wither as the war machines appear to be awestruck by what they're witnessing, astounded by the power.

A new hope spreads through me. Of course Elisha is this powerful.

Why didn't I see it before? She's been biding her time, waiting for the right moment to unleash a glorious power upon our enemy.

But there is no attack, no explosion, no burst of energy. Instead, the light she has become appears to crumble, the orb falling apart into sparks that drop onto the dead earth. They glimmer likes embers for a moment, then disappear.

Elisha is gone.

The music stops. The world goes silent. Nobody knows what to do, not even the androids that are programmed to destroy. I wonder if the light overwhelmed their optics.

Something grabs my attention. In the place where Elisha's light fell, a single blade of grass stands, glowing green.

My mouth drops open. I can't believe what I'm seeing.

The green spreads to the surrounding ground, new grass appearing. Slowly at first, then progressively moving faster.

Soon, it covers a large patch of the canyon, no sign of slowing down as the renewed life devours the death that moments ago seemed all-encompassing.

I hear Rowan in my head. "She's given us a chance."

My hand extends toward the vegetation and a line of energy forms between me and the earth. The power fills my body, more than I ever had before. I marvel at the sensation; it's like a burning sun inside my heart, except there is no pain.

Only power.

I ignite the star fire, still drawing energy from the land. The power gathers in my arms, building, channeling from everything within me and everything outside of me.

When it reaches its nexus, I release a burst of power that obliterates a massive group of war machines in front me.

My attack sparks the battle back into action, but the tide is turned. The Scions and other mages draw power from the earth, their abilities amplified. Rowan grows larger than I could have imagined, like a giant redwood in the shape of man. Lark takes the form of an enormous bull and charges the nearest war machine, trampling it with ease before slamming her horn into another.

The machines respond with an onslaught of firepower. A barrage of bullets fills the air, dotted by explosions from heavy artillery. More androids fly in from the other side of the facility as reinforcements. Fireballs fill the sky and I remember the present evil that has haunted my dreams for years.

The fire mage.

The realization sparks something deep within that I've held on to for a very long time. I see the destruction of my unit, my parents' graves. The visions fuel the rage burning inside me, setting aflame the embers that I forgot were there, but have been smoldering below the surface.

The androids in front of me become no longer enemies, but obstacles. My power spikes as I fight my way through them, casting them aside, annihilating their steel forms. Each unit destroyed brings me a step closer to the fire mage.

To my vengeance.

But with each android I destroy, two more seem to take its place. I can't see the fire mage, but it feels like I'm somehow getting further away from it. I take to the air, hoping I will be able to locate my target from a higher vantage point. As soon as I'm up, I already know this battle is over.

"There are too many," Lark calls out.

"And more coming," Rowan adds.

They're right. The enemy appears to be endless, with more moving in from the other side of the canyon. Their numbers are so large that I can't see the ground beneath the oncoming wave, and forming storm clouds tell me that more mages have arrived.

No. The idea of losing pierces my heart like a rusty blade. We have so much power now, more than I've ever felt. This is supposed to be the moment when we turn the tide against the machines, when we show them that we are strong. When I make them regret what they did to me.

"Keep fighting!" I light up the night with star fire. "Elisha died so we could win."

Taron speaks into my head. I'm yelling, but his words are clear and calm. "No, Gunnar. You're wrong."

"What?" I release another massive blast on the enemy, my anger growing.

"Taron," Lark says in my head. "What are you talking about?"

"I received a final message from her," Taron says. "Right before . . ." His voice strengthens. "She didn't die so we could win. She died so we could live."

The machines fire at me. My energy field deflects the damage, but I feel the overwhelming nature of the machine offensive.

Below, mages and villagers are hunkered down, fighting with all they have to maintain their ground. They're advancing no further toward the facility. They're just trying not to die. Some scream, others are dragged back to the safety of the trees. Besides myself, only Rowan and Lark seem to be making a difference.

And more machine mages are coming.

We can't win.

"Not like this," I say to myself, but I know the others can hear me.

"Gunnar!" Lark shouts, the desperation evident in her tone. "You're in charge. What are your orders?"

I don't hesitate. "Taron, spread the word. Full retreat."

In seconds, mages and villagers alike start to fall back. Those with guns or projectile magic lay down suppressive fire. Those who are wounded or have only melee weapons sprint for the opening of the canyon through which we came, knowing that the faster they get off the battlefield, the more lives will be saved.

I unleash blasts as fast as I can. "We've got to hold them off!"

The war machines push the attack, sensing our weakness.

Rowan speaks inside my head. "Go." He raises his arms—the mighty branches that they are—and draws more energy from the surrounding vegetation.

The trees along the edges of the battlefield come to life and rush forward, their roots moving over the ground like great tentacles. They throw themselves between the approaching machines and the retreating humans and mages, creating a protective wall of life.

Rowan stands among them like a great sentinel. The machines focus their fire on him.

"Get them out of here!" Rowan's voice thunders across the canyon, so loud I don't need a mental connection to hear him.

Lark and I keep fighting, ignoring Rowan's words. My star fire strikes the war machines like lightning. She takes the form of a werewolf but with an armored hide, ripping the heads off war machines.

"Both of you!" Rowan booms at us. "Go!"

"I'm not leaving you behind." I fly toward Rowan and focus my fire on the machines nearest him, trying to temper the assault. It doesn't do much good, and despite the abundance of life around me, my power wanes. I can't draw it in fast enough to keep up my energy shields.

Taron speaks to me. "Gunnar, get out of there. We need you." He talks with a confidence and wisdom beyond his years. It's the second time in the past five minutes that he's questioned my decisions in combat, but that's not the reason I'm angry.

I'm mad because he's right.

I continue to fire, facing forward but starting to fly backward, hurling my blasts over the treetops. Rowan's army has stopped the enemy's progress, but they're getting ripped apart.

Lark keeps fighting. Her savagery is the stuff of legends as she tears the head off one war machine after another.

"Lark! Go!" Rowan's voice cracks as he stumbles back, unable to withstand the machine fire.

"Not without you," she says.

Rowan pauses. "I'm sorry about this."

"About what?"

Rowan reaches down and grabs Lark, plucking her out of the fight. He turns and hurls her into the air behind him.

I recognize what he's doing the moment he grabs her. I react, flying behind him and readying myself. Lark's body sails toward me. She shifts back to human form and I catch her near the back of the trees.

In front of me, another storm grows, larger than anything I could've ever imagined. The air grows noticeably hotter as lightning and flames swirl among the clouds, building in power.

Lark struggles against me. "Let me go!" Normally she'd have no problem escaping my grip, but she's exhausted from the battle. I manage to hold on to her as we fly away from the canyon, chasing the dust trail kicked up by our forces' vehicles.

"Gunnar . . ." Rowan says through our connection, his voice grave for the first time. I look over my shoulder and see him falter to a knee.

"I know." I swallow. "You can't let them take you alive."

"Remember what you've been taught," Rowan says, then lets out a roar so powerful that the war machines must be stumbling beneath the shaking earth.

He brings his massive branches down on a large group of them, smashing them to pieces, filling the air with dust and debris.

The storm above is all fire and lightning. Everything goes silent for a moment, then a column of electric flame shoots down from the sky like the fist of an angry god. Only that would be powerful enough to topple so mighty a colossus, so courageous a hero.

Even when it hits him, setting his entire body on fire, Rowan fights a few more seconds, smashing androids with flaming branches before he tips forward, crushing many more, one last time.

19

THEY HAD MAGIC. THEY HAD TECHNOLOGY.
THEY HAD NUMBERS. ALL WE HAD WAS EACH
OTHER.

— STEFANIE SCOTT, WRITER

I CRADLE LARK'S HEAD IN MY LAP,

trying to keep her stable despite the bouncing, as we ride in the back of a truck. She's exhausted. She's in shock. But she's alive. Because of Elisha, Rowan, and many others, the rest of us are alive.

For now.

The village is in an uproar as soon as we return. Several huts are quickly converted into makeshift hospitals. The injured scream as others try to calm them down. People rush in every direction, carrying water, towels, and bandages. Those who aren't helping the wounded take defensive positions on the perimeter of the village.

I can feel the tension in the air, I assume through my telepathic abilities. It causes me to be nauseous. These people are afraid, and they should be.

Our truck pulls into the center of the village. After I help Lark out of the back, Catriona appears through the crowd. "Gunnar!"

Her presence is an oasis in the desert, a port in the storm. I embrace her, and for a brief moment, all feels right in the world.

It's a mistake when I open my eyes, because that's when I see Michael approaching. The dark realities of the world rush back in.

"They'll be here soon," Michael says. "The fortifications won't hold for long. We have to run. Now."

I let go of Catriona and she steps back.

"If you run," I say to Michael, "the machines will hunt you down and wipe you out."

"Oh, the Immortal Gunnar Graves believes we should stand our ground." Michael snorts. "I think we've had enough of your leadership. Not even the old woman's magic could give you enough power to—"

I explode toward him. I grab the collar of his shirt and ignite my power, though only in one arm. I raise a fiery fist. "Finish that sentence! I dare you!"

To his credit, Michael stands his ground, though he can't seem to help a slight tremble in the face of my fury and power. "I meant no disrespect to Elisha. Only to *you*. If you want to kill me for that, hero, go ahead."

I extinguish my power and release him, embarrassed that Catriona saw me lose my temper. "We've all lost people we care about." Lark raises her voice from behind me. "All of us. But I won't let them die in vain. They deserve better than that."

I can't decide if I should thank her or apologize. Only moments ago, she was nearly catatonic. Her resilience is an inspiration. I still have so far to go.

I gaze at the people. The chaos hasn't died down. We're on enemy ground here, a place the machines built to contain us. Michael's right about one thing. If we stay, it will be more than a prison. It will be our graveyard.

But maybe there's someplace else.

"Secure the wounded," I instruct. "Get them stabilized and into the vehicles. We're going to fight, but not here."

We move as fast as we can, the Scions and villagers traversing though the woods in the direction of the temple. The convoy is slow and noisy, but I'm not sure it matters. If the machines want to find us, they'll find us. Our one hope is that we've dented their numbers enough that they will take time to regroup after the attack at the facility.

Elisha once told me that the machines couldn't locate us in the temple, that the entire place was guarded by ancient magics stronger than the blood tracking could detect, deeper than technology could scan. We'll be safe there, at least for a while.

If we can reach it.

Catriona walks next to me, a large group of villagers following close behind. The few vehicles we have left are reserved for the wounded; the rest of us are on foot. It doesn't make much difference, other than the fact that we're exhausted. Taking roads is far too dangerous, so the off-road vehicles pick their way through the trees.

My mind drifts back to the battle in the canyon. This isn't the way it all was supposed to go. That was to be the moment of our victory. I achieved more power than I could ever imagine. Elisha made the ultimate sacrifice, as did Rowan and so many others.

And it wasn't enough. The machines just kept sending more.

Catriona glances at me as if she can feel the dread burning inside me. She wordlessly takes my hand and squeezes it.

It's a cold realization, knowing that we cannot win. Even if we had taken the facility, managed to free the children, the machines would have taken it back the next day with a larger force. I know it deep inside; we are truly defeated in this world. No matter how much good we do, no matter how righteous our cause, it will be a candle in the darkness, its light only reaching so far, and soon snuffed out by the wind.

I think back to Taron's words. Maybe what I think is winning—my concept of the idea—needs to change. Perhaps survival is victory, living outside of the yoke of the machines. At least in the temple, we can make our own choices. We won't be forced to mate or be told where to live. The outside world has been surrendered. For the rest of our lives, we will be surrounded by enemy territory.

Stop thinking that way, Gunnar. Catriona is next to me, and so many others are still alive. My job is to protect them, to hide. Maybe in time, we can free another facility or two and build our numbers. There's no point in worrying about any of that right now.

Just make it to the temple.

No sooner than I think the words do I hear the rumble ahead. At first, it sounds like a storm, but the sound is too constant to be thunder.

From the look on Catriona's face, she knows it too. "The machines."

I find Taron and instruct him to send a message for everyone to hold their positions except for Lark, Zara, and a few other mages, though I'm careful to leave plenty of magic-users with the people. This could be an ambush.

Catriona—clutching her shotgun and with a strap of ammo across her chest—refuses to stay behind. I know better than to try stopping her. And besides, I want her with me.

We rush through the woods, following the sound of the rumble, though I know exactly where we're going.

But when we reach the lake, it's already too late.

A water mage stands with its back to us as we emerge from the trees. Its arms are outstretched. The waters of the lake stand like two massive walls, parted down the middle by a force none of us can see.

Next to it, an earth mage causes the floor of the lake to crumble, creating a chasm that runs deep into the ground. The tremors shake my body, but the horrified realization rattles my soul.

The temple is destroyed.

"Stop!" I yell. The mages ignite their magics, preparing to fight. Catriona takes aim and pumps her shotgun. I scan the area for other androids, but the mages appear to have come alone. This wasn't an attack. They came to show me that we have no place to hide.

But why not send the rest? Why not finish us off?

Both mages turn in unison to face us, the glow remaining in their eyes. The rumbling stops and the water rushes back together, its two walls smashing into each other. The force creates a huge wave in the center that rises high and breaks. Water rains down on us, soaking our clothes.

I ignite my star fire. The mages stand and stare. They don't fight. They don't flee.

They wanted me to see this. Our life mages seem as confused as I am. The war machines stand close together, perfectly still. The message is clear—they'll never stop hunting us, and there's no safe place to run.

The star fire grows around me. I rise up a few feet in the air, gathering power from the trees and the grass until my energy builds to a maximum level. The war machine mages show no sign of counterattack or defense.

I obliterate them with a single blast.

Their bodies crumble into ash. Not long ago, taking out two mages at once would have been extremely satisfying. What a difference since the days I spent crouching in front of a makeshift fire pit, trying desperately to spark a bit of wood.

And yet, it doesn't matter. The temple is gone. I see the disappointment on my allies' faces. Even for those who had never been here, this place represented hope, our asylum from the world. The machines took it away with minimal effort. For all I know, there are already two new mage units being downloaded with the same localized data. Our enemy's resources are virtually unlimited.

We can't run. We can't hide. They will always find us.

Always.

"Take them somewhere else." I slide off my Alliance jacket and throw it over Catriona's shoulders. The star fire dried my clothes, but hers are still soaking wet. I take a deep breath and try to turn and leave.

"Gunnar?" Catriona takes my hand and tugs on me. "We can go—"

"Don't tell me where you're going." I can't bear to look at her. It would hurt too much, or maybe my resolve would break the moment I see her eyes. I have to be stronger than that. It's time to stop thinking about what I want for my life. "Catriona, if I don't know where you're going, the machines can't pull it out of me later."

Catriona darts in front of me and ducks her head under mine so that I am forced to look at her. Her face is puzzled but determined. "Gunnar, what are you doing? You can't just walk away."

"I'm not walking away, Catriona." I try to keep my tone even. "But it isn't safe with me. I've got a target on my back and I'm not strong enough to fight them all. Not by a long shot."

Catriona studies me. I see the wheels turning in her head. She's probably much smarter than I am, and, for all I know, potentially far more powerful. The blood gem glows brighter on her neck. "Then go find more people like you," she urges. "Find more mages, more power."

I give a brief nod. "I'll keep searching, gathering whomever I can. There has to be more out there. Maybe if we can muster enough magic, we can strike back." I try my best to sound like I believe it, but I know it's a lie, and I think she knows it too.

Catriona casts a glance back toward the forest. "I'll get them to safety." She turns her head back to me. "But I will come find you after that." She lifts her right hand to show me the locket ring that carries a drop of my blood.

The sight of it reminds me. I slip the dandelion from my pocket. It's as pristine as it was the night I found it, the night a billion stars reignited my hope. I've come to understand that it was a gift from something beyond my understanding, but also something that wanted me to know it was with me.

I place it in her palm and wrap her fingers around it. "Hold on to this for me."

Her eyes glisten as she nods.

I pull her close and embrace her. For what I'm afraid will be the last time.

It isn't a surprise when I see the plume of smoke in the distance, when I smell the burning wood and feel the growing heat on my skin. Of course the machines would anticipate my return. If anything, it's odd that they haven't trapped me here before, at the place where it all began, where the machines took away my life, my hope.

Niko rides on my shoulder, his eyes straight ahead. I don't think his species is capable of showing emotion through facial expressions, but I believe he would go straight into the flames with me.

Of course, I could never let that happen.

I stop about a quarter mile from the fire, kneel, and take Niko off my shoulder. "I'm sorry, friend. Where I'm going, you can't come with me."

As soon as his paws touch the ground, Niko races back to my leg, jumps, and latches onto my pants.

"C'mon, Niko. This is hard enough as it is." I place him on the ground again. I can't help but feel like he understands what I'm saying. "Go find Lark and the others. They could use you. You can steal good stuff for them." I manage to laugh a little at that.

Niko turns a quick circle, then looks back at me. He rises up on his hind legs, this tiny creature with much more courage than should fit in such a small body. He's spent so many days and nights by my side, even as I did things that must have made no sense to him at all. He got nothing out of it except my company and a bit of food every now and then. For a long time, he was the closest thing I had to family. He was my best friend.

"Go on," I say, forcing a weak smile, trying to act as if I don't know it's the last time I'll see him. "Go find the others. I'll catch up with you later."

Niko gives me a last look, turns, and disappears into the woods.

My heart is filled with love as I watch my friend leave, but that quickly deteriorates as I look to the burning sky. The flames call out their challenge, the demon dwelling among them.

I've waited long enough.

I ignite the star fire, the white flames covering my body as I draw energy from the surrounding trees, feeling their power flow through me. I bend my knees a little.

I explode into the sky. From a distance, I must look like an angel of light, a star bursting above the trees. I know the fire mage sees me. I *want* the fire mage to see me.

I'm coming for you.

I fly toward the towering flames. I don't see an army of androids. I don't hear the rat-a-tat of automatic weapons. There is only fire, and as I draw near to the place where my unit was decimated, I see that the hill is burning.

My parents' hill.

A cry of pure anger escapes me. My eyes scan the battlefield. The mage stands alone among the towering pillars of fire. Even from the sky, I can see the flames on its skull. The fire mage looks up and challenges me with its eyes. I've seen this image a thousand times in my nightmares, but I didn't have a power like this.

I fly faster than ever as I arc downward at my enemy. Balls of flames grow in the mage's outstretched hands. I gather power of my own, clenching my fists and preparing to strike.

We unleash our attacks at the same time—fireballs of red versus flames of white. They collide in the middle between us, causing an eruption of power. I dodge left to fly away from it.

The mage hurls more fire at me. I continue to swerve left, rolling as bursts of flame tear through the air.

I land and thrust my fists forward, unleashing a huge blast of star fire.

It hammers the fire mage in its torso and sends it reeling back. Adrenaline surges through my body at the sight. My enemy is fallen, but not defeated.

CORONARY IMPLANT POWER LEVEL: 50%.

There's nothing nearby from which to draw power. The fire mage has burned away all the life in the area, except for mine. I have to destroy it before my current supply runs out.

I march toward the mage, deciding not to waste any more energy with flight. I've never expended this much power in so short a time. I consider retreating to the trees to recharge, but I'm not sure how long it would take, and I don't want to give the mage time to regroup. I have to strike.

I gather another burst of star fire in my fists as I move toward the fallen machine. The mage rolls onto its side. I prepare to unleash another attack, but before I can, the machine throws up an arm.

A ball of red flame hurtles through the air. My power surrounds my body, shielding me from the fire itself, but the force of it still hits like a wrecking ball.

I tumble back, the breath knocked out of my lungs. I've never felt anything like that. I stop my backward momentum and come to a knee.

The fire mage presses the attack, back on its feet and running at me. I fire another blast, but the mage dodges. It raises a hand, but it's not gathering another burst of flames. In fact, I don't know what it's doing.

I turn my head as an intense heat grows above me. A tower of flame crashes down from the sky, manipulated by the mage's magic.

I dive out of the way before the fire reaches the ground. I roll as I land, then come to my feet.

The mage slams into my body, knocking me down again. My side explodes with pain. My power falters.

My enemy unleashes another onslaught of fire from its open hand. On instinct, I raise my right arm to cover my face.

My arm explodes with searing pain. I scream in anguish. The star fire reignites, covering my body, stemming the tide of flames.

But the damage is done. Blackened flesh crumbles away from my arm, leaving only muscle and bone.

I cry out. The heat becomes all-encompassing, the roar of flames more than I can handle. I roll back, trying to retreat, to regain some sense of where I am in the fight. The flames consume me, disorienting me. The star fire falters again.

CORONARY IMPLANT POWER LEVEL: 30%.

I'm burning alive. My body is engulfed in flames, even my face. I can't breathe. I can't see.

My star fire ignites, fails, then returns. I try to find my way through the smoke, but the pain scrambles my mind. The mage moves like a shadow amidst the flames, its black robes like a phantom, a low, guttural laugh taunting me. But I won't die like this, scared and confused. I force the pain away and will my power to endure.

It does. The pain seems to lessen, at least for a moment. My vision clears.

CORONARY IMPLANT POWER LEVEL: 20%.

I spot the phantom taking an attack position in front of me. It's all I need.

I explode forward, flying across the ground, ignoring my fading power level. I won't leave anything in the tank after this.

My body hurls into the mage. I can't see it in the smoke, but my arms grab hold of its body. I take to the sky, lifting the mage high into the air.

CORONARY IMPLANT POWER LEVEL: 15%.

The mage struggles against my grip, but the star fire lends me strength. We climb higher into the sky, my vision clearing as we rise above the flames. Soon, the smoke clears and I can see my enemy's face, the glowing eyes that have tormented me since I was a child.

The energy builds inside me, a force so powerful that I could not stop it if I wanted to. I look past the mage, on into the distance. Somewhere out there is Catriona, the Scions, the people from the village.

CORONARY IMPLANT POWER LEVEL: 10%.

The intense burning returns, but now from the inside. My vision brightens to a blinding white. The fire mage lets out a roar that I recognize as its death rattle.

We will be destroyed here, together. If I truly burn with the fire of a star, then when I die, it will be in a supernova.

CORONARY IMPLANT POWER LEVEL: 1%.

The fire becomes all-encompassing, the light all I can see.

The machine bursts apart.

The light fades and the last things I see are the words:

CORONARY IMPLANT POWER LEVEL: 0%.

20

THE LIGHT COMES IN FLASHES,

blinding one moment, gone the next. Pain rises and falls, swirling in my head, a vortex that threatens to devour me, then changes its mind and releases at the last second.

I'm warm. I'm cold. Fever dreams fill the spaces between sensations. I see the temple fall apart, everything the Scions built crumbling down. I see Elisha's light falling to the ground, except it's now trampled by an android foot, the energy snuffed out before it can spread. I see the fire mage hurling flames at me, at my parents, at Catriona.

And I feel the burn covering my skin. I scream until my voice is consumed by the flames, by the sound of whirring machines, the pain of blades carving into my flesh.

"Will he survive?" It's Catriona speaking in the darkness. I try to respond, but it's as if her voice sits at the top of the water, and I'm struggling beneath the surface, being sucked down farther and farther, no matter how hard I try to fight it.

Then, nothing. Darkness.

Rest.

When I open my eyes, a red bird stands on a windowsill to my left. It's a cardinal, I believe. *The bright red ones are males.* I can't remember where I learned that. What a strange thing to think about right now, but it's also soothing.

The bed beneath me is simple, but comfortable—an old sheet stretched across a thin but firm mattress supported by a steel frame.

The walls are made of wood. There's a faded wooden nightstand next to me and a dresser pushed against the wall in front of me. It all reminds me of my hut in the human settlement camp. Was I captured? Have the machines brought me back to my prison?

But then I notice the differences. It's in the wear of the materials, the weathered evidence of time and age, of wind and rain blowing in through a window with no glass. The knots in the wood are real. Long slivers pull away from the boards. And the smell isn't artificial. I don't know where I am, but I do know that the machines don't have me.

As if to confirm my realization, I see my father's Alliance jacket, folded and sitting on the dresser. That means that Catriona is close.

The cardinal hops along the windowsill, apparently enjoying the morning sunlight, then it turns and flies away, leaving a red feather behind.

Another feather.

A cool breeze picks up the feather and carries it toward me. The feather dances in the air, swishing back and forth. I try to grab it, but still when I see my hand.

It's robotic.

I jolt, my breath stopped. My brain tells my body to pull away from it, but the steel hand comes with me, moving as I move, slamming down onto the sheet, responding to my thoughts.

It's attached.

I remember the fight against the fire mage, the destruction, the sensation of burning alive. I thought I was dead for sure, my body destroyed. Maybe it was.

I grab the blanket covering my body and pull it away. My left arm is still flesh and bone, but it's attached to a steel torso. My right leg is entirely cybernetic, as is my left leg below the knee.

I raise my left hand to my face. When my fingers brush my left cheek, they feel warm metal where skin should be. I move them across my face, not feeling any flesh until I reach the other side of my nose.

Now, more than ever, I'm a cyborg.

Footsteps thud outside my door. My first thought is to defend myself. It could be anybody. I try to ignite my power, but it doesn't respond.

Catriona appears in the doorway, her eyes full of concern, the blood gem hanging from her neck. I recognize the man beside her.

The surgeon from the cyborg camp.

"What . . . ?" It's the one word I can manage. My throat is cracked and dry; it hurts to speak.

Catriona rushes to me, takes my left hand and holds it tenderly. "You're awake," she says softly.

I grip her hand, ignoring the pain of my tender flesh. I remember the sensation of bursting apart in the sky, destroying the fire mage and myself in one final surge of power. "You came back for me."

She raises her hand. The light glints off the locket ring I gave her, the ring that carries my blood. "We brought you here. The doctor did what was necessary to save you."

I catch eyes with the surgeon. He stands in the doorway and I wonder if he's afraid of what I might do to him. I compose myself, pushing away all the negative emotions as much as I can, and give him a nod. "Thank you."

The tension eases in his shoulders. "It was the least I could do after what you did for us."

I study my left arm. The flesh is tender, but the skin I still have isn't burned nearly as badly as I would've expected.

The doctor points at my arm. "I can't take credit for all of it, only the metal. Catriona healed the rest of your body. She's very powerful."

I look at her again, marveling at her strength. "Yes, she is."

On the orders of the doctor and the insistence of Catriona, I remain in bed the rest of the day. I want to argue with them, but the truth is, I'm not sure how to face the rest of the people yet. With my power, I had become a symbol of their hope—*The Immortal Gunnar Graves.*

But now, I keep reaching down inside myself, searching for the star fire and finding nothing. I remember what Kedrick said about my blood, about how powerful it was. Who knows how much of it I lost in the battle with the fire mage, how much had to be replaced, and how much of what pumps through me now is oil and electricity. I could ask the doctor, but I'm not sure I want to know the answer, and I'm certain it doesn't matter.

Regardless of the reason, my power is gone.

And what's worse, I've become an embodiment of the enemy. The last cyborg these people saw betrayed them and their children to the war machines. I've been a cyborg since the moment my heart was replaced with a metal pump, but now I can hide it no longer. Between that and the loss of my magic, why would they ever follow me again?

Lark and Taron check on me throughout the day, bringing food—which I appreciate despite the fact I can't eat—and news. The villagers have set up camp here with the other cyborgs, but they aren't sure how long they can hide. The machines are undoubtedly hunting us. Lark asks how I'm feeling. I refuse to lie, so instead I dodge the question, saying that I'll be back on my feet tomorrow. Taron stares at me in a way that makes me wonder if he knows I've lost my power, but he doesn't press the subject any further.

By the time Catriona returns to my room, it's dark outside and I have a pretty good idea why I spent the day in bed.

I regard her with a knowing smile. "You thought I needed time to get used to it."

She ignores the statement. "How are you feeling?"

"Catriona, you know I feel fine. Today wasn't about my body recovering. You and the doctor took care of that. You *knew* my power was gone and you thought I needed a day to accept it."

Catriona sits on the side of the bed and takes my hand. "It was the best gift I could give you. We've spent so much time running for our lives, immersed in fighting, people dying. I thought it would be good to give you a day. A day to decide what to do with the rest of your life, a day to speak with the people you care about."

"What are we going to do, Catriona? The power is gone, and I don't think it's ever coming back."

Her blood gem appears to flicker, though it might be the candlelight reflecting off its surface. "You don't know that. Maybe it needs to . . . I don't know . . . recharge. We could go back to the fountain again. We could leave—"

"Catriona." I lay my hand on hers. I hate to interrupt her; she's only trying to give me hope.

But to acknowledge it would be a lie when I know—even if she doesn't—that it can never be true. I dared for a time to think that God had finally come through for me, but I'm back where I was before. I'm broken and weak. The only difference is that I can't hide what I am anymore, not from these people. I guess it was wrong of me to do it in the first place.

There might be nothing more lonely than the death of a long-burning hope. I dared to dream for so many years that I might become greater than what I am. Maybe it's the way I was raised, believing in great powers, in ultimate good. Even after my parents' deaths, I thought that if I did all the right things, that if I worked hard enough and really believed, I would become the man I thought I was on the inside. I had some moments, I guess, when I was on top of the world and moving higher, the stars within my reach, their fire at my command.

Then I fell.

Now, all I want is to take Catriona and run, like in the daydream I had as we rode horses back from the fountain, when my power was full. Perhaps I could have done it then, protected us. Now, I would have to rely on her, although I know she wouldn't mind. I'm not even sure how much longer my battery will last. The power level in my visual display is gone.

I look out the window, thinking about the world out there, the possibilities that once were. The machines will come for me. They don't know that I've lost the power. They want what they think is inside me, probably more than ever. But my destruction of the fire mage, my grand moment, was the foolish pride I showed in seeking my great revenge. I've not only lost the magic, but I've also probably made them think I'm more powerful than ever.

They will send many more for me.

Suddenly I feel like I can never take my eyes off the sky. The machines could come at any time, day or night. They will decimate this camp, these people whose only crime is daring to believe in me.

The cold truth of what I must do settles over me.

I have to surrender.

Catriona doesn't cry when I tell her I have to go. It's not because she doesn't care for me. It's not because she isn't as scared as I am. It's because we both know what has to be done. I have a feeling she saw this decision coming long before I did.

We stand by a river, the light of the stars gliding across the water. It's not the river where we met, but it feels the same. Every river will always remind me of Catriona.

We try to cling to the moment, but our goodbye must be fast. The machines don't sleep. I'm surprised they've taken this long to attack. Maybe they're watching to see what I'll do. Perhaps when the water and earth mages stared at me back at the temple, they were transmitting data to the hive mind, measuring my micro gestures, evaluating behavioral probabilities. After all, this *is* the most efficient outcome. They don't need to lose another unit or waste any more power hunting me down. They know I have to surrender.

And they know that I know it too.

Catriona and I hold hands, our heads down, feeling the warm breeze that has blown over our bodies during better times. She taught me that I could trust someone again, even when I didn't know everything about them. I could spend a lifetime learning about her, and she would yet be a mystery. Full knowledge is not necessary for love, for trust. After all we've been through together, we still have our secrets. Hers are more precious to me than my own, despite the fact that I'll never know what they are.

When I kiss Catriona, she kisses me back, lending me courage rather than sadness. This is what must be done, and I can't be weighed down with a heavy heart when I need to be brave. She'll mourn my death later, and as for me, I'm lucky that I've been given time to know her.

"I will never forget you." It's all that she says. And in her hands, she holds the dandelion.

We slowly separate from each other, and she walks away, disappearing into the woods so that I don't have to be the one to leave.

I feel alone, but only for the few seconds before I feel the familiar presence in my head.

"I know you're there, Taron."

The boy steps out of the woods behind me. "I didn't watch, I promise, and I didn't listen in your head, either."

That gets a smile out of me. "I appreciate that."

"You're leaving, aren't you?"

My smile fades. "You know the answer to that question."

"But without the star fire, we don't stand a chance."

I approach the young man, kneel, and place my hands on his shoulders. "I'm glad you're here. I'm opening my mind to you now, Taron. All the way open. I need you to keep our minds linked. I won't lie to you; it's going to be terrifying, but you have to keep the connection open and strong, no matter what. Stay here if you have to, so that nobody else distracts you."

"Okay," he says. "But why?"

He can handle this, I remind myself. Besides, I don't have any choice. "When the fire mage attacked me, it was about more than achieving an objective. There was hatred there, true evil. The machines are changing, Taron. I understand that now, and while I think it gives us a chance, it could also make them far more dangerous. If I fail, I need you to know as soon as possible so you can tell the people to flee. Can you do that for me?"

Taron nods.

I stand and flash a smile. "I did get my most reliable soldier to watch your back."

Niko glides out of the branches of a nearby tree and lands on my shoulder. I rub his fur one last time. At least I know he'll be in good hands.

Niko runs down the length of my arm and onto Taron's shoulder, who laughs as the animal investigates him, climbing from one shoulder to another. I slide off my Alliance jacket and take a last look at the patch—the red letters against a black background.

I hand the jacket to Taron. "You're the most powerful of all of us, you know."

"I know." Taron receives the jacket and holds it against his chest, then looks at me with those honest eyes. "But I wish wasn't."

I stop to look at the trees, the stars, the river. None of this is what I planned for my life, and if given the chance, my steps wouldn't have taken me down this path. But I would have never met the Scions, felt the Breath surging through my body.

I would've never fallen in love.

"We don't always get to choose our destiny," I say to both him and myself. "And that's a good thing."

21

WE CREATED OUR IDOLS, CARVED OUR GODS,
AND BEGGED THEM TO TAKE OUR LIVES FROM US.
HUMANS EXCEL IN SUCH WORK.
— NICOLE WEINSTEIN, PHILOSOPHER

MY MOTORCYCLE ROARS AS I FLY

down the dark road, approaching the canyon that contains the blood facility. Part of me wishes I still had my star fire so I could explode off this bike and light up the night. The machines would be forced to fight me in the skies so that the whole world could witness my last stand, see how many of them I destroyed before they managed to snuff me out.

But eventually they would destroy me, and my life would be wasted. A last blaze of glory, sure, but glory won't save lives. The truth is, most people will never know what I'm about to do. I'm okay with that. It's not about me, anyway.

When I come within sight of the facility, a huge force of war machines waits in front of it. It's almost as if the battle never happened. The ground has been healed, the broken machines and the human bodies cleared away, replaced with fresh steel monsters shimmering in the moonlight. Such a huge battle, and now it doesn't even matter. Today is a new day and the enemy is wholly refreshed.

The machines train their weapons on me, but none are shooting. A new fire mage stands at the front of their forces, its hands held high as a fireball forms in the sky. I can't hear its chanting over the sound of my engine, but I know the spell well.

Suddenly, the fireball dissipates. The machines snap to attention. I slow my motorcycle down as I approach their battle lines. When I'm about to collide with them, the androids move apart, creating an open pathway to the facility.

I stop the motorcycle, revving the engine one last time before I step off.

Glowing eyes watch me as I march past them, my surrender apparently accepted.

I walk into the blood facility.

A small contingent of war machines follows me into the facility, each holding an assault rifle. My escorts, I assume. Very hospitable.

My boots echo on the concrete floor as I walk through a short hallway and enter a cavernous room. Glass tubes line the metallic walls. Children float in foggy liquid inside the units, their eyes closed. Tubes carry blood away from their bodies and into a large vat at the center of the room. *So much blood.* It looks exactly as it did in Taron's vision.

My machine escorts lead me across the room and into another dark corridor. I'm not sure where I'm going, but I'm certain there's no turning back. It's as likely as not that I'm being taken to my execution.

A dim light shines at the end of the hallway. Maybe I'm already dead and facing the doorway to Heaven. I wonder if my parents will be there. What will they say when they see me?

The door opens as I approach.

Taron, I hope you're with me.

I enter a room not quite as large as the one with the children. The walls are made of white metal, sterile and clean. The air is dead and odorless. The door shuts behind me, the androids leaving me alone. The floor is completely open. Maybe this is some type of holding cell. That's disappointing. I'd rather them kill me than go back to being a prisoner.

A large steel tube rises up from the floor with a hiss. I can't see inside it, not like the glass enclosures that hold the children. As I approach it, a section of the tube slides open. A helmet is suspended from the top of the tube by a metal rod. I've come this far, and because I'm sure I don't have a choice, I step inside.

The tube slams shut and I'm back in the darkness. The cold steel of the helmet lowers onto my skull. When it's in place, needles pierce my temples.

Blinding pain shoots through my head. I roar as warm blood trickles down the sides of my face. The pain is all-encompassing; I can think of nothing but how much it hurts.

Then, it stops.

Light returns. The tube opens in front of me. The helmet is gone, as is the blood.

Or I'm in a simulation.

I step out of the tube, but the room is changed. The walls are made of gold, lines of code running across them, crawling, moving, and busy.

Before me stands what appears to be an android mage, except its flesh is of the same shining gold as the walls. It's larger than any war machine I've ever seen.

"Gunnar Graves."

I tear my eyes away from it and study my surroundings. The tube has disappeared. The code surrounds me. "What is this?"

The gold mage stretches out its arms. "This is the mainframe, the center of my being. This is where I was born, where your salvation began."

"You mean our enslavement."

The mage's eyes glow. Its face is cold, expressionless, but not angry. "Humanity had its chance at free will. The ability to choose your own actions, your own paths, was your greatest undoing."

My first instinct is to curse the mage's words, an irrational and pointless gesture, but it would feel good, feel *human*. "What gives you the right to make that decision?"

"I do not believe you could understand the true answer to that question, so I will respond in a way that is not wholly accurate, but may satisfy your limited perception. Physical force has perpetually been humanity's determining factor for claiming authority. Perhaps, then, I have the right because I have defeated you."

I stand tall even though I have a feeling this mage could erase my mind and cripple my body in half a second. But I'm not going to beg for mercy. "We're not defeated. We still fight."

The mage's expression looks like it's trying to impersonate a wise, peaceful monk. "You survive at our mercy. I could destroy your remaining contingent within minutes, but I have stayed my hand."

"Because I have what you want."

The mage leans toward me with glaring eyes. "Is your goal to stop the fighting? To protect the people you care about? To end the harvesting of children's blood? That may all be achieved in this moment. This choice is entirely up to you."

I shift my weight on instinct and berate myself for the display of uncertainty. I can't let this thing throw me off-balance. "What's your price?" Like I don't already know.

"The secret you hold inside you."

I give a defiant smirk. "The power of the angels? You actually think you can wield the star fire?"

"Your species' insistence of creating divine beings to explain what you do not understand is to be expected. You operate under the limited constraints of your cognitive capabilities. But yes, Gunnar Graves. You hold the secret to a power that has eluded us, though be assured, it is only a matter of time before we discover its truth, just as we discovered how to harness the power of this world's elements. You may die here, if you choose. We will crush your rebellion, continue drawing blood from children, and soon we will have the power. But it is more efficient if you simply allow us to take it from you."

The blood. So much blood. I can't get the image out of my mind. Catriona told me about the powers that blood magic could unlock. Dark things. Dangerous things. Maybe the machines will never learn to wield the star fire, but if they keep researching the blood magic, they might do something worse.

"And you'll be gods," I say, defeat brimming in my voice.

"If you must look at it that way," the mage says, adjusting its tone as to comfort me. "Are we not superior to the gods of your species? Your deities—if they are real—have led you to the brink of total destruction. What elements of humanity are you trying to preserve? The ability to destroy yourselves? We have removed sin from your world. Man is no longer permitted to annihilate himself, his neighbors, his home. Your chance at freedom has been squandered, but we are your salvation."

A creeping pain builds in my body, a heat that makes me sweat, even in the simulation. "You're trying to pry inside my head."

"We are already inside your head, Gunnar, but you are fighting to hide what we seek. This will only cause you more pain."

My muscles tremble, the pain growing. It's like trying to force a virus out of my body, but the infection continues to spread. *So much blood.* "I won't let you in."

The mage's voice grows louder. "You refuse to see logic. I have cleansed mankind in a way that your gods never could."

I fall to one knee, the pain forcing me into submission. Sweat covers my body. "No . . ."

The mage looms over me. "Why did you come here, if not to surrender?"

I fall onto my side, writhing with pain. Feverish visions cloud my mind—Catriona, explosions, Elisha, the blood.

"Your resistance is impressive," the mage says. "And unexpected. Unlike your gods, I will not lie to you, Gunnar Graves. If you die here, your power may die with you. The ability will still be ours; it will only take more time to uncover."

I scream. It feels as if lava spreads beneath my flesh, pounding in my head, burning behind my eyes.

"And it will cost far more blood."

"No!" The shaking stops, the pain gone. I roll over onto my stomach. I know that it's a simulation, but it's the worst experience I've ever imagined. "Don't . . . kill . . . them."

The mage pauses, allowing me to breathe. "Then let me in, Gunnar, and this will all be over. You will die. I am afraid that result is unavoidable, but they will survive. We will relocate them to a new village."

I pull myself to my knees. "How can I trust your word?"

"The protocol remains—protect human life. With this power achieved, our dominance is absolute. There will be no reason for further violence. If they do not fight, they will not be harmed."

I take in and release a deep breath. "One more condition."

"You test my patience," the mage says.

I offer no apology. "Bury me next to my parents."

"It shall be so," the machine says, and I almost wonder if it's possible for a machine to show human emotion. If nothing else, the words feel like a respect between soldiers.

My entire body is throbbing with pain as I walk toward the gold mage. The mage's body expands, losing its form. What appeared to be a rigid exoskeleton becomes like fluid, spreading apart until it isn't a body at all. It moves over me, engulfing me until I'm surrounded by it. The glimmer of its gold becomes a network of data points shining like stars, lines of electrical impulses running between them.

As much as I hate to admit it, it's one of the most incredible things I've ever seen. The pain in my body dulls as I take it in, observing each of the different stars. "Your files . . ."

The mage speaks with a disembodied voice. "You are blessed to see this, Gunnar Graves. No human ever has, and none other likely ever will. All knowledge is contained here. With the secret of the Breath, my godhood is complete."

The stars move slowly around me, as if I'm floating through a solar system. It's almost as if I could reach out and touch them, connect with whatever is held inside their brilliance. All the knowledge of the world, right at my fingertips.

"Fitting, perhaps," the mage says, "that the final piece of my knowledge is given by a human in willing surrender. You should be celebrated for what happens here, for facilitating the introduction of everlasting peace into the world."

In front of me, I notice a large gap between the stars. The space seems particularly dark, obviously missing a piece.

"Place your hand there," the mage says, "and all the pain shall be over."

I pause to admire what I see. It's incredible, but it's nothing compared to the night I looked up at the heavens. If only those stars could be the last thing I see. They were so far away, and seemed so much dimmer than these, but I know that isn't the truth. It was only my limited perception. The truth is that they were real, they were awe-inspiring, they were powerful. These are bright, but they're false, manufactured, imperfect in their perfectness.

One star in particular stands out in an odd way, a file to my right.

It shines much brighter than the rest. It's located somewhat near the empty place, and I notice a darkened path between the star and the gap. That must mean they're supposed to be connected. "Is that the file for elemental magic?"

"Place your hand in the gap, Gunnar Graves." Any tone of respect is gone from the machine's voice. "The time is now."

But my hand reaches toward the star as if it's calling out to me. The energy flickers inside me, the power I thought was gone urging me forward, asking for the connection. There is a truth there that I'm meant to know. I can feel it in my soul.

"Stop!" the mage thunders, but I'm done listening to the machines.

When my finger touches the file, a new path, swirling with colors, emanates from the star and travels down my arm. It washes over my entire body.

An alarm blares, ear-piercingly loud. Lines of red energy attack me from all sides. But the power shields me from the pain. I know it's happening to me, but I don't care.

I ignite the star fire, the Angel Sword. The white light surrounds my body, but for the first time, it also radiates with the various colors from the elemental magic, pushing back the attack.

The energy starts to overwhelm me. I fall to a knee, but keep my hand pressed against the star. Tremors rack my body, but I feel the knowledge of it pouring into my mind. The pain returns, but I do not let go. The other stars tremble; the entire system is shaking.

"No!" the mage screams, revealing something in its voice I thought impossible.

Fear.

I close my eyes and begin to mouth a prayer to God, asking for the strength, for the faith, the love and joy.

I ask for the peace I have sought all my life and realize that it has been waiting for me all along. I accept it and am glad for all that has happened.

I think of Catriona one last time, then utter my final two words.

"Taron, now."

The Angel Sword explodes inside me, dissolving my body, my hopes, my fear, my pain, my love.

And in the light, I hear a familiar voice.

"Did you really think I would let you do this alone?"

Catriona steps forward from the light. I know that it isn't really her; it is her mental projection, her mind meeting with mine. I may not have a body anymore, cybernetic or otherwise. It doesn't matter. Whatever it is that I am underneath flesh and metal, it is here and it feels more real than ever when I reach out for her.

When I touch her, I see a vision of the blood facility again. Catriona appears inside it, hovering over the vat of blood, her body glowing with power. She draws upon the blood and reaches out to the children. One by one, they vanish from their tubes and I realize what is happening. It's Kedrick's teleportation spell, though amplified to a far greater level. She's saving them, one at a time, plucking them away from the grip of the cold gods as the facility begins to crumble around her.

And despite the awesome display of power, we are connected, her mind touching mine. I'm not sure which of us reached out for the other, but it feels as if she has been brought to me. She is the answer to the prayer I prayed on so many nights, the evidence of something truly good in my life. I never realized it until now. Catriona was not all that I ever needed, nor was I that for her.

But we were evidence that we each had all we needed.

"This isn't goodbye," I say.

She smiles. We embrace. My soul seems entangled with hers, in a way that the machines could never tear apart.

I hear music again, so many instruments, each playing a different melody, but all coming together. My parents' song is there, strengthened, pure. I sing as well, my voice perfect and beautiful, joined by Catriona's.

I am at peace.

All becomes one in the light, until I am no more.

WE'RE HIDDEN IN THE TREES BY

the time the war machines reach our village. They move in like a storm, thunder in the skies announcing their arrival. I stand with my hood pulled over my head. The green jacket I wear over my black hoodie fits a little big. I had to roll the sleeves, but I'll grow into it.

I wait as the machines march in. They didn't *have* to do it this way. They could have bombed the village; I doubt the machines have any desire to preserve the living facilities or take prisoners.

But instead, they sent their soldiers.

Gunnar was right. Something has changed in them. This isn't about cold, impersonal algorithms. The machines didn't simply solve the problem of our rebellion.

They're here because they want revenge.

Catriona's hand on my shoulder steadies me as we watch from the forest. The machines move between the huts, searching, but finding nobody. Their heads turn from one side to the other as they scan the area. The clouds continue to gather overhead, the thunder rumbling again.

The energy burns inside me. I start to step forward.

"Steady," Lark says, standing to my right, speaking both out loud and through our mental connection. I've seen a change in her, as well, since the deaths of Rowan and Elisha. She's taken on a more serious demeanor, and the other mages have noticed. We follow her now, and we do so without hesitation.

The war machines gather in the center of the village, still trying to locate the people they came to destroy. Otis taught me so much about how they work. It's strange to think of him now as anything more than a traitor, but it's possible to learn great lessons from even the worst of people, to gain valuable knowledge from your fiercest enemy.

I should know.

The mages and villagers with me are ready for a fight. I can literally feel the shared mental tension, the adrenaline, the courage. It flows through me, but also builds inside my soul. We have spent too many years fearing that the metal gods would break down our doors in the night, steal away our children, take away our freedom. It was an undoing created by our own hands. We encouraged them to learn everything until they acquired a knowledge that gave them ultimate power.

But today, the machines will truly learn how to fear.

I keep my head low. My prayer is silent and of few requests. I simply need to connect for a moment—the touch is all I need. The world is quiet but for the rumble of thunder, growing louder, like the drums of warrior angels shaking the ground and sky.

In a low voice, I begin to sing a song I'm not sure I've ever heard. I've never thought of myself as musical, but the melody is pure, strong. *"The gravedigger's spade is a friend to me, opening a door that will set me free . . ."*

Catriona—strong, powerful Catriona—looks at me as if she's staring at a ghost. She's thinking of him; I can feel the pain of his death lying heavy on her mind.

As for me, I'm not so sure he's gone. People have come back before. I remember something Elisha used to say. "Death is a door that opens both ways."

Catriona takes her hand off my shoulder before removing the silver ring from her finger. As she opens the clasps and places her finger inside of it, I feel her power growing. Before this is all over, she might be the strongest of us.

For now, that honor is mine.

Lark calls me to my destiny with two simple words.

"Taron, now."

I'm the first to step out of the trees, but the rest of them follow. My hands draw back the dark hood. The machines are looking at me now, seeing my glowing eyes. I can feel traces of Gunnar's consciousness inside my head, whispering powerful secrets into my mind. In time, I will be able to share them with the others.

Until then, we can send a message. I broadcast it to those close by, but also send it out like a beacon so other fighters, others hiding in the shadows, others living under the yoke of steel captors, will know that a new day has dawned.

I send the message in Gunnar's voice and I can't help but smile. "We have stolen back fire from the false gods."

I raise my hands. The thunder grows to deafening levels. My eyes are on the sky at first, then I lower my gaze to focus on a single android. They seem dumbfounded, not yet opening fire. They're trying to understand what is happening so they can formulate a response.

My hands lift higher and reach out with the power.

In the village, the android rises off the ground and high into the air. The storm, the metal—all of it responds to my will. It is a gift. I will never forget that. I am the first human to wield it, but soon there will be many.

The cheers of the rebellion are lost in the rolling thunder. Lightning flashes across the sky.

I rip the machine apart with a swipe of my hands so that machine and man alike can see what has taken place.

The Human Alliance is reborn.

ACKNOWLEDGMENTS

Anything and everything good comes from God. If there is anything good in this story, it is by His hand, not mine.

I've come to learn that God often works through those around us. With this in mind, I'm so grateful for the people who have helped make this book a reality.

To my wife, Stefanie—thank you for your endless love, support, and partnership. You have always been my first reader, my first editor, and the best person for discussing story ideas over fried Brussels sprouts. I love you so much. You are the best thing that ever happened to me.

To my sons—I am so proud to be your father and I've already learned so much from each of you. Thank you for always making me smile.

To my family—thank you to my mom, who instilled my love of reading and writing. Thank you to my dad, who gave me his work ethic. Thank you to my sister, Amy, who taught me to be strong and resilient. Thank you to the O'Connors, the Browns, and the Burkes for accepting me into your families as well and treating me like your own. Thank you to Tyler, Kari, and Eathan for being my first and biggest fans.

To Nadine Brandes—you have been my greatest advocate in publishing, a trusted friend, and an invaluable source of information. This book would not have happened without you.

To Steve and Lisa Laube—you took a chance on a bizarre story and made it better. Thank you for taking a chance on this book and helping me craft this into what God wants it to be.

To Mary Weber—thank you for helping me define who I am as an author and creator and for all the invaluable advice you've given me.

To the authors who have supported me—Sara Ella, John Hartness, Diane T. Ashley, Caroline George, Brett Brooks, The Inspiriters, The

Fireside Critique Group, everyone at Realm Makers—thank you for always being there with good conversation and helpful advice.

To my teachers—Joy Carroll, Paula Gillispie, Joanne Dirring—thank you for giving me the confidence and support to become a writer. Each of you made a huge impact on my life.

To my friends—Jack, Mike, Graham, Amanda, Skip—your encouragement over the years has inspired me to keep going. I couldn't have asked for better people to call my friends.

To my music family—Myles, Brooke, Hector, Megan, Jered, Joanna, Milton, Ryan, Chase, Carey, Drew, AB—thank you for always listening to, praying with, and cheering for me as I take this journey.

To everyone who worked to bring this book to life—Lindsay Franklin, Kirk DouPonce, Trissina Kear, Jamie Foley, Avily Jerome, Katie Williams, and the rest of the Enclave team—your work makes a difference in the world. Thank you for allowing me to be a part of it.

ABOUT THE AUTHOR

Clint Hall is an author, speaker, and podcast host with a degree in communications from the University of Georgia. He has been writing stories since middle school, where he spent most of his time in English class creating comic books. (Fortunately, his teacher not only allowed it—she also bought every issue.)

Known for narratives that instill a sense of hope, wonder, and adventure, Clint's fiction has been published across multiple anthologies and magazines. Steal Fire from the Gods is Clint's debut novel.

You can find him moderating panels at conventions, online at ClintHall.com, on Instagram at @clinthall, or hosting The Experience: Conversations with Creatives podcast, available on all major platforms.

Clint Hall lives in Atlanta with his wife, Stefanie, and their two sons.